*An Alexis Snipperdoom Novel*

*Book 2*

JD BROYHILL

**Disclaimer:**
The characters, places, events, and items portrayed and defined in this work are fictitious. This book is the work of the author. Any similarity to actual definitions is by coincidence and not intentional. All artwork is the property of the author. The author holds all copyrights to the art displayed in or on this book.



ISBN: 9798992673272

Library of Congress Control Number:
2025905547

Printed in the United States of America

**Cover art by:**

**Gombar Cover Designs**

**Star Ceptre art by:**

**Anthony Conley**

# DEDICATION

To James, Jeremy, and Stephen—
Love you to the moon and back!

To Rick—And then…

Mom—You are my light and refuge.

"At the end of the day, there is only one victor—ME!"

~Alexis Snipperdoom

JD BROYHILL

# CONTENTS

JD BROYHILL

Alexis stood before Aerianna's chamber. Without knocking, Alexis pushed open the creaking, heavy door. Across the room, she spotted Aerianna sitting on the bed. She looked pale, white as a ghost, fidgeting with the sleeve of her robe. Aerianna looked up, her eyes glazed over, obviously deep in thought. She laid eyes on Alexis, contemplating the bad news she was about to share with her.

"Aerianna, what is wrong? Everything worked out as we planned. We had a remarkable evening. Why is your face like that? What is happening? Please, tell me! You look dreadful." Alexis frowned as she observed Aerianna. Instantly, a wave of panic hit her.

Aerianna reluctantly jumped off the bed and approached Alexis. She reached for her hand, ready to share the news. She swallowed hard and took a deep breath. Now was the time!

"I do not know how to tell you this, but we have a problem. A very, very, big problem! You are not going to like it, not one bit! Perhaps you should sit down, My Queen," Aerianna insisted, pointing to the chair in the corner of the room. Aerianna quickly released the Queen's hand, noticing her nose flaring as anger built.

Alexis puckered her lips as she stepped back, trying to get a better look at Aerianna. She placed her hands on her hips, scowling. Outraged, Alexis continued to observe Aerianna, wondering why she acted strangely. Something was amiss, and she assumed it was disastrous.

"What are you saying? I do not understand! Speak up, you stupid girl. I am not in the mood for guessing games. Hurry and get to the point before I lose my patience!" Alexis bared her teeth, snarling at Aerianna, realizing horrible news was about to be shared, and she was ill-prepared.

"Alexis, you'd better sit down. This may take a while…"

Alexis stared at Aerianna in disbelief. She rolled her eyes in an irritated manner. "How do you know this? Who told you?" Alexis demanded a speedy response. She was skeptical, hearing such news, assuming it was pure gossip and lies.

"I overheard Carmin talking with a security member. Carmin explained that a note was left in the Palace stating you would DIE!"

"I do not believe it. It is a bunch of crap. Who would do this? Most of all, why?"

"Alexis, the assumption is that the threat against you is direct retaliation for Loggane's death and Yarlen's imprisonment. I do not know much more. I am frustrated that Pauto did not tell me this himself," replied Aerianna, waiting to see how Alexis would respond.

Alexis stood up and looked down at Aerianna. "Well, so someone believes they can make death threats against me? Really? Wow, I am shocked. I am also greatly perturbed that this information came to light under such casual conditions. I would assume someone would have taken this much more seriously. Am I wrong?"

"No, Alexis, I wholeheartedly agree. I feel it has been handled rather poorly. I plan to find Pauto and get to the bottom of what he knows. Please allow me some time to investigate this matter. Let's not jump to conclusions. I just wanted you to know right away once I found out," replied Aerianna.

"Okay, I understand. I suppose there is no need to be alarmed until we know more. Please locate Pauto and report back to me."

"Yes, My Queen. I shall." Aerianna excused herself and expeditiously left the chamber to find Pauto. She knew Alexis was dismayed and wanted to reassure her that the rumors were nothing to fear.

Alexis followed Aerianna and departed the chamber to head back to her own. She contemplated the information Aerianna shared with her. It made no sense, and anger began to build.

After some time, she impatiently started pacing around her room, awaiting Aerianna's return, hoping for more information about the supposed rumors. *'Where is Aerianna? Sometimes, she is more of a heartache than she is worth. Unbelievable!'* Their conversation was not over, and Alexis demanded an update. *'Why is it taking so long to speak with Pauto?'*

Alexis grew more frustrated as time passed. She checked the large, black clock hanging over the door. It had been two hours. Glancing out a window, she wondered what was happening in the rest of the Palace. Alexis was in a foul mood, and waiting for Aerianna seemed to fuel her negative attitude. She tapped her finger on the windowsill as she stared out into the valley below, wondering about her fate.

Aerianna found Pauto exactly where she assumed he would be. He stood next to a Torrin near the stables. He brushed the majestic animal and smiled as he noticed Aerianna approach.

"Ah, I see you found my secret hiding place," he joked.

"Ha-ha, right. I know where to find you. I have seen you here numerous times, and it seems to be your favorite hangout spot. I need to speak with you about an urgent matter related to security, and I trust no one else with this issue. Since we are friends, I hope you will allow me to confide in you. I am asking for your discretion."

"Absolutely. You know how I feel about you, Aerianna. We are more than just friends, and I will always be there for you. How may I be of assistance?"

She blushed slightly and smiled. "Well, after Yarlen was sentenced and placed into the High Tower, there have been a lot of rumors circulating. I am sure you have heard them. Alexis and I are worried there may be some truth to the threats that have recently surfaced. I am not sure what to think. The worst part is that Alexis constantly nags me to find out what's happening. I know she is upset, but it is not my fault."

"Of course not. It is not your fault," Pauto reassured Aerianna as he lightly touched her hand.

She smiled. "You're just saying that because we are friends. I would appreciate it if you could investigate the situation as a member of the Security Command. As the new Council Security Command Chief, I kindly request that you gather more information for me. I want to put the rumors to rest or determine what needs to be done to end these threats. I am also confused about why you did not tell me about the situation. Why did I have to hear about them from Carmin?" asked Aerianna, flustered.

"First off, I would have told you if I had more information. I did not want to alarm anyone until I knew if we had a serious problem on our hands. I do agree with you that I need to dig deeper. Up until this point, I have just let things go. I assumed they were just rumors, and there was nothing to worry about yet. Now that Alexis is aware of the potential threat and rumors, I must be on top of it and find out what I can. I am sorry you feel I was less than forthright. I honestly did not want to worry you."

"It is okay, Pauto. However, I must update Alexis. She will be relentless until she has more information. So, do you have any idea where you will start the investigation?" she asked, hoping he actively formulated a plan.

Aerianna gawked at Pauto, finding him very handsome and too distracting. Her heart fluttered every time she looked at him. Pauto was of average height and had a full head of thick, blonde hair. His hazel eyes changed color depending on the light. Sometimes, they were a deep green, other times a light brown. She found them beautiful. Pauto was also rather lanky and trim. She loved watching him, especially when he was tending to the Torrins.

She could tell he loved them. Occasionally, she caught him talking to his Torrin, Maizzeh, rubbing her face and giving her a gentle kiss on the cheek. It warmed her heart to see his display of affection.

"I have some general ideas. I will round up my team, and we will determine where to start. I will also visit Yarlen. Perhaps he may be behind this scandal? It seems obvious, but sometimes it is just that simple," he said with a smirk. He winked at Aerianna, running off to begin his investigation.

*'Wow, he is so smart and handsome,'* she thought. *'Okay, okay, get your stuff together,'* she said to herself under her breath. She

knew Alexis was eagerly awaiting her return, probably huffy and upset that it had taken her so long to update her. She turned around and walked back toward the Palace, ready to face the Queen.

Loftily perched above the Palace grounds was the High Tower, a prison for those convicted of the most severe crimes in the kingdom. Yarlen had been sentenced to spend the rest of his life confined in a tiny room at the top of the brick structure. The view from his cell was breathtaking, yet he would never have the chance to escape or experience freedom again. This was the cost he incurred for betraying Alexis, who had made certain he would remain captive forever.

Initially, Alexis contemplated taking Yarlen's life, but she realized that would be too merciful. It would grant him an easy way out, and he didn't deserve such leniency. She wanted him to endure pain each day. Instead of death, she ensured he was stripped of his Ceptre, his magic, and everything that could aid him as a Warlock.

In an instant, his life as he knew it came to an end. It was a harsh lesson for him to grasp. Once Armbruster's trusted right-hand man, he now faced the grim reality of living as a prisoner for all eternity.

Alexis sat on her favorite chair in the chamber, still irritated over Aerianna's absence. She held her Ceptre, which always made her feel better and more in control. She ran her long fingers mindlessly up and down the Ceptre, scowling. Alexis wondered what was taking Aerianna so long, as her patience dwindled. She would impress upon her that her prolonged absence was unacceptable, and it better not happen again!

Alexis tried to remain calm, though the constant negative thoughts in her mind made it difficult. She held her Ceptre tight, causing her hand to ache. Realizing it was causing pain, she threw it toward its stand.

The Ceptre placed itself into the rack upright as its bottom began to glow red, indicating it was locked down. She stared at the Ceptre, thinking about wanting to head to the dungeon and work on her secret project. At the moment, it may not have been the ideal time, but she was looking for something to occupy her and distract her from the present circumstances.

Aerianna knocked on the door hesitantly, knowing Alexis would be upset with her. Yet, she realized it was not wise to return to Alexis without sufficient facts.

Instead, Aerianna chose to speak with several security officers before talking with Pauto. She felt it was better to have more information for Alexis than none or very little.

Alexis would consider Aerianna's lack of attention to detail irresponsible. Aerianna knew better than to upset Alexis. She was in one of her moods – demanding and less than tolerant of any nonsense or lack of initiative. Aerianna hoped Alexis would understand and appreciate all she had done to collect information for her. However, she was not stupid and figured it was unlikely. Alexis would probably start their conversation in a firm tone, followed by screaming.

"Enter," shouted Alexis. She knew it was Aerianna, but wanted there to be no question that she was annoyed by the tone of her voice.

"Your Majesty, I bring you news," she proclaimed with delight, hoping to appease Alexis.

"Oh, really? Well, I certainly hope so. It took you long enough. I have no idea what you have been doing or where you have been, but you better explain your lengthy absence," Alexis growled, watching Aerianna with disgust, still rubbing her sore hand.

"Yes, I know. I apologize, but I wanted to be thorough. I did not want to return until I knew I had done all I could to gather information for you."

"Very well, sit. Tell me what you have discovered," Alexis motioned for Aerianna to sit on her bed, and she complied.

"I hunted down Porti and a few of the other Security Command Team members. I wanted to see what they knew about the threats and rumors. I found Pauto by the stables and talked with him at length. He will start his investigation immediately. I believe he is the perfect person to handle this task for us," she said, beaming.

"Of course you do! It has nothing to do with the fact that you are infatuated with him, huh? I see how you act around him, and it is quite apparent. It seems he likes you, too. However, I do not need you, lovebirds, getting in the way of the investigation. Am I making myself clear?"

"Yes, I understand. I would never let my feelings for Pauto get in the way. He is an absolute professional, and I fully trust him."

"Good. That is a great start," agreed Alexis, now sitting with her hands folded.

"Alexis, Pauto suspects Yarlen. He does not know if Yarlen started the gossip or if he just planted the seed. Still, Pauto believes that he is somehow part of this entire problem. I think he may have a point. I know it seems obvious, but perhaps there is more."

Aerianna observed Alexis, attempting to read her face. Alexis did not show any emotion. Instead, she stared at Aerianna without batting an eyelash. Finally, after a few minutes, Alexis stood up.

"Okay, then. How do we proceed? Will Pauto update us or what?" Alexis shouted, getting irritated.

"Yes, of course. Pauto will meet with his team and then speak with Yarlen. He plans to report back to me later this evening. Once I hear more, I will share the news with you. Is that acceptable?"

"It will have to do, won't it? It's not like I have a choice," Alexis sarcastically responded.

Aerianna made her way to the door, pausing to excuse herself before she headed to her chamber. Keen to delve deeper into the threats, she felt it was essential for her to ensure that the news was relayed to Alexis in a much swifter manner in the future.

Once she closed the door to the chamber, Aerianna paused briefly in the hallway. With caution, she glanced down the corridor to check for any nearby presence. Then, she forcefully brought down her Ceptre, which had a glowing purple stone at its center, encircled by a radiant sun. Instantly, a vibrant green haze enveloped her, and she vanished from sight.

Alexis sat in her chair, reminiscing about the traitorous Yarlen, grinding her teeth angrily. Suddenly, she jumped up and walked to the window.

She craned her neck to look off into the distance, grinning at the High Tower to the right. Alexis noticed the flickering lights in the small, round windows. The High Tower stretched far into the sky. It was the tallest of all buildings on the Palace grounds. There was only one way up to the top of the High Tower—a long, winding, circular staircase. Yarlen was at the top of the tower, his chamber small and practically empty. A simple cot, table, and chair filled his space.

He would spend eternity in a prison of his consequences. Alexis smiled. *'All is well,'* she thought, feeling pleased and knowing she was responsible for his imprisonment.

Alexis secretly wished to see Yarlen but figured it was best to stay away. Honestly, she did not trust herself around him. He would probably say something to irritate her intentionally, and she would lose control and harm him. That would not be wise. So, she would have to restrain herself from visiting the High Tower. In time, she would face him and take some time to discover why he betrayed her.

Pauto contemplated the details of the threats against Alexis. He agreed with Aerianna that someone knew more than they were willing to divulge. Pauto could only assume the rumors were fabrications courtesy of Yarlen.

Ever since his imprisonment, Yarlen was extremely vocal about his unfair, one-sided trial. Yarlen wanted revenge. There was no doubt in Pauto's mind. Pauto wondered how Yarlen planned to execute his vengeance. He did not believe Yarlen would be stupid enough to lash out directly at the Queen.

Yarlen did not have that kind of support or power of his own. Someone was pushing the plan through and actively working on it. Maybe Yarlen was kept out of the actual plan to protect him? Pauto knew only one thing—he would have to work quickly to get to the bottom of the allegations and ensure the Queen's safety.

Approaching the rest of the Command Security Team, Pauto informed the other members of his plan. He demanded that an investigation be initiated, but did not want anyone to become suspicious. Pauto recognized that being discreet was vital.

Aerianna emphasized the importance of swiftly addressing the alleged threats. Pauto speculated that something was wrong with all the facts he had already gained. They did not add up. The threat, explicitly aimed at Alexis, was not specific, which seemed odd.

The note found on the conference table inside the Command Chamber read: ***The Queen will die!***

It was just an unsupported warning so far, and no other reliable information had been discovered. The more Pauto contemplated the situation, the more he came to believe that it was all a hoax. However, he was unwilling to risk his life by saying this to Alexis without further proof.

Pauto scoured over his transcripts. He was very thorough and kept excellent notes. So far, he had little to go on. Pauto wanted his reports to be complete and in sequential order for when he met Armbruster. They met daily, and Pauto provided him with security updates and other Palace news. Armbruster was kind but relentless when it came to the safety of his family. Pauto decided he would ask his Command Scouts to speak to commoners in the village to ascertain what they knew about the Queen's threats.

★*.★*.★*.★*.★

Armbruster sat silently behind the ornate table in his chamber. His room was dark and cold, and the light flicker from his fireplace was the only light in it. His window curtains were closed, as he wanted complete darkness and silence to allow him to think. He played with his new, scraggly beard, scratching his right cheek. He was not yet accustomed to it.

Nonetheless, he believed it would add a look of sophistication. Now, he regretted the decision as it bothered him. He considered shaving it, but decided it was best to see how he felt about it in the future before taking any impulsive action.

As he sat in silence, Armbruster reminisced about his friend Yarlen. He assumed Yarlen was upset with him because he had not visited. Feeling ashamed, Armbruster barely looked at Yarlen at his trial. He regretted not standing up for Yarlen but realized it was in his best interest. He was not stupid. Armbruster figured Alexis would have been vengeful, which would have resulted in trouble. Armbruster felt it was better to side with Alexis and avoid her wrath.

Armbruster walked to the window and pushed back the heavy, black drapes covering his window. Wanting fresh air, he unlatched the lock, and both sides of the window popped open. A cool breeze entered the chamber. He stood, hands on the windowsill, admiring the scenery. It was a beautiful and relaxing sight. He sighed as he continued to reminisce about Yarlen, walking toward his bed. Just as he was about to sit on his oversized canopy bed, draped with dark, red velvet curtains, there was a loud knock on the door.

"Sir, may I enter?"

"Yes, come in," replied Armbruster, finally sitting on the edge of the bed.

Aerianna entered the room and bowed. "Sir, I need to speak with you."

"What is it, Aerianna?" curious as to why she was there. It was rare for her to visit him.

"I believe we may have a problem. I am sure you are aware of the rumors, specifically the death threats against the Queen. I am highly concerned."

"Of course, I have heard them. Even so, I doubt there is any truth in them whatsoever. Many facts are missing, causing me to believe they are idle threats. I would not worry," said Armbruster, looking stern.

"Sir, I beg to differ. The rumors seem to be specific retaliation for Yarlen's imprisonment and Loggane's death."

"I am aware," scowled Armbruster. He stood up, walked to a nearby table, and sat on a red, tufted, high-back chair, looking directly at Aerianna.

"I believe Yarlen knows something about the gossip, and he may have an accomplice, maybe even more than one. I spoke with Pauto, and he is planning to interrogate Yarlen."

Instantly, Armbruster stood up and pounded his fists on the round, black table. "Why would he do that?" he bellowed at Aerianna, an aggravated look on his face, his big nose flaring.

"Sir, I asked him to do so. I assumed it would be less obvious if our Security Officer asked questions. If I were to speak with him, it would seem suspicious," Aerianna quickly replied, defending her actions, glancing nervously at Armbruster. She remained focused on his face, wondering if she had made the right decision to speak with him. Now, she wished she had stayed away.

Armbruster calmed down. He allowed himself to fall back into the chair, placing both his arms on the armrests and gripping the front with his fingers. He cringed at the pain, his fingernails now deeply embedded in the soft material. He appeared furious. To Aerianna, it looked like he had a death grip on the chair. His fingertips turned red, probably from the pressure he applied to the armrest.

"Okay, I suppose you have a point. I wanted to speak with him first, though I doubt Yarlen would have said anything to me anyway. I am sure he is still quite angry with me. When is Pauto planning to speak with him? I hope it is soon. We must resolve this situation as soon as possible. It is spreading like wildfire. We must contain it! I can only imagine how pissed off Alexis is at the moment. She hates rampant lies more than anything, and the uncertainty of the danger undoubtedly upset her even more." Armbruster shifted around in his chair, unable to find a comfortable position.

Armbruster relaxed his clasp on the armrests. He allowed his right hand to drop onto his leg as he stared at Aerianna.

"I agree. She is very exasperated right now. There will certainly be repercussions once we know more, and she will not sit idly by and continue to take threats. Alexis will seek revenge, and you know that, Sir." Aerianna shrugged her shoulders. She hoped he would agree.

"Yes, I do know her all too well. Though I am surprised she has not discussed this problem with me," Armbruster added, moping. He hated it when Alexis kept things from him, especially when she became silent, as it usually meant something was wrong.

When Alexis started acting secretly, it was a signal that something was bothering her. He wondered why she always confided in Aerianna, yet she kept him out of every aspect of her life. The more he thought about her lack of communication with him, the angrier he felt.

"I plan to speak with Alexis once I leave from here. I am sure there was no intention to keep you out of anything. I believe she is just frustrated and on edge. As you know, she does not like to admit any form of weakness," added Aerianna, wishing Armbruster would calm down. She watched, noticing his death stare.

"True. Thank you for speaking with me. I appreciate your candor, and I am grateful Alexis has you," replied Armbruster, pretending all was okay. He wanted to scream, feeling furious.

There was no denying it. Armbruster felt betrayed. Alexis left him out of another critical conversation and chose Aerianna's loyalty over his. Aerianna bowed politely and excused herself, eager to head back to speak with Alexis. Aerianna closed the door quietly as she exited the King's Chamber.

Outside the room, she leaned against the door for a second, wanting to catch her breath. Armbruster did not take the news as well as she hoped. Instead, he was outraged. Slamming his fists on the table caused Aerianna to jump in place, making her a nervous wreck. She did not know if he intended to hurt her or was violently angry at the circumstances.

At this point, Aerianna wanted to find Alexis quickly and update her about the conversation with Armbruster. Alexis would not be happy about Armbruster's reaction. Nonetheless, Aerianna would be sure to tell Alexis everything. The last thing she needed was Alexis accusing her of withholding vital information.

Back on Earth, Lorthana stood in front of the kitchen counter, preparing dinner the old-fashioned, human way. She liked cooking. It relaxed her and made her feel good. She disliked using magic unless it was for something important. As she chopped up the vegetables, she reminisced about Alexis and Zandorah.

She pondered what they were doing and if they were speaking to each other. *'Where is Gardone?'* she wondered. He had been away a lot lately, which was quite unusual. Lorthana could only hope Gardone would be home soon, and she would be able to ask him what was going on. She became increasingly annoyed over his constant absence from home without any explanation. Her instinct told her he was involved with something he shouldn't be.

At times, he became rather aggressive, turning the situation around and making it seem like Lorthana was overly suspicious. Lorthana was not stupid. She knew what he was doing. He was using reverse psychology on her, and it was not working. She knew his game and planned to continue pushing until she received the desired answers.

Gardone was still livid over Yarlen's imprisonment. He put a lot of effort into helping Yarlen with his acquittal. However, the final verdict was not in Yarlen's favor. No matter how tirelessly Head Legal Counsel Shorttar worked to help Yarlen, Alexis and her team ultimately prevailed. Yarlen was found guilty of treason and banished to the High Tower for the rest of his life.

Gardone was appalled by Alexis's dramatic exaggerations of events. When needed, she was a great actor and knew how to put on a show in front of others.

Alexis was a genius. She managed to spin every situation to make herself look like a victim. Sure, Yarlen had not made the best decision on how he handled Alexis. Nevertheless, Yarlen's intentions were clearly aimed at protecting Armbruster. There was no evidence presented to suggest that Yarlen had any intent or malicious behavior, although Alexis and her legal team attempted to portray it that way.

Alexis gloated when the verdict was announced, laughing and clapping, despite disregarding Yarlen's feelings. She glared at him with her usual sanctimonious smirk.

The Court Chamber erupted with instant chatter. Armbruster sat silently, unable to look at Yarlen as Pauto and his security team escorted him to the High Tower. Gardone was left speechless and looked shocked.

Gardone did not predict Yarlen would lose the trial. Though he assumed it would be a fight to win, Gardone had been hopeful Yarlen would be acquitted of the crime due to a lack of concrete evidence.

All the testimony presented appeared to be pure hearsay and crazy speculation. Gardone vowed to appeal the verdict on

Yarlen's behalf. However, the appeal would take strategic planning and time, and Gardone knew it would be an uphill battle.

Yarlen rested his head on the chilly stone wall of his prison cell, which was devoid of any furnishings. As he looked up at the ceiling, he noticed several cobwebs and big Cuvveys, resembling earthly spiders, making their nests in them.

These Cuvveys were of different shades, but they all had elongated, slender legs and glossy, oval-shaped bodies.

There were a few venomous varieties, though the purple Farwoh was the deadliest. One bite would produce instant death. The Cuvveys in Yarlen's prison chamber were harmless. They were the black Hoppie, identifiable by its cushioned and round feet on the end of its long legs. Alstromia also had a few spiders, since Alexis had brought some with her from Earth, as she adored their appearance.

The tiny window in Yarlen's cell was permanently sealed, making the room musty. The only source of fresh air in the room came from several small, square holes allowing airflow in and out of the chamber above the door. The floor had a rough gravel texture, which was also very dusty. Most of the walls were covered in sharp, pointy rocks to deter anyone from getting near them.

The only smooth wall was the one behind his bed. It allowed him to lean against the wall without cutting himself. He sat upright, with his hands by his side, his lunch tray on his lap. He heard a rustling noise, recognizing it was a set of keys unlocking the door. Yarlen opened his eyes as Pauto came through the door with a Security Commoner, looking stern.

"Hello, Yarlen," Pauto announced, looking at Yarlen, feeling powerful.

"Well, well. To what do I owe the pleasure of your company?" asked Yarlen sarcastically.

"I am here to ask you questions about the threats against the Queen."

"Why would you think that I know anything about that?" asked Yarlen, clearly without care.

"Let's see, maybe because of the verdict at your trial," retorted Pauto.

"You assume I know something. I do not. I have nothing to do with the rumors or the threats. Prove it!"

"My, my...aren't we defensive, Yarlen?"

"You give me too much credit. I am stuck in this prison with no means to communicate. How would I ever start any trouble for the Queen?" Yarlen rebutted, staring at Pauto.

"I find it hard to believe that someone as resourceful as you cannot make that happen. I am sure you have found a way."

Yarlen glared at Pauto, trying to hide his smile. He assumed someone would blame him somehow for the rumors and threats. However, he could honestly say he was not the one responsible, though he wished he was in a small way.

"Perhaps you have an accomplice? Maybe you are using someone on the outside to help you get your revenge?" continued Pauto.

"Again, you are reaching. I do not have that kind of power. I wish I did," replied Yarlen, starting to get annoyed at the line of questioning.

"Why can't we just cut the crap? Tell me what I want to know. I do not have time for this game. The Queen demands answers," screamed Pauto as he moved toward Yarlen, becoming increasingly aggravated.

"Tell the Queen: Too bad. I am not the one responsible. She is fishing in the wrong pond. I am innocent of the charges brought against me and was wrongfully imprisoned. Now, she wants someone to blame for this fiasco. It's amusing how she keeps pointing the finger at me for everything. You should be looking at others. Perhaps someone else holds a grudge? Did you ever contemplate that, Pauto?"

Yarlen was not interested in being labeled as the scapegoat for every negative situation. When the first threat surfaced, he knew instinctively he would be blamed for it. Now that the questioning had begun, Yarlen was getting annoyed. He would once again be in the position of having to defend himself. *'Such injustice!'*

The old Wizzard closed his eyes and let Pauto scream as he reminisced about the trial. Yarlen recalled looking at Alexis in her Red Robe of Tears, portraying the innocent victim. Her hands were folded as her fake tears ran down her face. Yarlen wanted to laugh at her phony act, but decided it was not the time or place. Instead, he turned his head away and tried his best to remain calm. Indeed, she was the worst being he had ever encountered, and he wished she would pay for her lies and deceit. Yarlen opened his eyes and glared at Pauto.

"Why don't you just leave? I have no information to give you. Honestly, even if I did, I wouldn't. I have nothing to gain either way. Just leave me alone," Yarlen yelled, now fuming.

"Very well. If that is how you want to play this," responded Pauto. He observed Yarlen waiting for him to say something else. He did not. Yarlen moved the food tray off his lap and rolled his eyes at Pauto. It was apparent that Yarlen was done talking.

"Anything else? I think we are done," announced Yarlen, kicking a few rocks on the cell floor and watching dust billow under his foot.

"This is not the end, Yarlen. I will be back again. I know you are hiding something. In time, you will tell me," Pauto reiterated, shaking his head and turning his back to Yarlen. He walked toward the door, stopping for a second to see if Yarlen was watching him leave.

On the contrary, Yarlen looked out the small window, ignoring him. The tall and burly Security Commoner opened the door, allowing Pauto to exit. He then followed, closing and locking the door.

Once the room was quiet and Pauto left, Yarlen contemplated their conversation. He folded his arms and closed his eyes. Yarlen knew this would not be the end of the investigation, and Pauto would be back. He would use force next time, probably even torture. Pauto was intelligent and resourceful. It was unlikely he would back down.

The Queen would continue to push him, and he would do what was necessary to get answers. Yarlen was sure this was just the beginning of a long and unpleasant situation.

Regardless, the inquisition would continue. Yarlen would need to prepare himself physically and emotionally if he wanted to survive.

Pauto stomped out of the prison chamber, infuriated. He did not believe Yarlen. He saw how nervous Yarlen acted and noticed his lack of direct eye contact. The old Wizzard was hiding something. Perhaps Yarlen was not the guilty party, but he knew who it was and protected them. Soon, Yarlen would give up his secret. He would see to it. Pauto would get the information. There was no doubt. Yarlen had no clue how miserable Pauto could make the interrogation if he chose to.

As Pauto exited the High Tower, his frustration grew even stronger. He came to the unsettling realization that Yarlen was fully aware of the reason for his visit and had actively worked to hinder the investigation. It was clear that Yarlen had no intention of cooperating. In fact, he would likely prefer death over assisting the Queen. Yarlen made his intentions known—he relished the idea of watching them struggle and would take pleasure in their discomfort.

In the Palace, Aerianna kept an eye on Alexis. She behaved cynically and curtly. Her impatience and irritation were obvious. She made huffing noises and pursed her lips, conveying her displeasure.

"When will Pauto provide us with an updated report? I want to hear about his conversation with Yarlen. Everything is taking too long. Maybe you should go find Pauto?"

"Alexis, Pauto needs time. I am sure he is talking with Yarlen as we speak. Give it a bit," Aerianna said, clearly defending Pauto.

"It is not fast enough. Are you sure Pauto is capable of getting the job done?"

"Yes, My Queen, he is your humble servant. Pauto will do what must be done to protect you," Aerianna responded, attempting to make the situation less tense. She could see the anger building in Alexis. She was on the verge of an outburst. Aerianna did not want to experience that. She did not wish Pauto to become a victim of her tongue lashings. Pauto was a loyal member of her staff. He deserved better.

"You're saying that to protect him. I told you, you cannot stay neutral. You care too deeply for him. Maybe you need to step back from this, and I will find someone else to work with me."

"No, I am perfectly capable of keeping my feelings for Pauto out of this. I will not let them interfere. I promise you. My loyalty is to you and all of Alstromia," retorted Aerianna, feeling slightly guilty. Yes, her feelings for Pauto probably did play a role in her decision-making, but she knew he was the only one capable of finding the truth about the culprit behind the rumors. She would never risk her life, or Pauto's, for that matter, by allowing her feelings to get in the way.

"Very well. If you think you can control this situation, then you handle it. Just remember, I will be watching both of you. I will also hold you both accountable. I will not tolerate you two lovers acting irresponsibly because you are infatuated with each other."

"Of course, I understand. I will discuss this with Pauto once I see him," Aerianna said. She was nervous, realizing her job was on the line. She could not afford to make any mistakes, as it could cost her too much. She stood by the door, about to leave.

"What are you doing, Aerianna? You're not leaving! We still have much to discuss," Alexis yelled, insistent.

"I assumed our conversation was over. I thought you wanted me to find Pauto and gather more information. Am I wrong?" asked Aerianna, her hand still on the door handle.

"Yes, completely wrong. I wish to discuss this in further detail. We have not resolved a thing. Also, why are we not searching for an accomplice? I doubt Yarlen could start this drama on his own. He is very clever, but his ability to do anything spiteful against me is limited. He must have magical powers or ways to communicate with the outside."

"Alexis, I concur. Pauto is probably already working on that, too."

"I was thinking about who would want revenge. Unfortunately, I cannot think of anyone other than Yarlen. I am astonished. Who would want to risk their lives to go against me?" Alexis vehemently declared.

Aerianna considered the possibility of an accomplice, but no one came to mind. She agreed with Alexis. There had to be someone else. Yarlen was currently powerless. He did not have many resources to help him. *'Who would be crazy enough to take on Alexis?'* she thought.

Alexis watched Aerianna as she mindlessly played with her hair. She gazed off into the distance as if in a trance. "What are you thinking about, Aerianna?"

"I think that we must dig much deeper. Have you spoken with Armbruster? I spoke with him earlier, and he was extremely upset that you hadn't discussed the rumors with him. I can only assume he is starting his investigation."

"I don't have the time, nor the energy, to worry about Armbruster. He is just trying to get in the way. It is what he does. I wish he would stay out of it, as it complicates everything unnecessarily. Armbruster is nosy," Alexis responded, aggravated. She shook her head, hands on her hips, ensuring Aerianna would see she was displeased. Alexis planned to address Armbruster and his need to meddle in her affairs. He forced his way into every situation, acting like a child constantly needing attention, and she was sick of it.

"Alexis, please let me locate Pauto. It may be useful to find out what he has gathered on your behalf. Once we know more, we can formulate a plan of action to take the next step in the investigation."

"You're right, Aerianna. Let's do that. I'll wait to hear from you. Please come back as soon as you speak with Pauto."

Aerianna excused herself after agreeing to return with news. She left the chamber expeditiously on a mission to find Pauto and gather information, so Alexis would temporarily back off. She walked quickly down the long and narrow corridor, her dark, purple cloak dragging on the ground behind her.

The corridor walls were made of dark gray bricks, and their surface looked smooth and shiny. Tall Ozar lanterns on the walls lit up the corridor, emitting a warm glow. The floor was glossy, and its unique purple shade seemed to change color as one stepped onto it, causing a distinct clicking sound.

Aerianna smiled, reminiscing about Pauto, but then her grin faded as she thought about Alexis. Alexis was forever needy and pushed everyone beyond their limits. Aerianna was tired of continually being the buffer between others. She knew technically it was her job, but it was getting old.

Arriving back at the Palace, Pauto set off to locate Aerianna. He wanted to tell her about his experience with Yarlen. Pauto assumed she was under pressure from Alexis to act quickly. He had every intention of shielding Aerianna from the Queen and her violent outbursts.

Standing in front of Aerianna's chamber, Pauto took his right hand and used his fingers to comb through his hair. He stood before the door with slight hesitation. Nervously, he straightened the collar of his shirt. He considered seeing Aerianna and informing her that Yarlen was useless. Pauto intensely disliked the idea of being unable to give her something, knowing Alexis would throw a fit when she found out he had not been able to force Yarlen to confess.

After pausing for a minute in front of the door to weigh his options, Pauto finally mustered the courage to knock.

"Come in," Aerianna announced. She was anxiously waiting to see him.

Pauto entered the chamber hesitantly. Aerianna sat in a chair near her bed, attentively studying a map and focused on a task.

"Hi there! What are you doing?" he asked, glancing at the map in her hands.

"Trying to figure something out. Nothing to worry about," Aerianna placed the map on the table next to her chair, her eyes still focused on the chart.

"Oh, okay. I just returned from speaking with Yarlen," began Pauto, hoping she would become interested in what he had to say. She seemed focused on other things. "He was of no help. I'm not sure he is the one responsible."

Pauto waited for a reaction. However, Aerianna continued to stare at the map, not listening. "I sat down and had a drink with him, and we sang songs," joked Pauto, thinking she would laugh or perhaps look up long enough to take her eyes off the object.

"Oh, right, interesting. Good job," Aerianna replied, not paying any attention to his words.

"Aerianna, are you even listening?" he asked, getting frustrated.

"I'm sorry, pardon me?" she responded.

"Never mind. I said Yarlen was of no help. I'm not sure he is responsible for initiating the threats. I do believe, though, he knows more and may even have some outside help."

"I am sure he does. There is no way he could develop a plan on his own. He has someone aiding him. I hope we can figure out who it is before something happens to Alexis. She continues to be relentless, barking out orders and acting nasty."

"Isn't she always?" Pauto laughed. He knew it wasn't funny, but he saw Aerianna's seriousness and wanted her to smile.

"I am sorry, I'm not myself today. I am under so much pressure from Alexis, even more than usual. I'm not sure why she is acting so super bitchy right now. I wonder if she is anxious?"

"Aerianna, Alexis is always that way. You know this. I do not know how you can work for her. You are much braver than the rest of us. I could not work so closely with her as you do," Pauto said, feeling bad for Aerianna. He knew exactly what she meant.

Alexis was a challenging being, and he tried to avoid her at all costs.

"It is okay. Some days, I wish I could quit and walk away from Alexis and the drama that seems to follow. However, I like my job, and I do care about Alexis. She is a different breed, that's for sure," she winked at Pauto, laughing.

Her facial expression said otherwise. He did not believe her and felt mystified as to why she stayed by her side.

The two sat in silence, deep in thought. Aerianna wanted to say something, but felt compelled to stay quiet. Pauto wished to hold her, reassuring her all would be okay.

Eventually, they would identify the guilty party and address the situation. Sadly, Pauto did not know where to start. Yarlen's reluctance to give any clues frustrated him.

Pauto was agitated, realizing the investigation was stalled. He wanted to figure out who to talk with next, but had no idea. It would require more information and more time. Sadly, getting valuable information took too long. He did not like the way the situation was turning out. Pauto felt as if his hands were tied at the moment, and he disliked the feeling. Usually, he was able to extract information rather quickly from his suspects. He could only hope some new clues would emerge soon.

"Aerianna, I believe we are finished for the day. There isn't anything we can do right now. I plan to speak with Armbruster and then retire for the night. Do you need me for anything else?" he asked, hoping she would ask him to stay for a while. He enjoyed her company, but she seemed too distracted to care, or so he thought. Pauto felt it was best to leave her alone. Maybe he would be able to think more clearly once he was not near her.

"No, there is nothing we can do. You should speak with Armbruster. It is getting late. I am tired and must update Alexis before heading to sleep myself."

Aerianna got up, hoping Pauto would leave. She was not in the mood for company. He saw her face and understood. He walked to the door slowly. She decided to follow. As he was about to leave, she walked up behind him and hugged him. Surprised, he turned around.

"Do you want me to stay?" he asked, wishing to be close to Aerianna and desperately wanting to remain in the room with her.

"No, but thank you. I appreciate all you have done today. It means so much to me." She blushed as she said it. Pauto embraced her and planted a kiss on her lips. She pulled back and looked at him, shocked.

"Sorry, I can't do this right now. We have to stay focused on the job. You do understand, right?" Aerianna asked, feeling embarrassed. She hated to brush him off, but she did not want to let their emotions interfere with the investigation. Later, hopefully, they would be able to figure out their feelings and discuss any future they might have together.

"Oh, of course, it's no problem. Have a good night," he briskly responded. He let her go and walked out the door without another word. He felt utterly rejected and distraught. There was nothing else he wanted to say to her. She had made it clear she did not want him.

Aerianna walked to the door and watched him as he strolled down the hall, his head down low. She felt awful. It was not her intention to turn him away. Aerianna liked Pauto very much, but promised Alexis to treat Pauto like any other staff member. Alexis was adamant, ordering Aerianna to keep her personal life out of the situation.

Aerianna refused to give Alexis any reason to reprimand her. She would figure out a way to speak with Pauto once he calmed down and explain why she backed off. The last thing Aerianna wanted was for Pauto to think she did not like him.

Nonetheless, he had to understand her reasoning. It was imperative that they remain professional until this crisis was averted. Somehow, she still wished she could have told him why she pushed him away. She felt guilty. Aerianna knew she should have talked with Pauto and explained the need for the distance between them.

Now, she realized he would probably avoid her, feeling awkward about what had happened between them. She took a deep breath and closed her chamber door, deciding to speak with Alexis so she could eventually sleep. She was tired and mad. Alexis would be waiting for her, and Aerianna was not in the mood to defend herself yet again.

Pauto headed toward the west wing of the Palace to speak with Armbruster. His feelings were hurt, and he felt awful. He shuffled down the corridor, letting out a heavy sigh. *'How did I misinterpret my relationship with Aerianna?'* He was sure she liked him, but her abrupt dismissal left him feeling glum and confused. He knew it was best to let it go for now.

His focus must be on the Queen's safety and the investigation. His relationship with

Aerianna would be put on hold. He rubbed the back of his head, walking and thinking, still utterly upset. He contemplated why Aerianna acted in such a way. It was not like her at all. Something must have happened. He could only assume it had everything to do with Alexis. The evening turned out to be quite abysmal and not the way he had envisioned it. He could only hope his conversation with Armbruster would go more smoothly.

Alexis sat on the long, stone bench on the Landing Deck, overlooking the valley. Two security guards stood in the background, keeping a watchful eye. Armbruster ordered extra security for Alexis due to the threats. She had her legs crossed under her cloak, attempting to stay warm. Her hands were on her lap as she stared ahead.

It was a chilly night, with a cool breeze that gently moved her hair in the wind. She brushed a few stray strands behind her ear, irritated.

Alexis looked up at the moons and speculated why someone would want to kill her. She realized not everyone liked her, but found the timing of the threats strange. It had been months since Yarlen's imprisonment and even longer since Loggane's death. *'Why now?'* she pondered.

None of it made any sense. She could not help but wonder if her child, Lilah, was also in danger. *'What about Armbruster?'* she thought. *'Is he safe? What should I do?'* Alexis felt helpless, and that was something she hated. She took pride in her ability to maintain control.

Alexis heard a noise. Startled, she turned around. Armbruster approached, looking concerned, with a snarl on his face. He appeared tired. He had big, dark circles under his eyes. His new beard looked scruffy. All in all, Armbruster looked like she felt inside—worn out.

"What are you doing out here, Alexis? Are you okay?" he inquired lovingly, gazing at her. His wife looked exhausted and preoccupied. She seemed stiff as she sat on the bench.

"Yes, I am fine. I had to get out of the Palace. I felt as if I was suffocating. I am tired of sitting around, waiting for something dreadful to happen. It is not a pleasant way to live."

"I am so sorry, dear. What can I do for you? Do you want to talk about it?" he asked, hoping she would elaborate on the subject. Her statement was quite unclear, which he found worrisome. He favored having open discussions, sharing his emotions, and working through issues together. Alexis was not inclined to share any of her feelings. She kept her thoughts to herself most of the time. Alexis gave him a fake smile, hoping to ease his worries, but he failed.

"Not really. I'm not sure what we should discuss at this time. I want to find out who is terrorizing my life. I always knew this day would come. I just never believed it would bother me so much."

"Honey, it is a serious matter. Everyone is quite concerned. Believe me. I am doing my best to find out who is responsible. We will find answers, I promise," Armbruster said with reassurance. He placed his hand on her shoulder.

"I know. Thank you for your concern. It will be alright. I am probably just tired. Perhaps after I get some rest, the circumstances will bother me less. There is so much uncertainty about this situation, and it is causing me too much stress." She turned her head away from him, embarrassed. Alexis did not like to display any form of weakness. It was not in her nature. She hated Armbruster witnessing her vulnerability.

"I plan to meet with Pauto and gather more information," declared Armbruster. "Have you had a chance to speak with Aerianna yet? I assumed she had a conversation with Pauto already."

"I have been out here for a while. I wanted to clear my head. I have not received an update from her. I assume I will shortly."

"Alexis, you should go to bed. Please, get some rest. I know you are tired and nervous. I promise that tomorrow, we can start fresh. There is no need for you to be out here in the cold alone," Armbruster said, smiling, trying to give her some hope.

"I am not alone," she replied with a slight laugh, pointing to the two security guards protectively watching. Alexis loathed having someone following her every move. It took away her privacy and independence. She was irritated but understood the reasoning behind the increased security.

Armbruster turned around, looked at the security detail, and nodded in agreement. "Yes, you are absolutely correct. I do not want you to be unattended. Someone will always be with you until we find out who is attempting to harm you. It is my job to protect you and Lilah. I will not fail. Since you don't want to talk, I think I'll head to my chamber. You know where to find me if you need me or anything." He bent down and gently kissed her cheek.

Alexis winked at him and squeezed his hand in response. Armbruster nodded and turned to head back inside. He planned to locate Pauto before calling it a night. Armbruster was exhausted but knew he would not be able to sleep until he had met with Pauto. *'Hopefully, he will have some good news to share,'* he said to himself.

Alexis remained on the bench for a while. Armbruster was greatly concerned. His demeanor was serious, and his smile was phony. She knew he was not feeling secure and probably worried about her and Lilah. Alexis stood up and walked to the edge of the barrier.

She braced herself against the stone railing, reflecting on the current situation. Alexis caught a glimpse of the High Tower, wondering if Yarlen was still awake. She shrugged her shoulders, not caring one way or the other. Finally, she turned around to head back to her chamber.

The security guards followed, watching her every move. Alexis wished to sleep and forget about the day. She hoped Aerianna had done her job and worked diligently to gather more data for her. Alexis demanded answers and wanted to know without a doubt if Yarlen was involved. If he were, she would make sure he would suffer. This time, he would perish. She would not allow him to get away with anything.

Pauto met Armbruster in his chamber. Armbruster rested his left hand on his cheek, waiting for Pauto to begin the conversation. Pauto sat across from Armbruster, sitting up straight and attentive. Both stared at each other, neither knowing how to begin the discussion. Pauto decided he would start, making it easier.

"Sir, my conversation did not go as I had hoped. Yarlen was quite evasive with his answers. He remained firm in his position that he was not guilty. He declared he was not the source of the threats. I tend to believe him, but he seems to be hiding something. There was minimal eye contact, and he acted fidgety throughout most of our conversation. These actions raised more suspicions for me."

"Is that so? What do you believe he is hiding?" asked Armbruster, intrigued, now rubbing his chin.

"I think he is attempting to throw us off track. He is diverting the conversation so that we will look elsewhere. Yarlen is shrewd and will not provide us with useful information that can ultimately help us in any way. Sir, we cannot underestimate him."

"True, Yarlen is a Warlock of few words. He has never felt the need to elaborate on any subject unless pushed. Perhaps he actually does not know who is responsible?" Armbruster added, wondering if there was any truth to the statement.

"No, he knows. I will find out. It may take a bit of time, but I will. I need your guidance in this matter. How far do you want me to go to get the information?" Pauto wanted to follow established protocol. All prisoners faced interrogation and torture if necessary. Pauto did not want to take the next step in his cross-examination of Yarlen without expressed permission from Armbruster. He observed the exhausted King, making a note of his facial expression and reaction.

"Pauto, follow protocol. We both know what needs to be done. I am looking for the truth."

"Sir, I understand. Thank you for your guidance. I will move ahead and initiate the process," Pauto responded. He felt relieved that Armbruster supported his plan to interrogate Yarlen, regardless of how painful it would be for him. Yarlen would be forced to speak and tell the truth.

"Sir, may I be excused? I want to discuss this with my team and make the necessary arrangements. If that is okay, I plan to start the next phase with Yarlen tomorrow."

"But of course, do it. We do not have the luxury of waiting. We must learn more about this situation to ensure the safety of my family. I will not tolerate Yarlen playing games with us. Pauto, thank you for your time," Armbruster stood up and extended his hand. Pauto shook it, nodded, and turned to leave the chamber. Pauto felt relieved that his conversation with Armbruster had gone well. He headed to the Security Command Chamber to brief his team. The day wore him out, and he was eager to get some well-deserved rest.

Pauto marched down the corridor with his arms crossed in front of his stomach. He reached his destination and entered the Security Command Chamber to address the security group. He intended to lay out the plan to force Yarlen to reveal what they wanted to know. Pauto assumed it would not be a difficult task. However, he also knew they needed Yarlen alive to serve the Queen better.

Pauto's team—five elite security members, sat silently, awaiting further instructions. Pauto took a seat and folded his hands. He nodded to them and began divulging his plan.

After his lengthy meeting, Pauto set off for his chamber to retire for the night. As he approached his bedroom door, he stopped and realized how extremely exhausted he felt. He rubbed his eyes and shook his head, trying to stay awake. Once inside his room, he eyed his bed, thinking about how great it would feel to sleep.

However, he quickly realized that his mind was way too active to rest. He removed his clothes, dressed in his long sleeping shirt, and crawled into the small bed.

His room was very bland. It contained a small desk with twisted Trimber legs. A plain black chair stood in front of the desk. His one nightstand stood beside the bed on the right side. The nightstand was square, black, and featured two small drawers. A tall, gold-colored standing lamp was next to the other side of his bed. Pauto used it when he read in bed at night. It was very bright, and the top was flexible, allowing him to bend it over the bed for better lighting.

In the right corner of the room stood a black wardrobe closet. It was arched, with two doors and three drawers. Pauto did not require much storage as he lived meagerly.

His uniforms were lined up meticulously in a row in the closet. His drawers held his undergarments, tunics, and sleeping clothes. He had very little need for casual clothing and owned very few. A large, black-framed, standing mirror leaned against a wall. He received it as a gift from his mother many years before. Though Pauto was far from vain, he did like to ensure he looked well-dressed in his uniform before starting his job every day.

He lay on his back with his hands at his sides, reflecting on the events of the day. Although he wanted to sleep, he found it difficult to do so. For a moment, he thought about Aerianna but chose not to linger on her or their relationship. It would keep him awake. Pauto wanted to concentrate on the process of interrogating Yarlen. He realized his eyes were finally getting heavy as he lay on the bed. He was glad soon he'd be asleep, his day done.

Armbruster sat down and crossed his arms as he rocked back and forth in a chair. *'So, Yarlen thinks he can lie? What is he hiding? Does he have an accomplice? What does he gain by retaliating against Alexis?'* Armbruster wondered, shaking his head. Yarlen underestimated Pauto and his team. They would do what was needed to extract the information from Yarlen. Unfortunately, for Yarlen, it would not be a pleasant experience.

Armbruster disliked the idea of torture but felt it was a necessary evil. The process would be excruciating for Yarlen, but it had to happen. It would all stop if Yarlen provided Pauto with what they wanted. It was simple enough. Armbruster was beginning to hate Yarlen. He was shocked that the stubborn, old Wizzard and Warlock had refused to aid them. It was clearly in his best interest.

Armbruster thought about how long it would take for Yarlen to succumb to the pain Pauto and his team would inflict upon him. Armbruster chuckled. He knew it would not take much. Yarlen was getting old and fragile. Armbruster contemplated speaking with Yarlen to encourage him to reveal all he knew, but realized it was a moot point. He was a determined Warlock, set in his ways.

*'At this point, why would he help us? We will not release him. Maybe Yarlen hopes he can work out a negotiation.'* Armbruster decided to share these thoughts with Pauto in the morning.

Aerianna picked up the fragile map. *'Where is the cave?'* She could not recall its exact location. She wanted to think in private, away from others. It was one of the places where she still felt safe. The cavern contained many of her items, including secret Spellbooks from her mother, Agnessa.

She cherished the few items she still had of her mother. Alexis was responsible for her mother's tragic death. Aerianna still felt bitter resentment toward Alexis for her mother's demise in many ways. Those feelings would need to remain buried for now. Aerianna would deal with that issue at a later time. She attempted to forget the tragic and life-changing event.

Still, every time she admired her mother's belongings, it opened the old wound and ached like a Cuvvey's bite. The emotions became too much to bear. It was one reason she kept her mother's things locked away in the cave. If the items were easily accessible in the Palace, it would become hurtful. She preferred to keep her life in balance as much as possible.

Now, she yearned to touch Agnessa's belongings, reminiscing about her deceased mother. She missed her so much. Also, she knew some of the Spellbooks could be helpful during this trying time. Aerianna planned to read and inspect the books privately, looking for anything useful. Perhaps she could find a way to help Alexis uncover the mysterious person who initiated this tragic and mysterious event.

Aerianna stared at the map and found the cave. It was small and inconspicuous, located on Tullah Mountain, off to the east. She planned to fly there soon, but now was not the time. She wanted to give the impression she was actively involved in finding the person making the threats. In some ways, Aerianna did not care. She felt that Alexis had made the situation what it was through her actions.

Alexis never thought about anyone else and believed it was okay to continue acting like she did. Aerianna realized Alexis would answer for her actions in time, and Aerianna did not feel sorry for her. Though loyal to Alexis, Aerianna also felt devoted to the rest of Alstromia. The Clan deserved a better person in charge, someone less selfish.

Alexis was probably the vainest and most selfish being she knew. She admired her will but was disgusted with her actions of late. *'Is Alexis capable of caring for someone other than Lilah? Probably not,'* she assumed.

Aerianna placed the map back into the desk drawer. Then, all of a sudden, the urge to leave hit her. She decided she would fly to the cave in the morning. Aerianna packed a bag and stuffed it with numerous books and other necessary items. Finally, she took her wand and placed it in the bag. It would be cumbersome to take her Ceptre.

The other day, during her visit to town, she overheard a few commoners discussing the rumors while walking along the river. She stopped to chat casually with a small group. They appeared nervous and tense about the situation. Aerianna spent a long time reassuring them that the Palace was secure and everything was okay. She promised them the Queen would be safe as well.

Unfortunately, she had a nagging feeling that the commoners did not believe her. They stayed quiet but looked away as if they thought she was lying. Aerianna disliked having to fib to them. Regardless, she knew it was her job to reassure everyone that all was well on Alstromia. She would do whatever it took to put on a brave face and pretend everything was under control. Aerianna understood that Alexis would not allow the rumors to continue spreading throughout the Clans.

Alexis lacked patience and felt no one should ever question her or any of the leaders. It was Aerianna's job to do her best to convince the Clans that the stories were just rumors. Aerianna hoped she succeeded, even if only for a while.

After packing, she placed the heavy bag beside her table and walked to the bed. Her gray padded headboard was very tall, almost reaching the ceiling. The bed was covered in a lavender blanket with six large pillows.

Aerianna loved her bed, which also stood very high off the ground. A three-step stool stood next to the bed, allowing her to climb into the bed easily. Once on her bed, she pulled back the fluffy, lavender velvet comforter and crawled in. With the sheet pulled up to her chin, she reminisced about Pauto. She wondered if he was thinking of her as well. She stared at the ceiling, noticing the shadows, contemplating whether Pauto was still mad at her. She attempted to dismiss the negative feeling nagging at her.

Aerianna concluded she was not ready to start a serious relationship with him. It would complicate their working relationship. He was a fantastic and understanding Wizzard and Warlock, though she feared getting too close. If things backfired, Alexis would surely harm him, and Aerianna was unwilling to take that chance. Aerianna pushed the thoughts of Pauto aside and tried desperately to fall asleep.

Then, suddenly, Alexis and Yarlen came to mind. Frustrated, she tossed around in bed, refusing to allow Alexis into her brain this night. That was more of a nightmare than a dream.

Aerianna chuckled to herself and rolled onto her right side. Deeply under the blanket, feeling warm, she approved of the silky, cream-colored sheets beneath her body. *'Tomorrow is another day,'* she said under her breath.

Feeling restless, she rolled onto her back again and stared at the ceiling. Without warning, she dozed off to sleep, dreaming of Pauto. Aerianna was deeply sleeping, blissfully unaware of what horrible event was about to occur.

In a small New England town on Earth, four Warlocks met in secrecy. The location was kept secret to ensure the privacy and safety of all involved. The room was small, and the door was locked. The shortest of the four stood up and began speaking in an authoritative voice.

"I believe we have to move quickly. The Queen and her security detail have started an investigation, and it appears Pauto is in charge. We cannot lose the opportunity. Why are we not implementing the plan?" he asked, staring at the other three. They remained silent for a moment. The oldest of the four then stood up to reply and make a point.

"Timing is everything. Some things are not complete or ready. We must remain vigilant. I did not expect anyone to take the hints seriously. I assumed we would have more time. Let us remain patient and continue with the strategy. Does anyone have a problem with this?" he asked firmly. He observed the others, awaiting a response, but the group shook their heads and remained quiet, not wanting to cause trouble.

At the same time, in the Palace on Alstromia, Alexis turned over in bed, feeling restless. She could not sleep. It had been a stressful day, and the Queen was in a sour mood. She did not know what to do, wondering, *'Should I meet with Yarlen by myself? Should I allow Pauto to take the lead in forcing Yarlen to reveal potential information?'*

Irritated, she turned over to face the window. The rain was falling, and a smirk spread across her face. Alexis adored the rain, and it brought her a sense of safety and comfort. Nothing thrilled her more than a thunderstorm with plenty of downpours. The soothing sound calmed her. As the water ran down the window, her eyelids grew heavy. She was aware that sleep was overtaking her. With a soft sigh, she surrendered to slumber, a smile gracing her lips as the thunder rumbled in the distance.

Across the Palace grounds, lightning flashed across the sky, illuminating Yarlen's cell as the rain came down loud and hard. Yarlen lounged on a rusty cot in the small, cold chamber, shaking. He craned his neck to look out of the tiny tower window, staring in the direction of the west wing of the Palace. He assumed Alexis was asleep, as well as the others. Yarlen theorized about Pauto and his team. He believed they would be coming for him soon.

There was no doubt that Armbruster had already ordered Pauto to do whatever was necessary to gain information from him.

Armbruster was a changed Warlock. He was no longer his ally. It was apparent at the trial and now even more so. Armbruster stayed away from him and stopped all communication. Yarlen assumed Pauto would be here soon. *'Will it be today? Will I be able to stand the pain and torture Pauto will inflict upon me?'* he wondered.

Yarlen felt sick to his stomach. He rubbed his head and gently rocked back and forth on his cot. His head throbbed, and he was tired. He pulled back the thin, gray blanket on his bed. As he looked at it, he shook his head with disgust. It was the lightest and most worn blanket he had ever seen. He wanted to cry.

Not too long ago, he slept in a large bed with a layer of thick, luxurious blankets. He remembered how wonderful it felt after a long work day, sliding under the top sheet and pulling the blankets up to his chest, feeling warm and secure. He missed his pillows and recalled plopping his tired head down on the plush cushions, feeling the layer of thick fluff under him. Now, he had a small, scratchy, tattered blanket that barely kept him from shaking in the frigid chamber. His life changed so quickly and drastically.

Yarlen understood that something needed to improve. He was unwilling to spend the rest of his life in prison or endure such miserable conditions. He yearned for his luxurious lifestyle back, convinced that he deserved it. His trial had been manipulated, filled with countless lies. He had been painted as the worst traitor imaginable. Yarlen recognized that he had been set up. Alexis twisted every word and scenario to benefit her case, completely disregarding his well-being.

Unfortunately, Yarlen came to understand that his hatred for her had only grown stronger. He recalled seeing her in the Council room, gazing at him with her fake tears, desperately attempting to win the sympathy of the Council Jurors. They had fallen for her performance. He remembered watching the Jurors' reactions as they were captivated by Alexis and her dramatic web of lies. Seated in her testimonial chair, she looked stunning while effortlessly playing the part of the victim.

She sobbed, intentionally staring at the Council Jurors, wanting to ensure they saw her heartache and pain. Then, hoping they would realize Yarlen's betrayal devastated her, she staged her biggest acting event yet. She grabbed her chest as if she had a massive heart attack, her eyes fluttered closed, and she fell hard to the ground, shaking. Instantly, there was an enormous commotion, and all attention was on Alexis, just as she so cleverly planned.

The trial was put on hold for a few hours while they allowed Alexis to regain her composure. After her medical team conducted an exam to ensure she was okay, Alexis bravely returned to the chamber, looking frail and scared. Alexis held Armbruster's arm, pretending she needed his support.

She strolled toward her seat, showing everyone that she had been even more traumatized by the trial. There was no doubt that Alexis was the award-winning actress that day. She gained the trust and sympathy of all Council Jury members. It took them less than five minutes to convict Yarlen of treason.

After the verdict announcement was read, she looked relieved but managed a coy smile, pretending she was still under duress. As Yarlen was removed from the trial chamber, he remembered staring at Alexis. She displayed a conniving smirk, though she tried to hide it. Instantly, he knew he was doomed.

The sound of the roaring thunder outside the Tower brought Yarlen back to reality. He closed his eyes, attempting to sleep and trying to forget about the trial, though it was difficult.

Unexpectedly, he heard the lock on his cell door click. Startled, he sat up. Instantly, he worried that Pauto and his team had arrived to begin the torture session. Yarlen felt his hands shaking as he stared at the door, waiting to see who was about to enter.

He felt tiny beads of sweat forming on his forehead. Yarlen noticed the chamber door open halfway. Then, he saw him standing in the doorway, smiling. Immediately, Yarlen grinned, threw the blanket on the floor, and stood up. He realized his friend was about to help him escape this horrible place.

Yarlen quickly approached the door with an approving smile. In the hallway, Yarlen turned around one last time to look at his tiny prison. Freedom was just seconds away. His face radiated delight as he confidently left his cell behind forever!

# CHAPTER 4

Yarlen strolled out of his prison chamber, as if he did not care whether or not he was caught escaping. Gardone turned around to glare at him with a disapproving look. Yarlen pretended not to notice Gardone's impatience. It seemed odd to him that Gardone had arrived alone, making Yarlen wonder why, but he would not question his actions.

Yarlen assumed Gardone would come to break him out of his prison. However, he expected others to accompany him to ensure his safe escape, especially since the High Tower was very well guarded, and he was never left unattended.

"Yarlen, come on, we must hurry. We do not have time for this. You are moving way too slowly," Gardone reprimanded Yarlen as he stared at him. Gardone preferred not to get caught freeing Yarlen from his prison chamber. The plan was in place, and he had every intention of ensuring it was executed flawlessly.

"I do not understand the urgency. There is no one around. You need to relax," Yarlen replied, continuing to stroll at a leisurely pace.

Before Yarlen could say anything else, Gardone grabbed Yarlen by his sleeve and slammed down his heavy Ceptre. The two disappeared into a red haze while the chamber door remained slightly ajar after Yarlen's escape.

The security guard appeared moments after their departure. He looked cautiously at the door before pushing it open all the way. Once the door opened, he panicked and stared at the empty room. *'Where is Yarlen? How did he manage to escape?'* he pondered. Scared, he bolted from the chamber and headed to find Pauto. He knew there would be trouble. It was going to be a long, long night!

Alexis was sleeping soundly until a ruckus in the hallway woke her up. Annoyed, she shot a glare at the door, curious about the commotion happening outside her room. Sitting up, she glanced out the window and noticed it was still dark outside. Frustrated, she tossed the heavy blanket aside and leaped out of bed. She made her way to the bathroom and looked at herself in the mirror as she washed her face. Dark circles were evident beneath her eyes, and Alexis felt concerned about her appearance. Her hair was tousled, and her lips appeared chapped and dry—signs that she had been neglecting her self-care due to stress and worry.

Once she finished drying her face, a sense of foreboding washed over her, as if something terrible was unfolding or had already occurred. Shaking off the feeling, she stepped out of the bathroom and headed to her wardrobe to select a cloak. After getting fully dressed, she resolved to speak with Aerianna, anticipating that she would have a handle on the situation and could update her.

Aerianna woke up to the sound of pounding noises on her chamber door. She looked around, confused, still not fully awake. *'What is happening?'* Her heart raced as she tried to force herself to wake up. She glanced at the door and yelled, *'Come in.'* Pauto appeared in her room, looking disheveled and anxious. He looked dreadful. Something was very wrong.

"I am so sorry to bother you, Aerianna, but we have a situation. I do not know how to break the news, so I will just say it…it seems Yarlen has escaped. I wanted you to know first. You will need to determine how you want to inform Alexis. I know this is not what you want to hear, but I wanted to inform you immediately. I have already tried to share the news with Armbruster, but he is not in his chamber. No one knows his whereabouts."

"Are you kidding me? Yarlen escaped? How did this happen?" She glared at him and continued her interrogation. "Where was the security by his chamber? I was under the impression that someone guarded the room every second of the day?" asked Aerianna angrily, now fully awake and sitting straight up in bed.

"I ordered it. However, the guard was hungry and left to get food, as his replacement never showed up at the scheduled time. We have no idea what happened to him. I can only suspect foul play. I have already alerted our entire team to find the missing security guard member and Yarlen. They are searching the Palace, but I do not believe Yarlen is here. The door to his prison chamber is still completely intact. So, I believe someone broke him out of his cell, possibly using magic. Yarlen must have an accomplice. It is the only plausible explanation."

"Great. This will not go over well with Alexis, and you know this! I am sure she will be enraged once she hears of this fumbled mess. Not to mention, she will be scared as we still do not know if Yarlen is behind everything. I must get dressed and speak with Alexis right away. You should continue searching for Armbruster and figure out our next move. I know you wanted to do the right thing by telling me about the escape, but preparing for the repercussions is challenging. Thank you for sharing the information with me, but I need to get ready. Please, leave!"

"Umm, of course, I am so sorry. I will update you once I have more information. I realize Alexis won't take this well. I am sorry," Pauto replied as he turned to walk out of the chamber, closing the door behind him.

Aerianna shook her head. She knew Alexis would be furious about the blatant lack of security. Surely, she would blame Pauto and his team for the negligence. Severe consequences were forthcoming, and Pauto would bear the brunt of them all. Aerianna would have to formulate a plan to shield Pauto and find a way to locate Yarlen. She hopped out of bed, bypassed her stool, and walked to the wardrobe to find something to wear.

Once she managed to get dressed, she stood in front of her full-length mirror, staring at her reflection. *'How will I break the bad news to Alexis?'* Aerianna did not feel well, overwhelmed with worry. Her hands felt sweaty, and her heart raced. She took a deep breath and decided to head out to see Alexis, regardless of the consequences. It had to be done.

Apprehensively, Aerianna stood outside the chamber, unwilling to enter. She knew Alexis would be insane with anger, as she held onto the door handle with hesitation, staring at the door. She wondered what was about to happen. Aerianna bit down on her lip and mustered up the courage to knock before entering.

"Alexis, may I enter?" she asked as she knocked on the door. There was no reply, so she pounded on it a second time, waiting for a response. After a few seconds, she pushed the door open by the handle and entered the chamber.

Alexis was not in her chamber, which was quiet and cold. The fire was out in the fireplace, indicating she'd been gone for a while. If she had planned to stay in the chamber, Alexis would have kept the fire going to stay warm.

Frustrated, Aerianna departed the room and decided it would be best to find Armbruster and Pauto. Perhaps they would know where to find Alexis? Aerianna felt the last few days had been bad, but now it would become a nightmare. Alexis would be on a rampage, looking for someone to blame, making life miserable for everyone around her. She felt a burning sensation in her throat as if she was about to throw up. She swallowed hard and continued to make her way down the corridor, passing a few Security Commoners. They marched in a row, carrying their Mesmer Ceptres. They moved out of her way quickly when they realized it was Aerianna. She nodded, acknowledging them, and walked on, eager to find Pauto and Armbruster.

Lorthana wandered through the house on Earth, searching for Gardone, but he was nowhere to be found. After several minutes of fruitless searching, she resigned herself to summoning Zandorah. Something was off with Gardone—he had been acting mysteriously and not sharing his plans with her. As she stood by the window, contemplating when her daughter might arrive, she suddenly felt a hand on her shoulder. Startled, she turned around to find Zandorah smiling at her.

"You wanted to see me, Mom?" Zandorah asked.

"Wow, that was quick. I did not expect you to come for a while. I know you have a lot going on right now, trying to keep peace on Iriss. I need to ask you a question about your father. Have you seen him lately?"

"No, why do you ask?" inquired Zandorah, looking at her mother. She pondered why her mother would ask the question in such a way.

"I haven't seen him much lately. He tends to disappear without warning and comes back home late. He spends most of his time in his room and doesn't communicate with me much. I have a feeling that he might be avoiding me. The situation seems off, and I suspect that he might be involved in something that he refuses to share with me for some reason."

"Mom, he is always secretive, you know that. This is nothing new. Are you sure you are not overreacting? He could be busy with his team, and maybe nothing unusual is happening."

"No, I know your father. He has been very distant and elusive. When I do see and question him, he is very vague. He finds ways to avoid answering my questions by diverting the subject. Gardone fabricates flimsy excuses and leaves. I can feel it. He is up to no good. He has changed."

"Okay, maybe you are right. Let's assume Daddy is doing something he does not want to share with you. What would it be? He is not an evil Warlock, and he is highly respected. He would not jeopardize his future by doing something unethical. We need to give him the benefit of the doubt and assume he is busy with his team and the Clan," replied Zandorah, attempting to reassure her mother.

However, Zandorah felt uneasy and worried. Her mom would not have summoned her on such short notice if she weren't highly concerned. Therefore, she felt her mom's intuition was probably correct.

"I hope you are right, Zandi. Unfortunately, I have no idea what to do. Have you spoken with Alexis lately? Maybe she knows what is happening with Gardone?"

"I have not. Alexis has not given me any of her time. I have tried to reach out to her, but she never makes an effort to see me. I think she is mad at me for some reason, unless something else is going on?"

"Seems odd, but we are talking about Alexis. She does her own thing and does not care what anyone thinks. So, I would not worry about her lack of communication," said Lorthana, wishing to comfort Zandorah.

"Whatever! Getting back to Dad, where do you think he is? What do you want me to do? You must believe I can assist, or you would not have summoned me. Tell me what you need."

"I am not sure. I wanted to find out if you knew anything about this. I don't want to panic, but I just cannot let go of this feeling," Lorthana shook her head, staring at her daughter.

Zandorah pursed her lips, wondering what was going through her mother's mind. She probably suspected something, choosing to remain silent until she knew for sure what it was. This only made Zandorah feel more uneasy about the situation.

"Mom, I am heading back to Iriss. I will talk with my security team to see what they have heard. I am sure there will be some kind of information, even if it is just hearsay. I will get back to you as soon as I have more information. In the meantime, it is best to act normally around Dad so he does not suspect anything. You do not want him to think you are suspicious. That will only prompt him to devise a new plan to conceal whatever he is doing. Let's see if he accidentally lets something slip."

"You are very wise, Zandi. I appreciate your support. Thank you for visiting me. I do feel better, and I suppose you are right. We have to let this all play out and see what emerges." Lorthana pulled her daughter into her arms and hugged her. She was grateful for her love. It made her feel good knowing she had one daughter who cared about her. Alexis was another story.

Gardone and Yarlen arrived swiftly inside the disguised, old hut on Earth. It was deeply hidden in dense woods. The main room was filled with Warlocks from different Clans seated quietly. Yarlen recognized most but not all. They nodded as

Yarlen and Gardone entered the main room, remaining silent.

"Brothers! I bring you, Yarlen. He is now free from his unfair imprisonment. Our plan worked perfectly, as did the *Shielding Spell*. No one was the wiser. Thank you for your help. I humbly ask that you remain vigilant. We will be under scrutiny before too long. The Palace will be looking for Yarlen, and we must protect him. Your job is to ensure that we can proceed with the next part of the plan. I expect everyone is prepared," Gardone announced, observing the others in the room.

"Sir, I think we should split up. We should not be seen together. I am afraid it would raise suspicion," declared Weston, the short and stout Warlock from the Western Clan.

"Agreed. I ask you all to return to your homes and families. Act as you normally do. We cannot afford to make a mistake. We must stay on track and continue our rebellion. The Queen will fall. Her kingdom will be destroyed and replaced by our new empire. She will learn the hard way that she has made a grave mistake. She should never have underestimated Yarlen!" declared Gardone proudly.

"Gardone, what about Armbruster? Have you spoken to him? Does he know about Yarlen's escape?" asked Weston.

"NO! We cannot involve Armbruster in our plot. He stands by his wife, the Queen. He will not be of any help. We need to consider him an enemy at this point. He cannot be our ally. That time has passed. He made his decision by refusing to protect his best friend and confidant, Yarlen. It is apparent that Armbruster is weak and uncooperative. He is of no use to us."

"Understood," replied Weston.

The group of Warlocks disbanded and returned to their homes. Yarlen, Gardone, and a select few other sorcerers stayed behind. Once alone in the hut, Gardone reassured the small group that all would turn out well.

"Yarlen, we have prepared a room for you. I have placed your Ceptre and other items in your small chamber. My team retrieved them from the Tower, where they were secured. I am sure you will want to retire and relax. Please know I am available if you need me. Feel free to summon me if you wish. At this time, I will head back to my home as I do not want Lorthana to become more suspicious of my activities. Lately, I have been gone often, and I worry she will start to ponder the situation and reasoning behind my absence."

"Gardone," started Yarlen, "I want to thank you and everyone for what you have done for me. You have no idea how much that means to me. I am forever grateful and at your service." He bowed before Gardone.

"My friend, I know you are thankful. You did not deserve such unjust treatment. There was no way I could allow you to suffer in that prison chamber for another day. I am shocked at the audacity of the Queen. She has no clue what she has unleashed. She truly is ignorant or plain stupid." Yarlen laughed at Gardone's comment, though he felt the same. The Queen made a mistake in underestimating his loyal followers.

Yarlen was angry about losing his friendship with Armbruster. After all, he had been his best friend. It was not easy to think of him as an enemy. Yarlen was tired. The only thing that cheered him up at the moment was the idea of retiring to his room and having his Ceptre and magical items returned to him.

Now, he would be able to practice his magic once again. Yarlen grinned, envisioning the Queen and her security team scouring Alstromia looking for him, unable to find a clue. It gave him all the energy he needed. He was ready to move on to the next step of the plan.

Yarlen entered his new room, feeling refreshed. He sat on the bed, admiring his Ceptre, leaning against the wall facing him. It brought an evil grin to his face, forcing him to laugh out loud. He felt secure for the first time in months. It was amazing to be free, the prison chamber far away and gone from his life. He was tired and decided rest was the best remedy. He curled up on his soft, warm bed, hoping to fall asleep quickly. The bed felt great, almost as comfortable as the one at the Palace. As his heavy eyes began to close, he looked briefly again at his Ceptre, smiling.

In another room in the hut, Gardone met with a select group of Warlocks who stayed behind, discussing the master plan's next steps. Once their short meeting ended, Gardone boldly announced his departure. He pounded his Ceptre down onto the floor, chanting.

Within seconds, Gardone appeared in his private room of the home he shared with Lorthana. He removed the cloak and hung it in the tall, dark blue wardrobe. Feeling exhausted, Gardone fell into the chair behind the desk and contemplated the night's events. All had gone smoothly. Overall, he felt satisfied with the outcome.

However, he needed to convince Lorthana that everything was okay. Gardone worried that she would remain distrustful and doubt his explanations and actions.

Gardone was about to try to find Lorthana when he noticed her standing in the doorway of his room, leaning on the door frame. She wore an emerald green cleaning gown with an apron tied at her waist. She looked tired, and her eyes looked droopy.

Lorthana had pulled her hair into a bun, and she wasn't wearing her Ceremonial Ring, which seemed odd to Gardone. He wondered if she had removed it because she was cleaning or mad. He could not recall ever seeing her without it. Ever since they married and conducted the Ceremonial Exchange, Lorthana wore the ring even when she mixed up toxic potions.

Therefore, it seemed particularly strange to him that she was not wearing it. Her hand rested on the doorway frame. It appeared that she wanted him to notice she had taken it off.

"There you are!" she exclaimed, giving him a crooked grin.

"Hello, Hana. Were you looking for me? I just got home a bit ago. The meeting with my team ran a lot longer than I anticipated. I am so sorry. What are you doing?" he asked, hoping she would not inquire about the details of his supposed meeting. He felt guilty about lying to her, and he stared at her hand, still contemplating why she was not wearing the ring.

"You've been gone a lot lately. Is everything okay, dear? Is there something I need to know?" Lorthana asked, demanding answers. She glared at her husband, making him visibly uncomfortable. He squirmed in the chair.

"Oh, there's no reason for you to worry. All is well. We have so much going on right now. I promise everything is fine." He turned his head away, hoping she would not look him in the eye. She had a way of making him feel uneasy. Maybe it was the fact that he was lying to her? It did not matter to him. He had to keep her out of it. He did not want her involved, especially since the plot included their daughter, Alexis. The less Lorthana knew, the better. If she found out what he was up to, she would probably contact Alexis immediately and get Zandorah involved as well. It was far better to keep everyone in the dark and out of his master plan. No one would ruin this for him.

"Alright, dear. If you say so. Are you coming to bed?" Lorthana asked, assuming Gardone would refuse, citing some stupid lie. She stared at him while placing her hands in her gown's pockets.

"Of course, I am tired and need my rest. Come on, let's get our sleep." He stood up and walked toward her. He held her hand as they walked to the bedroom, staring at her hand, still thinking about the missing ring.

Once in the bedroom, both changed their clothes and crawled into bed. The bed faced a window overlooking the garden. Lorthana rolled onto her side, away from Gardone. He faced the opposite direction, hoping to avoid further discussion.

Lorthana tried desperately to hold back tears. She knew he was lying to her, hiding something. She did not want to start sobbing and then have to explain why, especially since she had promised Zandorah to act normally and pretend she was clueless about what he may or may not be doing.

Once Lorthana drifted off to sleep, Gardone jumped out of bed and approached her nightstand. Curious if the ring was in the small, black box, he quietly lifted the top and looked inside.

There, he saw the beautiful ring, with its sparkly, pink center stone, surrounded by smaller black ones, all-natural Earth diamonds. He handpicked them for her for their Ceremonial Exchange because she loved diamonds. Feeling sad, he closed the box and headed to his study to continue working on the master plan.

Slowly, all parts of the plot seemed to be falling into place. Soon, Alstromia would be under his control. He would take the kingdom that rightfully should have been his from the beginning. Loggane failed miserably, and now it was up to him to finish the plan. As for Armbruster, he made a terrible choice in aligning himself with Alexis. He would become another casualty of the scheme. There would be no mercy.

Years ago, Gardone received the Ceptre of Stainnard from his father, Prince Stainnard. He was elated at the prospect of owning one of the most powerful Ceptres. However, he felt betrayed when his father gave the Ring of Stainnard to Loggane, Armbruster's nephew. It seemed absurd to Gardone that Loggane should be entitled to such a powerful ring.

However, his father, Prince Stainnard, explained to Gardone that only Loggane knew how to control it and worked with him to learn its secret powers. Gardone knew one day he would retrieve the family jewel and be the one to use its magic.

Gardone sat in his chair, absent-mindedly playing with the ring on his finger. He began to recall the night he retrieved it. It was the night Alexis murdered Loggane. Gardone had been supervising Loggane's activity from afar, staying out of sight and ensuring he followed the formulated strategy. Gardone observed Alexis arriving outside the hut and entering the building. He knew there would be trouble the moment he spotted her. Gardone continued to wait in the woods, keeping a watchful eye on the area. Alexis never came back out of the building.

After waiting an hour, he figured she had used her Ceptre and returned to the Palace. Gardone knew he had to act quickly to retrieve the ring, assuming Alexis had left it behind. He entered the building, headed to the hut's dark cellar, and aimed his Ceptre at the wall. Instantly, the lanterns lit, allowing him to look around. In the middle of the cellar floor, he discovered Loggane dead.

Gardone inspected Loggane's lifeless body. He grinned as he bent down and lifted Loggane's hand to remove the Ring of Stainnard, the Protection Ring. *'Too bad for Loggane. He failed to use the Ring of Stainnard to protect himself from Alexis.'* Gardone hoped

Alexis left it on his body, forgetting the power it possessed. He felt a jolt and burning sensation the second he slipped it onto the ring finger on his right hand. His hand twitched. Gardone instantly realized the ring was his forever!

Moments before Gardone entered the cellar, Alexis stood over Loggane's dead body. Alexis gazed at Loggane, feeling elated that he had died so quickly. She grinned as she stepped away and walked out the door, leaving his body in a pool of blood on the dirty cellar floor, forgetting about the powerful ring.

A long time later, Alexis stood in front of Aerianna's chamber, waiting for her to answer the door. She had already knocked numerous times, knocking louder and louder, becoming increasingly frustrated. However, there was no reply.

Alexis decided she had the right to enter and proceeded to do so. Unfortunately, the chamber was empty, and Aerianna was not there. Her absence infuriated Alexis even more. *'Where is she? Does she know what is going on?'* Alexis wondered. Fuming, she slammed the door as she left. She was about to head back to the chamber when Aerianna appeared, almost running into her.

"There you are, Alexis. I have been looking for you. I need to speak with you. Something horrible has happened," she said, noticing the livid look on Alexis's face.

"I assumed as much. I heard yelling outside my chamber and knew something horrible must have happened for there to be such commotion. So, what is it?"

"I think we should step inside my room. We need to talk, and I do not want everyone to hear," replied Aerianna.

"Oh, for goodness' sake. Okay." Alexis opened the door and entered Aerianna's room. Once inside, she stood by the door, waiting for Aerianna to divulge the bad news.

"Alexis, I think you should sit down for this. You will be very, very upset. Please!" Aerianna pleaded.

"I am not in the mood to sit. Say what you must. Just get on with it. I am losing my patience."

"Very well. If you are sure…there is no easy way to tell you this…Yarlen has escaped!" Aerianna blurted out, stepping back. She worried about how Alexis would react to such news.

"Excuse me? Did I just hear you correctly? Are you sure? There is no way!" screamed Alexis, eyes flashing in anger.

"I am so sorry, but yes! He is gone. I just spoke with Pauto. Yarlen has vanished. We still do not have all the facts."

"THIS IS NOT ACCEPTABLE," yelled Alexis, feeling like she was about to have a heart attack. She raised her fists to her mouth, shaking with anger, her knuckles turning white from the pressure.

"Alexis, Your Majesty…please. Have a seat. Let's talk about this calmly," begged Aerianna.

"Calmly? Are you kidding me? This is not a calm situation. Do you realize what has happened? Your idiot boyfriend has allowed a traitor to escape! I expect Pauto in my chamber right away. I do not care how you get him here, but do it NOW! Do I make myself clear? I want zero excuses. I will hold Pauto personally responsible for this incident. Mark my words!"

Before Aerianna could reply, Alexis stormed out of the room, heading to her chamber. She could not believe what had happened. *'How did Yarlen manage to escape? Who helped him?'* Alexis would personally interrogate Pauto and not tolerate any of his nonsense. His team had failed. Yarlen was free. The responsibility was Pauto's, and he would pay for the escape, maybe even with his life! Alexis did not care what Aerianna thought. Her worthless boyfriend failed. He did not do his job, allowing Yarlen to find a way to escape. Pauto had no idea what was about to happen to him.

# Chapter 5

Pauto conversed with his security team, attempting to gain information about Armbruster's location. His Second-in-Command, Andreh, informed Pauto that a security commoner had reported seeing Armbruster heading toward the High Tower earlier that night. However, no one found this odd, assuming he planned to visit Yarlen.

Pauto found it alarming and unusual in every way. *'Why would Armbruster sneak around in the middle of the night, potentially heading to speak with Yarlen?'* Everyone assumed they were no longer friends, especially after the trial. Pauto demanded his team keep an eye out for Armbruster and, in the event he was spotted, inform him of his location immediately. He knew very well there would be accountability to Alexis for Yarlen's escape. He was anxious to discover what, if anything, Armbruster was aware of. Pauto realized the more answers he could provide Alexis, the better.

He did not want to die or deal with her threats toward him. Pauto sat in the chair at the head of the big table in the Security Command Team Chamber (*SCTC*). He folded his arms and placed them on the table. Worn-out, Pauto leaned down and allowed his head to rest on his arms, closing his eyes. He had a throbbing headache and was not prepared for the drama about to unfold.

★*.★*.★*.★*.★

Armbruster stepped into the library, aiming to avoid security. He realized this might raise questions about his presence at the High Tower. He couldn't comprehend how Yarlen had managed to escape. Armbruster's plan had been straightforward—he intended to talk to Yarlen to let him know he would ask Alexis to reconsider his imprisonment. Armbruster would cite miscommunication and point out numerous errors presented during the trial.

However, Armbruster panicked once he arrived at the High Tower and discovered that Yarlen was missing. Refusing to be implicated in his escape, Armbruster quickly fled the scene. He wanted to find a quiet place to sit and think before informing Alexis about Yarlen's escape. Armbruster began to fret, realizing he had neglected to use his Ceptre to leave, so no one could have the opportunity to spot him.

Instead, he panicked and fled. *"Did anyone see me?"* Armbruster marched to the back of the library. Once feeling secure in the room, he waved his Ceptre in front of the fireplace, igniting a roaring fire. The flames blazed, adding warmth to the room. Feeling drained, he sank onto the large brown leather couch. He glanced around, wishing for solitude, and fortunately, he found himself alone. Armbruster was puzzled and contemplated how Yarlen had managed to get away.

Armbruster propped his feet up and leaned back on the couch. The flickering flames had a soothing effect, making it hard for him to stay awake. He shut his eyes, hoping the throbbing noise in his ears would fade away. He felt utterly miserable.

Alexis stood beside the fireplace in her chamber, impatiently waiting for Pauto and Aerianna. She knew their confrontation would be a disaster. Though she did not care too much about their reaction, she did not want to distress Aerianna. She needed her, and upsetting her would make everything more complicated.

Alexis considered Yarlen's escape and concluded he had been planning this for a while. It would have required an elaborate strategy, along with considerable assistance, to make it happen. The only thing unclear was who had aided him in his efforts. She suspected a few individuals but had no evidence to pinpoint one specifically.

She wanted to speak with Armbruster but was still unable to locate him. She wondered where he was hiding and why he was not around. Alexis was tired of his lack of attention to her needs. He seemed too focused on other things and put her needs last on his priority list. It was precisely the reason why she chose Aerianna as her Second-in-Command. Aerianna was there for her, always ready to listen and help.

Aerianna entered the Security Command Team Chamber in a hurry. She planned to locate Pauto as quickly as possible. Alexis was adamant that she deliver Pauto directly to her as soon as possible. Aerianna did not like it, but knew she would have to oblige.

Pauto looked up from the table and greeted her with a smile as she entered the chamber. He seemed genuinely happy to see her. Knowing she was about to share the bad news with him only made Aerianna feel even worse. He would not be pleased to be summoned to see the Queen.

"Pauto, I must speak with you right now," she forcefully said, looking directly at him.

"What is it? You appear upset," said Pauto, noticing the strange look on her face, beginning to worry instantly.

"Alexis is distraught. She wants to see you in her chamber immediately. Please, come with me. I do not want any trouble," she begged him, though guilt nagged at her.

"Of course, I will come with you right now. Why is Alexis upset? Is it something I have done?"

"I can only assume it has to do with Yarlen's escape. I am not sure. Please, let's go. I do not want to deal with her fury," replied Aerianna. She remained firm in her stance, waiting for him to stand up from his chair and follow her.

Pauto observed Aerianna. He had an idea of what was happening. Most likely, Alexis was upset with him and his team, probably holding them responsible for Yarlen's escape. He knew his conversation with Alexis would have consequential implications. He did not look forward to it, but he did not want to place Aerianna in a position to defend him. Pauto informed his team that he would be gone temporarily and walked up to Aerianna to leave with her, facing the angry Queen.

Armbruster stirred, hearing voices. He jumped off the couch, wondering who had entered the chamber. Armbruster recognized her instantly, and he grinned.

"I have been expecting you," he said.

"I should have come earlier. However, I wanted to wait until everyone was asleep. I brought my aide, Catharinne. She will wait by the door to ensure we are left alone to speak."

"Very well. Did you know Yarlen was planning to escape?" Armbruster asked her.

"I assumed so. He was not guilty… you know it. He would never have betrayed you or Alexis. He gave his life to the kingdom and left me for you. Shame on all of you," she yelled angrily, shaking her head in disbelief, her arms firmly folded.

"Be quiet," insisted Armbruster, giving her a stern look. "I know you are upset, Sonia, but I ask you to please keep your tone down. I do not need Alexis to find out you are here."

"Fine. Who helped Yarlen escape? Was it you, Armbruster?" Sonia asked bluntly.

"No, it was not. I do not know. I assumed you had. Now, I must assume otherwise. You would not be here if you had, am I correct?"

"You are! I had nothing to do with it, though I wish I did. I have wanted to see him for months. I knew Alexis would not have tolerated my presence. Though I must say, I was under the impression she respected me."

"She has always admired your powers. She knows you are the most gifted of all. I also think it scares her. She believes in you, but maybe she is jealous of you and your powers?"

"Ha, doubtful. Alexis does not care for anyone other than Lilah. She does not admire you, Armbruster. Why would she respect me?"

"Because you gave her what she needed. The power to overtake the kingdom."

"True. So, where does that leave us with Yarlen? Where exactly is my husband?"

Armbruster gawked at Sonia. He was slightly shocked to realize she was not the one to help Yarlen escape. It was his first thought. Now, looking at her, he considered who else could have been his accomplice. It would take more time to solve the disappearance of Yarlen Granderview Raventon, II.

Pauto and Aerianna stood before the Queen's Chamber, reluctant to enter. Pauto reached for Aerianna's hand, but she pushed him away, shaking her head. He realized she did not want to be affectionate at the moment, especially since Alexis was probably about to teach him a harsh lesson. Aerianna knocked on the door and waited for Alexis to appear.

"Come in," came the reply from the other side of the door.

Nervously, Aerianna and Pauto stared at each other, hesitating. Aerianna nodded at Pauto and bravely led the way into the chamber.

"Well, it is about time," said Alexis, glaring at Pauto.

"Your Majesty, I bring you Pauto. Do you wish for me to stay?" asked Aerianna.

"Yes, stay. You should be here. It does involve you. Pauto, approach," Alexis ordered, waving her pointer finger at him. Pauto walked up to Alexis and bowed meekly.

"Your Majesty, how may I be of assistance?" Pauto asked, feeling his legs become rubbery.

"How may you be of assistance? Are you serious? Do you have any clue why I summoned you to my chamber?" she responded nastily. She stood near the window of her room, holding her Star Ceptre in her right hand.

"My Queen, I can only assume it concerns Yarlen's escape. Am I correct?"

"I would think so," Alexis replied, continuing to stare at Pauto, her bottom lip protruding. She was furious, and it took every ounce of effort to control her emotions.

He posed the question, already aware of her answer, "What is it that you would like to know?"

"What would I like to know? Really? How about...how did Yarlen escape? Are you and your team so incompetent that you let this happen under your watch? Do you find this acceptable, Pauto?" she screamed, now standing before him. He could feel her warm breath on his face, causing him to back up. He felt his hands twitch.

"You are about as lazy and useless as they get, Pauto. I expected more from you and your elite team. Why is it I am here now having to reprimand you? I do not like being put in this position. You are not new to this team. You are supposed to be the leader, with a wealth of knowledge and information. Why am I faced with having to ask you where our prisoner is located? Can you tell me this, Pauto?" She waved her hand in front of his face, almost touching him, becoming louder.

"Your Majesty, I know you are upset…" he started to say, but she quickly interrupted him.

"Stop it! I do not want your excuses. I do not want to hear anything but the truth. I want to know why I should not hold you personally responsible for this fiasco!"

"Again, My Queen, if I may…I had nothing to do with his escape. My team watched him every second of the day on a rotating schedule. However, the security guard on duty was hungry, and his replacement was hours late. He briefly left to gather a meal and come right back. When he returned minutes later, Yarlen was gone. The replacement guard is still missing. I assume he was harmed, possibly murdered."

"Is that so?" she asked snippily, backing away from him, her eyes squinted.

"Yes, it is, My Queen. It is all I know. I have no other information. Well, there is another fact I just learned," Pauto reluctantly added. He did not want to tell Alexis, but knew it was necessary.

"Oh, really? What exactly is that?"

Pauto cleared his throat, hoping he could say what he needed to. "A member of my unit informed me that your husband, Armbruster, was sighted just before Yarlen's escape. The King was heading in the direction of the High Tower. We assume he was headed to visit Yarlen. No one suspected anything unusual about the situation until now." Pauto stepped back, fearing Alexis would punch him.

"Are you blaming my husband? Did I hear you correctly? Pauto, you are walking a thin line. I am about to put an end to your life. Be careful..." Alexis warned him, moving closer, ready to slap his face or whack him with her Ceptre.

"Your Majesty, I am only the messenger. I am sorry if this upsets you. Would you rather I lie to you and withhold vital information?" replied Pauto, hoping she would not kill him.

Alexis suddenly faced away, angrily marching back to the window. She tapped her foot, making huffing noises, then screamed aloud, "What the HELL?" She turned around to face Aerianna and Pauto. Aerianna partially hid behind the Warlock, attempting to stay out of Alexis' way.

"Do you suspect Armbruster? Seriously? Why would he do that? There is no way that he would be involved." Alexis screamed. She made an effort to calm herself down slowly.

"No, I do not believe he is the accomplice. I am just curious as to why he was there. It is suspicious behavior."

"As am I. Armbruster should never have been near the Tower," replied Alexis, fuming. "Aerianna, what do you think?" she asked, seeking support.

Aerianna peeked her head out from behind Pauto's back. "My Queen, I do not know," she responded, bravely emerging to face Alexis. "Maybe it was an innocent visit. Perhaps Armbruster went to see Yarlen to make amends? Maybe he felt guilty about the trial's outcome and wanted to speak with him to clear the air between them. I simply do not know." Aerianna looked at Alexis, trying to read her face and reaction.

"Hmmm, I suppose. Nonetheless, I still dislike Armbruster's presence at the High

Tower just before Yarlen's disappearance. It does not look good for him. It shines a negative light on the circumstances," declared Alexis, still clearly irritated.

"It makes him look guilty, Your Majesty. It does," agreed Pauto, nodding.

"Very well, then. We must locate my husband, Armbruster, and ask him why he was there and what he knows about Yarlen's disappearance. Pauto, I expect you and your team to find him. I do not care how long it takes. Bring him to me. Okay?" she said, looking directly at Pauto, making her demands clear to him.

"Yes, My Queen. May I be excused so I may inform the others of the new mission?" replied Pauto, hoping for a quick exit from the Queen's chamber.

"Yes, be gone and do it now. I want him found immediately!" Alexis yelled.

Pauto excused himself and ran from the chamber. He was grateful that Alexis did not harm him. It could have ended badly. He would not fail Alexis again.

Aerianna remained in the chamber, waiting for Alexis to bark out more orders. Alexis remained silent and bit her lip, rocking back and forth on her feet. She looked odd doing this, and Aerianna tried not to laugh.

"Alexis, how may I be of assistance to you?" Aerianna asked, hoping to change the conversation.

"I want you to supervise this mess and keep an eye on your worthless boyfriend. I do not need him screwing this up. I expect updates, many updates. Do you hear me?" she asked Aerianna.

"Yes, I understand and will obey. I will be there to supervise and will report back to you. I am so sorry this has happened. I can promise you this...Pauto will get to the bottom of Yarlen's disappearance, and we will find your husband."

"He better. His life depends on it. You are dismissed." She turned her back on Aerianna, hoping she would leave. Aerianna got the message and fled the chamber to locate Pauto.

Alexis strolled toward her bed, frustrated and seething with anger. She slumped down on it, crawling up to the pillows. With a pillow firmly beneath her aching head, Alexis wondered, *'Why did Armbruster visit Yarlen? It does not make any sense.'* It was a foolish move on his part, and she hated him for doing that.

Alexis worried about those who were supposed to be in charge. *'Did Pauto deserve his rank and title? Is he competent to handle Yarlen's escape investigation? Can Aerianna distance herself enough from Pauto to perform her job well?'* Why was it always up to her to ensure everyone could do their jobs?

Tired of her command staff's lack of initiative, Alexis planned to deal with that another time after all this drama surrounding Yarlen's escape was over. She closed her eyes, hoping her headache would subside.

Pauto sat at the head of the long and wide Trimber conference table and laid out his plan to find Armbruster. The team listened attentively, refraining from interruption. Once Pauto finished sharing his strategy and relaying specifics, he waited for their input. No one seemed interested in speaking up first, so Pauto took it upon himself to clarify the plan.

"Okay, the initiative has been described in full detail. We divide up and search each room in the Palace. Some of you will search the outside grounds in an effort to locate Armbruster and Yarlen. I want them located. Sadly, my life is on the line, and I expect everyone to step up."

Andreh, his Second-in-Command, spoke up. "Sir, we will get it done. Rest assured. We will not allow you to bear the brunt of this situation. The Queen will have her husband in her chamber before morning."

"Great! You are all excused. Thank you for your help," responded Pauto. He knew time was of the essence. Alexis would not allow this to go on for too long. He had to find Armbruster and deliver him to Alexis as quickly as possible to avoid another confrontation with her. Hopefully, they would also uncover clues about Yarlen's escape while searching for him.

Aerianna entered the chamber as others were leaving. She saw Pauto standing at the end of the table. He tried to smile at her, but she saw he was scared and restless. He nervously tapped his finger on the table, probably not realizing his actions.

Aerianna approached and took his hand, pulling him close to her. She placed her arms around his neck, giving him a long kiss that surprised him. She backed away a bit and whispered in his ear, "I'll never let her hurt you. I hope you know that. I love you!"

His eyes got big. Did he hear correctly? Aerianna loved him? Before she could say anything else, he hugged her and said, "I love you, too!" The two stared at each other and smiled. Aerianna let go of Pauto and headed toward the large window. She admired Tullah Mountain, thinking about the upcoming Battle Races. Pauto followed and stood beside her. He reached for her hand and held it gently in his. They remained silent, both thinking about Yarlen, Armbruster, and Alexis.

Sonia took a seat on the couch next to Armbruster, anticipating his response. He shot a glare in her direction. Struggling to respond to her inquiry, he shrugged and grimaced, unsure of what she wanted him to say.

"Armbruster, do you know where Yarlen could be?" she asked again, hoping he would give her some idea of where to find her husband.

"No, I do not know. I wish I did. At this point, I believe Yarlen has left Alstromia."

"Why would you believe that, Armbruster? What makes you think he is no longer here?"

"It is what I would have done," he quickly replied.

"I suppose that would make sense. What will he accomplish by escaping? He must know he will be found, and it is just a matter of time."

"Absolutely. Maybe Yarlen wants time to think? He must be working on a plan to return and make a stand with Alexis. Regrettably, I believe he is making the situation worse for himself. The longer he stays away, the more extreme the consequences will be. It is a dire situation, Sonia."

Sonia considered Armbruster's comments. She could not help but wonder why Yarlen had chosen to escape. Furthermore, she felt it was a horrible idea to leave Alstromia. Alexis would ensure he faced a new trial. He would never be able to see freedom again. She felt uneasy about the entire situation. She knew Armbruster would do his best to help locate him. She hoped Armbruster would find Yarlen before Alexis and her team.

On Earth in the hut, Yarlen awoke feeling refreshed. He stretched in his bed and smiled, feeling free. It felt amazing to look around a room filled with comfort and warmth. His prison chamber had been cold, bare, and lonely. Yarlen slipped his feet out of bed and stood up, sliding his feet into the leather shoes in front of his bed. He yawned and heard his stomach growling, feeling famished. Immediately, he decided to find Gardone or one of the others and inquire about the next step in the plan.

Once he found his way to the main living area of the hut, he inspected it. Everything looked different in daylight. The inside was large and bright. The sun shone through the front windows, making everything warm and inviting. He walked toward the kitchen area and riffled through a food storage closet for something to eat. He found bread and canned fish. Yarlen sat at the table, devouring the meal while patiently awaiting the arrival of the others. Why was he alone? It did not seem like a good idea.

He heard voices outside the building as he grabbed an apple out of a bowl on the table. Unsure if it was friend or foe, he slid out of his chair and stood behind the food storage closet door. Instantly, he recognized two of the voices. He knew it was safe to emerge from his hiding spot. He returned to the chair. Gardone entered the kitchen with one of his staff members.

"Well, good morning, Yarlen. I hope you slept well. Our security team stated the night was uneventful, and you did not have any unwanted visitors," Gardone announced. He sat down across from Yarlen, watching him eat.

"Yes, I slept quite well. It was a much more comfortable bed than the prison cot I slept in before, that's for sure. Thank you for ensuring my safety. I did not realize anyone was around. It was tranquil," responded

Yarlen. He stopped eating to observe Gardone.

"I promised you...you would be safe. I would not help you escape only to have you captured in the same night," said Gardone sarcastically.

"How was the rest of your night, Gardone?" inquired Yarlen.

"It was fine. I wanted to get back here to speak with you as quickly as possible to discuss the remainder of our project," said Gardone, eager to accelerate the plan.

"Okay. What do you wish to talk about?"

"What do you see as the next step? I want to send out a scout unit to dig a little deeper into what Alexis and Armbruster know. I am sure Pauto has his team actively looking for you by now. I can only assume they will make their way to Earth before too long. We must be ready. I am not sure you will be safe here for an extended period of time," added Gardone.

"I feel the same."

"With that said, I believe we need to move forward and execute the next step. Here is what I think we should do next..."

# Chapter 6

Alexis walked onto the Landing Deck, her favorite place on Alstromia, and admired her kingdom. She had a good night's rest but still felt a bit uneasy. She contemplated the threats on her life and wondered why Pauto had not yet updated her.

Alexis assumed he was preoccupied with Yarlen's escape, wanting to find him. She had not seen Armbruster since the day before, which added to her frustration.

Perturbed, she looked over her shoulder and saw two of the Security Commoners watching her. It made her feel better, but she was tired of having someone always on her heels. She valued her privacy, which was compromised when the threats emerged.

As Alexis stared into the distance, she realized she wanted to escape the Palace. It felt like a jail. She was constantly locked in her room to ensure her security. She yearned for freedom and decided to head to the stables and retrieve her Torrin. Flying relaxed her and allowed her some much-needed alone time. She wanted to get away from everyone and focus on herself.

Isolated in her chamber, she felt a wave of gloom and fear wash over her. Nothing irritated her more than having to abide by someone else's rules and restrictions. At this moment, it was Armbruster and Pauto who dictated her schedule. The thought filled her with frustration, and she was done complying with their demands. After all, she was the Queen!

With renewed energy, Alexis rose from the bench and approached the Security Commoners, eager and invigorated to pursue her own desires. "I will be heading to the stable as I plan to take my Torrin and fly for a while. I need time to clear my head," she boldly declared, not caring if they approved of her decision. Immediately, she felt better and more refreshed.

One of the Security Commoners gawked at her with disbelief, then stared directly at the other guard with a worried look, eyebrows raised.

"Your Majesty, I am under strict orders not to let you out of my sight. I cannot allow you to get on a Torrin by yourself. It is not safe," he stated cautiously, observing the Queen.

"You cannot allow me? Who do you think you are?" she screamed at him. "You do NOT tell me what to do or what I cannot do. Do you understand? I make that decision," she replied, standing before the quivering Security Commoner. He looked away and instantly backed down, feeling a sense of fright. The other security member stepped forward to address Alexis with bold confidence.

"My Queen, I must insist. We will accompany you. We can fly far behind you. However, we must protect you. Pauto ordered it so. We cannot let you put yourself in any danger. Please understand. Allow us to guard you and do our job, I beg you," said

Korbin, the much more outspoken security member.

"Very well, if you must. Let's head to the stable. I am tired of everyone telling me what I can and cannot do. It is extremely boring sitting in the Palace. For goodness' sake, I am not a prisoner," she responded, shaking her head. Alexis left the Landing Deck, forcing the other two to follow her to the stable.

Aerianna woke up, hoping that Yarlen had been apprehended. She was concerned that Pauto hadn't gotten any sleep and was anxious about Yarlen's disappearance. She intended to get ready and meet with Pauto to gather updates for Alexis. Aerianna didn't want to show up at the daily meeting with the Queen without any fresh information to provide. Before heading to her meeting with Pauto, she requested that her chambermaid, Darnellah, bring her breakfast while she prepared for the day.

Once, she had eaten her breakfast, which consisted of peppered white Harrluh—a slice of tender meat marinated in a creamy sauce, served over a grainy pasta, with little Smotes—small, round vegetables that tasted like peas, she planned her day. Aerianna always ate a hearty meal for breakfast and a light dinner. She believed that the strict meal plan helped her maintain a slim body. Finally, Aerianna was ready to locate Pauto, as she had a million questions and hoped he had the answers.

Armbruster contemplated returning to his chamber. He noticed Sonia sleeping on the couch. She looked peaceful, resting on her back. Her long, salt and pepper-colored hair cascaded over the side of the sofa. He had fallen asleep in the chair next to her, providing her with the comfort of the couch.

Catharinne was sprawled out on a blanket near the fireplace, snoring, sleeping on her side. The room was dark and cold.

Armbruster started a new fire to warm the room and add some light. Sonia propped herself up on the couch and watched him as he made his way back to the chair beside her.

"Good morning. How did you sleep? I am so sorry I took up the couch. You must have been very uncomfortable sleeping in that chair," Sonia announced, feeling guilty.

"No worries, I slept well. We should leave the library. I do not believe it is a good idea to continue staying here. Eventually, someone will come into the room to conduct research and find us. I will return to my chamber. You and Catharinne should head back to your home. It is not safe for you in the Palace. If Alexis gets wind of your presence, she will be less than pleased," added Armbruster, hoping to imply urgency. He looked at her, wishing she would agree.

"I suppose you are right. We should depart, though I plan to keep in touch with you. If you hear anything about Yarlen, promise me you will send a message. I will do the same in the event I hear anything." Sonia approached Catharinne and nudged her gently.

Once her assistant was awake, Sonia informed her of their plan to leave immediately. As the two Witches talked, Armbruster excused himself and exited the Library. He walked back to his chamber, apprehensive about seeing Alexis and Pauto. Without a doubt, they had been looking for him. His absence would have raised suspicion by now. He wondered if they knew Sonia had entered the Palace. Probably not, or they would have appeared in the Library ready to begin an interrogation. Alexis would be perturbed if she knew Sonia had been bold enough to appear on Alstromia.

Armbruster was glad there was no confrontation. He did not want to explain why he was in the Library with Sonia or at the High Tower. At this point, he only wanted to discover what everyone else knew about Yarlen's escape.

Armbruster planned to keep quiet about Sonia and her visit, if possible. Somehow, he was afraid Alexis would find out. Once she did, a fight would erupt between them. He did not want to think about that possibility. Instead, he decided not to focus on that and concentrate on Yarlen and his continued absence.

Outside of the Palace, Alexis strolled down the long path leading to the stables. Once she arrived at the building, she entered and walked to the Torrin's stall. She opened the single-latched door and patted the Torrin's head. In return, the beast lovingly rubbed her head against Alexis. The Queen spun around, hearing someone approach. Essten appeared, holding a set of dark purple reins, nodding.

"Good morning, My Queen. Would you like me to prepare your Torrin for a flight?"

"Yes, please. Also, could you ensure my security has two Torrins at their disposal as well? We will be gone for a while. I plan to fly to Tullah Mountain. I wish to depart shortly," replied Alexis, still patting the Torrin's head, excited about the flight.

"I will take care of it. Why don't you sit on one of the chairs out front while I prepare the Torrins? I will bring them out when they are ready."

"Sounds great. Thank you for your help, Essten," Alexis responded, feeling happy. She leaned in close, kissed her Torrin on the side of the cheek, and walked to the stables' front area. She stared at the uncomfortable-looking chair but decided sitting was better than standing while waiting.

Once seated, she discovered the chair was horrible. It was narrow and hard as a rock. She looked around and admired the scenery, attempting to keep her mind off the painful chair and her now aching butt.

The rain had stopped, and it was clearing. The Trimbers lightly swayed from the gentle breeze. The twin moons glistened. One was brighter as it was daylight, radiating warmth like the sun on Earth. She smiled as she sat with her hands folded in her lap, thinking about her upcoming flight. She thought about why she felt happy to be out of the Palace. More so, she was elated to be able to fly. She missed having time with her beloved Torrin, Elannah.

Alexis assumed her Torrin gave her the feeling of freedom she desired, something she currently did not have at the Palace. She wanted to leave the Palace grounds immediately. Alexis felt like a caged animal, despising the feeling. She watched the two Warlocks, both quite animated, as they talked by the stable. She contemplated what they were discussing.

The shy one nodded at Korbin as he screamed at him about something. Once Korbin realized Alexis was watching, he quickly lowered his voice, not wanting to get into trouble with her.

Alexis continued to observe their interaction, but her mind was elsewhere. She reminisced about Armbruster and wished she had a chance to speak with him. It still bothered her that he had been previously spotted by the High Tower the night of Yarlen's disappearance. She sighed, ruminating about the situation, wishing she were flying without a care in the world.

Minutes later, Essten emerged from the stable with her Torrin, ready for flight. He beamed as he handed her the reins.

"Here you go, Your Majesty. I wish you a safe and fun flight. Your security is behind the stable, waiting for you," he said. "They are ready to go."

"Great, thank you so much!" she responded, happy to leave. Alexis stood on a nearby stool and mounted her Torrin. She looked at Essten briefly and then allowed the Torrin to walk behind the stable. Her security detail waited patiently. Once all three were together, Alexis took the lead and headed off into the sky with a glowing smile, feeling elated. Finally, freedom!

Essten watched the three depart, wondering why Alexis wanted to fly. She had not been at the stable or on her Torrin in a very long time. He assumed it was stress-related. Essten heard about the awful rumors aimed at Alexis.

Many commoners were upset and worried about the impact on the entire Clan. Some discussed leaving Alstromia to live elsewhere. Essten did not want to abandon his home. He loved his work, family, and friends on Alstromia. As he thought about the circumstances, he shook his head and returned inside the stable to tend to the other Torrins.

As he brushed one of the beasts, he reminisced about his dead son, Collan. He missed him dearly. It seemed like forever since he had last seen him. Collan's tragic death still weighed heavily on his heart. The bitterness of such a cowardly act made Essten angry. It was hard for him to comprehend why someone would kill Collan just to silence him. He grieved the loss of Collan every day. He could also see the sorrow in his wife's eyes, making him want to cry.

Essten decided to finish his chores in the stable and head home to his wife, Marittaz. He knew she grieved but pretended she was alright, only to make Essten feel better. However, Essten knew she was not okay. He heard her cry, sometimes in her sleep at night, and it broke his heart. Their lives would never be the same without their beloved Collan.

Gardone stood beside the large table, wondering why Yarlen kept his mouth shut. He looked at him with impatience. Yarlen seemed preoccupied, not paying attention to anyone or anything around him.

"Yarlen, we need to discuss our next step. Are you okay?" inquired Gardone, exasperated.

Yarlen continued to stare aimlessly at the wall, barely blinking an eye. "I'm sorry, Gardone. What did you say?" Yarlen asked, realizing he was not attentive. He reached behind his head and fixed his long ponytail, fidgeting.

"I said… we need to discuss our next part of the plot. What is happening with you today? You seem very distracted. Are you sure you are okay?"

"Of course. I was thinking, that's all," responded Yarlen, now braiding his long beard. He hated it when his beard became frizzy and wild.

"Well, we should discuss our strategy and how we plan to implement each step. You need to snap out of it. I would appreciate your undivided attention," demanded Gardone with a scowl.

Yarlen saw Gardone's facial expression and realized he had to focus, or dire consequences would occur. Gardone would only tolerate so much of his non-attentiveness.

"I'm sorry, Gardone. I was mentally replaying my escape, contemplating the plan and the probable search underway to find me. My mind is preoccupied, but I promise you now have my full attention."

"Great, it is about time. I have some fantastic news to share with you. Part two of our plan has accelerated. It is by sheer luck, mind you, but it makes no difference. We will have her shortly, and then we can move on to our next part of the plot."

"WHAT? How did you manage it?" asked Yarlen curiously, feeling excited.

"You'll never believe our luck. Let me tell you…."

Armbruster walked up to Pauto as he stood by the conference table, discussing security measures with his team. The second Pauto saw Armbruster's approach, he instructed his team to leave. Pauto preferred to speak with Armbruster alone. Finally, he would confront the King and ask him why he was near the High Tower.

"Sir," he started. "My team has informed me the Queen has left on a Torrin flight with two security members. I have not heard where they are headed. I do not feel good about that situation. Do you know what she is up to?"

"NO! Why would she do that when there are threats against her? It makes no sense. Most of all, why would you allow that, Pauto?" yelled Armbruster, clearly enraged. He pounded his fists on the table and stood inches from Pauto's face, his eyes enlarged.

Pauto stepped back, worrying that Armbruster would harm him. Panicked, he moved to the other end of the table, watching him cautiously, keeping a considerable distance between them.

"Sir, I had no idea. My Second-in-Command just informed me about her unscheduled departure. I would never have allowed it unless I accompanied her. You should know that. The Queen's safety is my number one priority. I promise you!" Pauto calmly neared Armbruster, who looked more relaxed, with his face less angry.

"I know. I'm sorry for my overreaction. I do not understand Alexis at times. She makes me so mad. I would assume she would be much more cautious, given the circumstances. It is irresponsible for her to leave in such a way. She should have shared her plans with all of us. I can only hope she is okay."

"I will discover who accompanied her and what their plans are. I'll have my team reach out to Essten. He will probably know something," replied Pauto, attempting to reassure Armbruster and himself. He decided now was not the time to address Armbruster's visit to the High Tower or his possible involvement in Yarlen's escape. Pauto chose to remain silent.

"Very well. In the meantime, I will speak with Aerianna and see if she knows what is happening with Alexis." Armbruster excused himself and decided to locate Aerianna. He assumed she would have more information about Alexis's whereabouts. His wife never told him anything anymore. He would talk to her about this when she returned.

Aerianna summoned Darnellah and requested that she deliver the bags to the stable. She wanted to leave for the cave and spend the day researching some of her theories. Darnellah acknowledged the order and proceeded to take the luggage to the stable. Aerianna contemplated informing Pauto of her plans, but worried he would try to stop or convince her it was a bad idea.

She chose not to inform him. Instead, she planned to share details about her trip when she returned. Pauto was likely too focused on other pressing security matters, and she didn't want to disturb him.

As she left, she grabbed her wand from its stand on the desk and made her way to the stables, glad that she would soon be at the cave.

★ ⁎ ★ ⁎ ★ ⁎ ★ ⁎ ★

Alexis tilted her head as she gazed down at the valley beneath her. A sense of joy and freedom washed over her as the wind whipped through her long, black hair. The day was stunning, and she felt invigorated. She turned around for a moment to check that her security team was still following her. Once reassured of their presence, she signaled the Torrin to head toward Tullah Mountain.

As she continued her flight, she ruminated about the Palace and the threats. She hated the idea of having no control over the situation. Her return to Alstromia was supposed to give her power. She wanted to feel in charge, which is why she moved to Alstromia. It was her planet, her rules, and her control.

Sadly, now she felt the opposite—out of control. The Palace was supposed to be her refuge and not her prison. She thought about it for a second more and then enjoyed the flight and trip to Tullah Mountain. She would focus on fun and the feeling of freedom rather than the negativity in her life.

Looking ahead, she speculated why she had waited so long to fly. She promised herself she would not wait so long to do it again. This moment made her realize how much she had missed it.

Someday, she planned to teach Lilah to fly. She speculated about how much fun it would be to watch her daughter fly and observe her on her own Torrin. Alexis felt hopeful and content.

Alexis looked forward to spending time with Lilah once she was old enough to fly. Instantly, she recalled her first flying lesson with her mother, Lorthana. Alexis had been four years old. Lorthana had been quite patient with her. She had given Alexis a Torrin and taught her how to properly hold the reins and control the strong animal. Alexis learned quickly, mastering it all and highly impressing Lorthana.

It seemed as if Alexis had an instinctive talent for flying and handling her Torrin. She naturally took to it all and beamed with pride as she showed off for her family.

Alexis smiled as she zoomed through the sky, thinking about those good times. She also recalled Zandorah's escapade of flying, continually tumbling off her Torrin, ending up bloody from her falls.

Alexis laughed at her, feeling superior. That was the beginning of the rift in their relationship, very early in their childhood. She could not remember the last time she had flown anywhere with Zandorah or Lorthana. Thinking about it made her a little sad, though she would not focus on that now. She steered her Torrin closer toward Tullah Mountain, ready to relax and forget about her past.

Aerianna arrived at the stables. Darnellah stood next to Essten, handing him the bags. He carefully loaded them onto the back of the Torrin for Aerianna, securing them in place. He looked up and spotted Aerianna approaching by herself. He considered the reasons why she did not have any security with her. That seemed odd.

"Greetings, Aerianna. How are you?" he asked, happy to see her. She wore long, black pants tucked into tall boots, with a dark, gray cloak draped over the top. She looked cheerful, and her long, curly blond hair was braided, falling behind her back. She smiled at him, revealing her pearly white teeth and the noticeable dimples on her cheeks. Essten could not recall the last time he saw her look so refreshed or happy.

"Hello, Essten," she responded politely. "How are you? I see you have my Torrin ready for departure. Thank you, Darnellah, for your help. Please return to the Palace and clean the chamber. I will be back by this evening. I should return at a reasonable hour."

"Yes, I will do so," replied Darnellah as she bowed and excused herself. She jogged back toward the Palace to complete her chores.

"So, tell me, Aerianna, where are you off to today? Is anyone accompanying you on your trip?" asked Essten, attempting to gain more information about her plans.

"No, I am leaving by myself. I need time to relax. I want some breathing room. I will be near Tullah Mountain for a bit. I feel stifled."

"Hmmm, Tullah Mountain seems to be a favorite destination of the day," said Essten, thinking about the coincidence.

"Whatever do you mean, Essten?" asked Aerianna, her curiosity piqued.

"The Queen just departed for Tullah Mountain as well. She left with two of her Security Commoners not long ago."

"Wait. What? Are you sure, Essten?" Immediately, Aerianna panicked.

"Absolutely. The Queen stated that she wanted to leave the Palace and have some alone time. I assumed you and Armbruster knew of her whereabouts?"

"No, I did not. I also doubt anyone else knows. Did the Queen give specifics as to where she is going? To the top? To the cabin?"

"I'm sorry, Aerianna, she did not give me specifics. She was evasive in her answers. I wish I knew more. Is there anything else I may do for you now? If not, I need to finish brushing the other Torrins and head to the house to eat lunch," replied Essten, becoming worried.

"No, I assume that Alexis is okay. I will be back by nightfall. Please do not tell anyone. I need to finish some things and do not want others to know. I am counting on your discretion." She wanted it to be clear that he needed to keep his mouth shut. She did not want company, nor did she want anyone coming to look for her, especially not Pauto.

"Of course, Aerianna. Be safe, and see you this evening." He excused himself and headed to the end of the stables to finish his work.

Aerianna mounted her Torrin and flew off in the direction of Tullah Mountain. As she soared above the Valley of Grandu, she wondered why Alexis had also chosen to fly to Tullah Mountain. *'Did she inform Pauto or Armbruster?'* She assumed not. Her stomach felt uneasy.

Aerianna now wished she had stayed close to Alexis so something like this would not have happened. She could only hope the Queen was safe. It seemed odd to her that Alexis would have chosen to fly, given everything that was going on at the moment. Even stranger was the fact that she did not inform anyone about her departure.

With the current threats against her, it seemed like a stupid decision by Alexis. Aerianna would try to forget Alexis for now and focus on her trip to the cave. She would question Alexis later that evening about why she had chosen to fly off without notifying anyone else. Indeed, Alexis would have to agree it was a horrible decision. *'Oh well,'* thought Aerianna as she continued her flight to the cave.

Pauto appeared at the stable minutes after Aerianna's departure, accompanied by two security team members. He shouted for Essten, and he immediately appeared.

"Essten, I need to speak with you. It is my understanding that the Queen has left the area on her Torrin. What do you know?" he asked in an authoritative voice, lacking patience.

"Sir, she left a while ago with two security members. I do not know them, but she seemed familiar with them. They headed to Tullah Mountain. It is the destination the Queen gave me. Unfortunately, that is all I know." Essten hoped Pauto would not ask any other questions. He did not want to lie to him or tell him about Aerianna's quick departure. Essten did not like that both the Queen and Aerianna headed to Tullah Mountain. Strangely, neither seemed to know the other was going there. It appeared suspicious and very odd.

"I do not like it," responded Pauto, looking directly at Essten.

"I'm so sorry. I wish I knew more. Is there anything else I may do for you, Pauto? I am heading home to eat lunch and spend some time with Marittaz."

"Wait a minute," he said, grabbing his arm and stopping Essten's quick departure.

"Yes, what is it, Pauto?" Essten knew what was coming next, and he felt ill-prepared.

"Did anyone else show up at the stables today?" he asked, releasing Essten's arm.

Essten hesitated, getting scared. He was reluctant to tell Pauto about Aerianna. She would be furious with him if she found out he had betrayed her confidence. On the other hand, if he withheld such valuable information from Pauto and he found out, Essten would be in serious trouble.

Reluctantly, Essten considered his choices briefly and took a deep breath. "Sir, there is something else I must confess," Essten stated nervously, crossing his arms in an attempt to keep from shaking.

Pauto did not like the sound of that. He glared at Essten, feeling apprehensive. "What is it, Essten? Who else was here today?"

"Sir, it was Aerianna."

"Okay…and?"

"She came to retrieve her Torrin."

"Essten, please elaborate on the subject. I am not in the mood to try to guess the rest," Pauto said, getting angry.

"She stated her destination was Tullah Mountain. She did not provide details about the actual location. Aerianna insisted that I keep quiet and not share with anyone about her abrupt departure. Other than that, she confirmed her return would be sometime this evening. That is truly all I know."

"Damn it," screamed Pauto. "Why did you not summon me the minute she left? Better yet, why did you not inform our security that both Alexis and Aerianna left the Palace grounds? I find this unacceptable, Essten. I am very disappointed in you and your lack of initiative. Go back home and wait for me. I will be coming to speak with you later."

"I am sorry, Pauto. I will do as you ask." Essten left Pauto standing by the stable door and walked toward his hut. He practically ran down the hill from the stable, his head down. He felt he had betrayed Aerianna, something he did not want to do.

However, Essten realized he had made the right decision in telling Pauto about her leaving. After all, Pauto had to know as the Head Security Officer.

Pauto instructed his security team to locate Armbruster immediately. He wanted to brief him about the situation. Pauto hated the idea but knew it was necessary. Armbruster would be angry that Alexis and Aerianna left the grounds without anyone knowing their plans.

Exasperated, Pauto proceeded to the Palace, hoping Armbruster would take the news well or not hold him accountable for their unexpected trips. Pauto pondered why both Witches chose to leave at the same time. *'What is at Tullah Mountain? Why did they go separately? Why did Aerianna depart without a security detail?'*

Suddenly, it hit him. He remembered Aerianna examining a map when he was in her chamber, talking with her. The map was of Tullah Mountain, and she had circled certain areas in red. Pauto decided to see if he could locate the map in Aerianna's chamber. Maybe it would lead to useful information.

At this point, any clue or hint would be valuable. In the meantime, Pauto had to prepare himself for his talk with Armbruster before he saw him. Undoubtedly, it would be a nasty confrontation. Armbruster would expect Pauto to have all pertinent information about Alexis and Aerianna's departures. Armbruster could be very demanding and ruthless when he was upset. Pauto hoped they were safe and nothing awful happened to Aerianna or Alexis.

The burden of responsibility weighed heavily on him, and the mere thought of any harm befalling either of them made Pauto uneasy. He dreaded the idea of anything happening to Aerianna, and the guilt of not being able to prevent it was unbearable. As he reached her chamber, he let out a deep sigh and entered, hoping to find some valuable clues left behind.

# CHAPTER 7

Carmin picked up Lilah from her crib and cuddled her. The little Princess looked around, attentive, reaching for Carmin's face. Carmin figured she would feed and bathe the Princess since she had not seen the Queen in a while.

After tending to the Princess, she dressed her in her royal cloak. The baby seemed content but sleepy, her eyes closing as she glanced at Carmin. Wanting the baby to sleep, Carmin sat on the rocker and sang to Lilah. She watched her as she cradled the young Witch in her arms.

Once the child seemed asleep, Carmin placed her back in the crib and covered her with a blanket. She looked at the child lovingly, wondering why Alexis had not seen Lilah since the previous day. Carmin decided it would be wise to find Aerianna or Armbruster and determine where Alexis was hiding or if something was amiss.

As she left the baby sleeping in the chamber, she asked the security member outside to keep an eye on Lilah while she looked for Aerianna and Armbruster. The commoner agreed and sat on the tall stool by the door to keep watch.

Carmin hurried down the corridor, eager to locate Alexis and the others. She felt a chill in the hallway and wondered why it was so cold. Carmin shivered slightly and wrapped her cloak tighter around her body. Standing before Aerianna's chamber door, she knocked loudly with her fist.

After several failed attempts to get an answer from within the chamber, she left to find Armbruster. As she briskly walked toward Armbruster's chamber, her heart started racing. She began to fear something was wrong, and her mind was filled with horrible scenarios. It was abnormal for Alexis to be absent for so long and not see her child.

Additionally, it seemed strange that Aerianna was not around either. Pounding on Armbruster's chamber door, she hoped he would answer, though he did not. This only fueled her fears as a tear trickled down her cheek. She felt beads of sweat forming on her forehead, and her breathing became labored.

Frustrated, Carmin decided it would be best to find Pauto and ask if he knew their location. If not, she would inform him of their absence. Carmin felt an odd sensation run through her. She knew something about their disappearance was abnormal. Within minutes, Carmin arrived at the Security Command Chamber.

She entered the room without knocking, only to find it empty. She shook her head, wondering where everyone was hiding. Now, she felt nauseous with fear. Carmin concluded it was best to head back to check on Lilah. She would wait to see if the others would reappear. As she approached the Security Commoner outside Lilah's chamber, Carmin remained upset and puzzled.

"Has anyone been around?" she asked sternly as she stood by the door.

"No, no one has been here since you left. Is everything alright? You look upset," he asked, worried, noticing she looked sweaty and out of breath.

"I cannot find Armbruster or Queen Alexis. I have not seen Aerianna either. I tried to locate Pauto and the rest of his team, but they were all gone! It seems very strange, and I fear something dreadful has happened!" she screamed, now crying.

"Do you want me to see what I can find out for you?" he volunteered, wishing to make her feel better. He questioned what was occurring in the Palace.

"No. I would prefer you to stay here with us, just in case. Stay with us. Please remain outside the door. If you leave, we will be unprotected," Carmin said, almost begging him.

"I agree. I will stay. When my replacement arrives, I will request that he contact Pauto to get an update on the current status. Do not worry. I will ensure the safety of the Princess. No harm will come to either one of you."

He smiled, patting her shoulder, hoping to reassure Carmin, though he could tell she was still nervous. He had known Carmin for a long time, and it was not like her to act so scared or out of control.

"I know. I thank you. I will tend to Lilah. Please let me know the minute you receive any information on their whereabouts. Thank you!"

Carmin opened the door to Lilah's chamber. She walked to the crib to observe the child lying on her back, quietly sleeping with her thumb in her mouth. Knowing the Princess was safe in her crib made Carmin feel better. Feeling drained, she decided to take a small nap while the baby slept. She lay on top of the bed, her mind swirling with disturbing ideas that made her restless.

The security guard remained seated on the stool outside the chamber while waiting for his replacement. He wanted to find Pauto, but he felt that leaving Carmin and Lilah unattended was unwise. He leaned against the cold stone wall of the corridor and closed his eyes.

Back on Earth, Lorthana bent down in front of the vegetable bed. She carefully plucked vegetables from the garden, placing potatoes, carrots, and herbs into her basket. She craned her head up to the sky, allowing the warm sun to beam down on her. She loved Earth and all it had to offer. It made Lorthana feel good. She stood up and walked to the flower bed on the other side of her large garden, proceeding to cut some roses and wildflowers to make a bouquet for the dinner table.

Lorthana planned a romantic dinner for Gardone and hoped he would be home soon. She would make Gardone's favorite Earthly dish—pot roast, dilled potatoes, carrots, and gravy. She knew he would love it and hoped it would evoke a conversation between them. Gardone had been away a lot lately, and she wanted to spend some quality time with him.

As she contemplated his absence, she thought about Alexis and Zandorah. She had not heard from either in a long time. Their staying away worried her more and more each day. She hoped they were well.

Lorthana returned home and walked to the kitchen sink, where she proceeded to clean the vegetables and herbs in a large bowl. Once done, she arranged the roses and wildflowers in a tall, clear vase.

She smiled, admiring the pretty flowers as she placed them on the kitchen table. She sang happily, preparing the meal for Gardone, hopeful he would be home soon.

Yarlen sat outside the hut with his eyes closed, lost in thought. Gardone left him alone to return to his home. He informed Yarlen that Lorthana was becoming irritated and suspicious about his constant meetings away from home. Gardone decided to spend time with her to keep her from snooping into his actions. It would appease her, if only for a while.

Meanwhile, Gardone entered the kitchen and smelled the roast cooking in the oven, making him happy. He loved eating a good, home-cooked meal. Lorthana stood in front of the kitchen sink, washing dishes. She turned around when she heard him enter.

"Hello, dear. I'm so glad you're home. How was your day?" She was happy he was finally home.

Gardone approached Lorthana and planted a kiss on her cheek. He walked to the nearest chair and pulled it out from under the table. He sat down, gazing at her, admiring her beauty.

"Mmmm, it smells so good. Are you making a pot roast? It sure smells like it."

"Yes, I sure am. I am also making you dilled potatoes and carrots, your favorites," Lorthana responded, beaming with pride. She was delighted that he looked surprised that she had cooked for him. She wanted nothing more than his approval. He never had time for her anymore. Lorthana often felt neglected and sad.

"Aww, thank you, honey. That is so sweet. I am famished and cannot wait to eat. I will change and sit in the living room. Please, let me know when dinner is ready," said Gardone, hungry and eager to eat.

"Go relax. It should be ready shortly," Lorthana said, opening the oven door to check on the roast and vegetables. She pulled out the large roast. The delicious smell made her drool. She closed the oven door, giving the meal a few more minutes to cook. She could have used magic, but cooking relaxed her and gave her a sense of purpose.

Gardone walked to the bedroom and changed into his favorite pair of pants and dark blue tunic. Right after, he entered the bathroom and washed his face. He looked into the mirror while drying his face and wondered what Yarlen was doing, hoping he stayed out of sight. Gardone hated leaving him there with the others watching him. He remained hopeful that everything would be okay until his return.

After changing and cleaning himself up, Gardone shuffled to the living room and sat on his oversized, cream-colored chair. He put his aching feet up on a stool and rested his head on the back of the comfortable, old chair. It occurred to him that he felt tired, so he closed his eyes to relax.

Lorthana placed the juicy roast on a platter in the kitchen, adding carrots and potatoes around it to make it look nice. She put two plates, napkins, and wine glasses on the kitchen table.

After the meal was on the table, she reached into the pantry and withdrew a Porting Wine bottle to complement the meal. Once everything was ready, she took off her apron and walked to the living room to inform Gardone it was time to eat.

Lorthana found Gardone sleeping in his chair, lightly snoring, his feet on a stool. She wanted to let him sleep, but had spent too much time cooking and refused to waste a delicious meal.

"Gardone," she said, gently shaking his shoulders. He woke up instantly and sat up straight, looking confused. For a second, he forgot where he was. Lorthana stood over him.

"I'm so sorry, Lorthana," he said, looking up at her. "I guess I fell asleep. I must have been exhausted. Are we ready to eat?" he asked, yawning.

"Yes, dear. Everything is on the table in the kitchen. Come, let's eat."Lorthana led the way.

The two walked into the kitchen. Gardone smiled as he admired the meal on the table. He felt hungry and could not wait to devour the delicious-looking roast and vegetables. The two shared their meal in silence. Gardone smiled at Lorthana as she watched him eat. She wanted to say something, but he seemed disinterested in idle conversation. Instead, she allowed him to enjoy the meal.

Alexis landed with her Torrin in the field adjacent to the cabin atop Tullah Mountain. The spacious, two-story building boasted four bedrooms and three bathrooms. Its exterior was a striking dark gray with white trim around the windows. The wide double doors were made of silver metal, featuring inlaid glass at the center. It had been custom-built for her several years earlier when she first arrived in Alstromia. The cabin felt like the ideal retreat. The thick woods behind it ensured privacy, while the front of the cabin faced a sheer cliff, offering breathtaking views of the River of Miccay and the valley below.

Alexis handed her Torrin's reins to one of the commoners and approached the front door. She reached inside her cloak pocket and withdrew a set of keys.

Abruptly, she stopped and giggled. She aimed her Ceptre at the door and unlocked it, laughing at the fact that she almost used keys to unlock it. *'Why am I so lazy about using magic?'* Alexis wondered. She pushed the door open on the right and entered the cabin. It smelled musty inside. The house had not been utilized in months.

In the main living area, Alexis started a fire with her Ceptre, and sat on one of the two large couches. She loved the cabin, especially the privacy and seclusion it offered.

Outside, the two Warlocks secured the three Torrins to the Rein Poles adjacent to the cabin by the stable. One of the Security Commoners whispered to the other. He nodded and walked toward the building's doors.

★*.★*.★*.★*.★

Not far away, Aerianna circled over the east side of Tullah Mountain on her Torrin, holding the map. She firmly sat on the beast, struggling to keep her balance. The wind picked up, and her Torrin attempted to fight the strong breeze while maintaining a safe distance from the ground. Aerianna almost fell off the animal twice, trying to lean to one side to gain a better view of the landscape below. As she gazed at the map, she recognized the bushy area below and steered her Torrin in that direction. The cave's opening was hidden by overgrown Grabbleberry bushes, recognizable by their hot pink leaves and dark purple fruit.

Aerianna directed her Torrin to the left side of the bushes, hoping she would be able to land safely. Her poor Torrin continued to struggle against the wind but managed to touch down without any issues. As they landed, Aerianna gently patted the animal's head, thanking her for a safe flight. The Torrin flicked her head and mane as if she knew what the pat on the head meant.

On the ground, Aerianna jumped off the Torrin and led her by the reins to the cave's entrance. A large Trimber stood to her right side. She tied the Torrin to the Trimber, allowing the animal to graze on the green vegetation below.

Aerianna walked behind the Torrin to reach up and retrieve her bags. Next, she walked to the sizeable Grabbleberry bush before the cave and parted it with her Ceptre, revealing the secret opening. Aerianna turned around one more time to ensure she was alone. She quickly entered the cave on a mission.

Alexis sprawled on the couch, watching the fire, feeling relaxed. She contemplated her current situation and was curious about what Aerianna, Armbruster, and Pauto were doing. Her eyes were closed, and she was listening to the crackling fire. She thought she had heard one of the front doors open and assumed it was one of the security Warlocks. Not worried, Alexis kept her eyes closed. It was not until she felt the sharp, piercing pain that her eyes popped open.

That was when she saw Korbin looking down at her. She felt a sickening, stabbing pain in her skull and unwillingly closed her eyes.

"There you go… off to sleep, My Queen," Korbin said as he watched her eyes flutter. He bent down to check on her, ensuring she was okay. Alexis was breathing, so Korbin assumed she was just knocked out from the blow to her head. He placed her Ceptre back in its stand by the front doors. Right after, he turned around and searched for the other security member.

Pauto boldly entered Armbruster's chamber, eager to share the news he had gathered from Essten. Armbruster sat attentively in his desk chair.

"Sir, I have spoken with Essten. I have to tell you… I am not happy. It appears Aerianna and Alexis have both flown off to

Tullah Mountain. I am not sure why," explained Pauto.

"I did not realize Aerianna had gone with Alexis. That is news to me," said Armbruster.

"Sir, she did not. They both left for Tullah Mountain, but separately. I do not believe either knew what the other planned. Essten was quite surprised. He said it seemed like a strange coincidence, and I must agree wholeheartedly."

Armbruster jumped up and started to pace around in circles frantically. "I do not like the sound of that. What do you think they have discovered? Why would they both head to Tullah Mountain? Why would neither of them inform us? It does not add up. We must investigate and dig deeper."

"Sir," started Pauto, "I am worried. Only Queen Alexis took security. Aerianna flew off alone. I am not even sure who accompanied the Queen. My team is checking the current roster to determine who it could have been. I assigned Korbin to her detail, but no one else was assigned. I do not know who the second Security Commoner is with her."

"Crap!" screamed Armbruster, even madder than before. He finally stopped pacing and stood in front of the fireplace, rubbing his beard.

"Sir, what are your orders?"

"I don't know, Pauto, figure it out. It is your damn job. DO IT. I cannot believe you allowed this to happen. I am furious. I am telling you—you better find them safe and sound. Get out of here and locate them!" he yelled at Pauto, acting belligerent.

Pauto bowed his head and, without a word, ran from Armbruster's room, heading to the Security Command Team Chamber to address his team. He assumed Armbruster would react that way. Though he hoped Armbruster would have been a little nicer, given that both Witches left without prior notice. Regardless, he did not blame Armbruster for his loud response.

Far away from the Palace grounds, Aerianna entered the damp cave and searched for the torch on the wall. The first torch was positioned immediately to her right. She felt it and lit it with her Ceptre. She walked further into the cavern, lighting one torch after another to ensure plenty of light.

After she lit the fifth torch, she found herself in an enormous open area. Along the back wall stood a large shelf filled with books and trinkets. She approached the table and chair and took a seat.

Aerianna dropped the bags next to the rack and opened one of them, pulling out the stack of maps. One chart depicted the cave's location, and the others showed the cabin on Tullah Mountain. She considered flying to the cabin later to relax, but she did not know how long she would remain in the cave. Aerianna started to wonder what initiated the threats against the Queen.

She jumped off the stool and pulled a few old books from the shelf. She nestled into the comfortable chair to begin her research, snacking on a handful of Grabbleberries she had picked up by the front of the cave. She loved the sweet and sour taste of the berries.

First, when you chewed them, they burst with sweetness. Within a few seconds, the surprising tartness followed. Depending on the ripeness of the fruit, some could taste quite sour, almost unbearably so.

Aerianna felt happy and approved of her decision to visit the cave, her favorite spot. Surveying the cavern, she still felt her mother's presence. Her mom, Agnessa, had brought her to their secret place for the first time when she was just a young Witch. Agnessa kept many of her potions and books in the cavern and its tunnels. Her mother lovingly referred to the place as Rianna's cave—her nickname for Aerianna. The two spend a lot of time in the hideaway.

It was in the cave where Aerianna learned a variety of fantastic spells from Agnessa. With a lot of patience and love, her mother taught her how to vanish quickly, cast a *Concealing Spell,* change her appearance, make potions, and many other skills.

Aerianna recalled sitting on her mother's lap while reading aloud from a Spellbook. She could still remember the way her mother smelled—like lavender. Perhaps that was why it was her favorite flower from Earth and her favorite color.

After Agnessa's death, Aerianna kept the cave hidden from everyone else. She did not want to share the valuable books, potions, or other magical items her mother stored there. Agnessa informed Aerianna at a young age that it would be their refuge—where they could work on perfecting their magic without any interference. Now, Aerianna valued the secret chamber hidden within the mountain even more than before. She would never reveal its location to anyone.

The Palace was abuzz. Security team members interviewed other Palace personnel, attempting to discover the reason why Alexis and Aerianna headed to Tullah Mountain. Armbruster returned to his chair and sat in silence. He was exasperated and could not comprehend why Pauto had not protected Alexis or Aerianna, keeping them safely at the Palace. '*How could he have been so thoughtless? Their departure was risky.*' Armbruster decided to head to the Security Command Team Chamber to ensure all was done to locate Alexis and Aerianna. He refused to leave it to Pauto.

At this point, Armbruster felt zero trust toward Pauto. He was starting to worry more and more about Alexis as the hours passed. '*Where is she?*' he wondered.

Alexis awoke with a pounding headache, which made her nauseous. She opened her eyes, cautiously attempting to survey the situation. Squinting, she saw the fireplace ahead of her. Alexis realized she was still on one of the couches in the main living area. She attempted to sit up, only to feel her hands and feet tied.

Frustrated, she squirmed around, trying to sit up to see where the Security Commoners had gone. In her attempt to sit, she fell off the couch and hit the hard Trimber floor, causing a thud noise.

A few seconds later, she managed to lean her back against the front of the sofa, facing the fireplace.

Suddenly, Alexis felt something warm running down the side of her head, assuming it was her blood. Alexis looked around, hoping she was alone. The two evil Warlocks seemed to be gone or outside. She spotted her Ceptre in its black stand by the front entry. Alexis knew she had to get to it somehow. Just as she was about to crawl to the door, she heard voices approaching, and she recognized one of them. She decided it was best to stay where she was, leaning against the couch.

Korbin entered the cabin alone, looking toward the couch where Alexis had been tied up. He found her sitting on the floor, wide awake as he approached. She glared at him with her head soaked in blood. She rolled her eyes, wanting to kill him.

"What the hell do you think you are doing?" Alexis screamed. The pounding in her head intensified, making her cringe.

"I see you are awake, Alexis," he said, ignoring her glaring stare.

"I am going to kill you once I am untied. I hope you know that."

"Of course, you will. Calm down. I could have killed you, but he wants you alive. So, we will sit here and await his arrival. It shouldn't be much longer."

"Untie me immediately. If you do, I promise I will NOT kill you," screamed

Alexis, causing her head to pound even more than before. At this point, she was feeling dizzy.

"Now, now... You really shouldn't exert yourself so much. I am sure your head hurts. I hit you pretty hard with your Ceptre. How ironic is that?" he said, laughing, feeling empowered. He loved that she was vulnerable and unable to move.

"Korbin, you have made a grave mistake. I am not sure what was promised for my life, but I guarantee you will be better off siding with me."

"Yeah, no! That will not happen. He said you would say that. I am perfectly happy with my decision. Do you want me to help you back on the couch, or do you intend to stay on the floor until he arrives? Oh, and don't even think for one second about summoning your Ceptre. Someone extraordinary cast a *Block Spell.* You have zero powers right now. I'm sure you probably already figured that out!" Korbin stated, smirking.

"I will stay here. Who exactly is *'he'*?" Alexis asked, wondering who would be so crazy as to try to harm her. "Don't tell me it's Yarlen," she continued, her eyes squinting as he observed Korbin. Yes, she realized her powers were not working.

Alexis attempted to retrieve her Ceptre, but nothing happened. What frustrated her the most was that she knew only a powerful Witch or Warlock could use the *Block Spell*. It was challenging and time-consuming. She wondered, *'Who cast the spell?'* Alexis contemplated it briefly but felt too nauseous to dwell on the subject.

"Why don't you stop? I won't tell you anything. Let it be a surprise when *'he'* appears. I think you will like it, ha-ha," he responded, feeling in control.

"You have made a mistake. Now you will live with the consequences," Alexis retorted.

"I'm not worried. I will be safe. He will ensure I am unharmed."

"Good for you," Alexis managed to say before throwing up. Her eyes darted toward Korbin as vomit dripped from her mouth. She hated him so much at that moment that she could feel her heart racing in anger.

Korbin shook his head, laughing as he exited the room. Alexis stared at the vomit in her lap, ready to scream. Korbin returned to the room with a white towel, looking smug. He handed it to her with a smirk on his face. She could not grab it since her hands were still tied.

Reluctantly, he bent down to wipe the vomit off her mouth. Alexis took the opportunity to bite his hand. She sank her teeth into him, feeling the bones of his hand crunch between her teeth. She tasted blood in her mouth. He pulled away, screaming, noticing the blood dripping from his hand. He snagged the towel and used the clean end to stop the bleeding. Alexis grinned at Korbin with blood-stained lips.

"Big mistake, Alexis. I wanted to be nice to you. Now, you can just forget it. I will not help you. You screwed up, big time." He left the room, letting her sit with the vomit on the floor in front of her.

Armbruster met up with Pauto in the Security Command Chamber. They inspected the maps on the stone walls. One of the security members circled areas in dark red ink on the chart. Pauto rose from his chair to scope it out. He ran his fingers across the map and stopped at a circled spot. It looked familiar to him. Earlier, he attempted to locate the map Aerianna had been inspecting in her chamber. Unfortunately, she hid it or took it with her to Tullah Mountain. Pauto smiled as he turned around to face Armbruster.

"I think I know where Aerianna went," he said confidently, looking at Armbruster.

Armbruster raised his head and said, "How do you know for sure?"

"Sir, I saw Aerianna's map in her chamber while talking with her. She had a similar map with a red circle drawn around this area." He pointed to the map on the wall and circled the spot with his finger, showing Armbruster. Filled with curiosity, Armbruster approached the map on the wall and glanced at the area, nodding in response.

Pauto pointed to the bushy area on the map. "Sir, I believe she went here," he announced.

"Okay, let's round up our team and head that way. We must find Aerianna. Maybe she knows where Alexis is," said Armbruster, feeling empowered.

The team assembled an hour later at the stable. Essten had prepared six Torrins ready for the flight. Pauto turned around to look up at Tullah Mountain. He spotted a green, glowing dome covering the entire top of the mountain.

"Sir," he said, pointing at the mountain, attempting to show Armbruster. "What is that?"

"What? OH NO! It is a *Protection Spell Shield.* Someone wants to keep others out. Who would have done that?" replied Armbruster. He continued, "I want to know what they are attempting to stop. It is an intricate and very complicated spell to cast."

Armbruster, Pauto, and four other Security Commoners mounted their Torrins and flew off in the direction of Tullah Mountain, hoping to find Aerianna, not knowing how they would be able to penetrate the *Protection Spell Shield*.

Lorthana watched as Gardone devoured his dinner. He looked content. Lorthana hoped he would enjoy the meal and her company. After some time, she initiated a conversation, which led to a lengthy discussion. Though, he did not share much information about what he had been doing or where he had been lately.

Lorthana felt he was evasive, keeping the details to himself. Gardone finished his meal and placed the napkin on the table.

"Hana, my dear, you outdid yourself. The dinner was delicious. Thank you for making such an amazing meal for me. It was quite a good surprise. I am also delighted that we had the chance to catch up and talk. I have missed you. I also wanted to tell you how beautiful you look today." He reached for her as she sat across from him, holding her hand.

"Thank you, Gardone. It was my pleasure. I'm so glad you enjoyed the meal. I liked it as well. It was nice to have some time with you. You have worked so much lately. Will you be able to stay home tonight with me?" she asked, assuming the answer would be *'no.'*

"I am so sorry, Lorthana, but I have to go. I still have one meeting tonight. Some of the other Warlocks are coming in from other planets. We have some critical things to discuss. I'm sure you understand," he replied quickly.

"I understand. I am just glad we had this time together. Why don't you get ready and head out? I will clean up and head to bed."

Lorthana stood up and started cleaning the kitchen, angry over Gardone's departure. She knew he was hiding something, which irritated her even more. She threw the dishes into the sink, accidentally breaking a plate.

Annoyed, she looked down at the shattered dish and began to cry. She wanted to speak with Zandorah, but figured waiting until the next day would be best. After carefully removing the sharp pieces from the sink, she continued cleaning, wondering what Gardone was preparing to do. She knew there was much more to his *'meeting'* than he would let on.

Gardone changed his clothes and dressed in his black cloak. He hated running late for meetings, especially one this important. He could not wait to see her in person and initiate the next step of the plot.

Aerianna spent hours in the cave conducting research. She was at peace and loved the lack of interruptions. As she read from the *Book of Insight,* she realized there were some valuable spells she could use to help Alexis pinpoint the source of the threats. However, it would have to wait until her return to the Palace. She packed the book and a few others, securing them in one of the bags. Aerianna decided to head to the cabin to read and relax before returning to the Palace.

As she left the cave, she extinguished all the torches and closed the entry with her Ceptre to ensure its location would stay non-visible. She packed the Torrin with her luggage and untied her from the Trimber. Once seated on the Torrin, she pulled back on the reins, directing the animal toward the field for take-off.

Quickly, she soared over the area. She would be at the cabin soon, relaxing and enjoying the rest of her day.

Alexis felt her back aching and experienced a massive headache. Her nausea finally disappeared. She stared at the vomit on the front of her cloak and the floor. *'Where is Korbin? Where is the other guard, and who is 'he'?'* She could not wait to meet the elusive person.

The flames in the fireplace were dying out, making the room feel cold. Alexis shivered and wished she were back at the Palace in her chamber. Suddenly, she heard voices, assuming someone was about to enter the cabin.

"She is sitting in front of the couch by the fireplace. She refused to move to the couch. I left her there," said Korbin.

"Okay, thank you. Please wait outside. If I need help, I will summon you," replied the other. He cautiously approached the couch, excited at the prospect of seeing her in such a vulnerable state. Alexis would be shocked to see his face. He knew it.

"Hello there!" he said with a crooked smile on his face, gloating.

"Are you kidding me?" she responded, unimpressed to see him standing there.

"Were you expecting someone else?"

"Gardone, you cannot believe you will get away with this, do you? What are you thinking? This will end badly for you. I would ask you to reconsider your actions," said Alexis, remaining aloof.

Gardone hated the fact that she seemed too calm and blasé about his presence. She did not appear hysterical or mad. Instead, she looked indifferent.

"I do not regret my actions. Implementing the plan took a long time. You helped accelerate the process by insisting on visiting the cabin. It was perfect, and I thank you for your stupidity," Gardone, her father, said, laughing.

"Daddy, I can only assume you are in cahoots with Yarlen. Where is that traitor? Is he with you? Just wait. Once I am free, you will both regret your actions. There is no turning back. You have sealed your future."

Gardone contemplated her words. He frowned at Alexis. He refused to provide her with any clues, wanting her to suffer and feel the frustration of not knowing what lay ahead.

Alexis continued to stare at him. She knew he would not share his plans nor give her information. He was a stubborn Warlock. Suddenly, she felt terrible for Lorthana, her mother. Did she know what he was doing? Surely not. There was no way Lorthana would have allowed such a betrayal. Why would her father do this to her? Did he not love her? It seemed ridiculous. Alexis wished Armbruster were there to witness Gardone's actions in person. Then, she thought, *' No one knows I am here!'*

Alexis started to panic. The reality that she had not informed anyone other than Essten of her plans made her nervous. *'Will Essten tell Pauto or Armbruster about my departure to Tullah Mountain? Will Aerianna begin to worry when she cannot find me? How long will it be before someone comes to my rescue?'* Alexis sighed but did not want to seem panicky in front of Gardone, who noticeably enjoyed her captivity.

"Alexis, I would like to get you on the couch. Please allow us to provide you with clean clothes and tend to your wound," stated Gardone, pretending to be concerned for her welfare.

"You know, DAD, you can just drop dead. I do NOT want anything from you or your damn minions. How can you betray your daughter? What kind of screwed up father are you?" she viciously screamed at him.

"Now, now, dear, calm down. There is no need to get so excited. Everything will be over soon. You will be fine. I do not plan on hurting you, Alexis. I do care for you. I need you out of the way. That's all!"

"Whatever! You are a pig! I feel sorry for Mom. What a worthless husband you turned out to be. She deserves better," responded Alexis, wanting to scratch his eyes out.

Gardone observed Alexis and considered her words. They meant nothing to him. He did not care what Lorthana thought. He had fallen out of love with her long ago and was going through the motions around her. She was simple, yet not the woman he had hoped she would be. He wanted someone powerful and relentless. She was neither.

"Alright. So be it if you want to sit here with vomit in your lap. I have other things to do. I will be back later. I had hoped we could sit down and discuss your future reasonably. I get the sense that you are not interested in engaging in a civil conversation. So, I am leaving. You can stay here until my return."

"Hold on…untie me. Let me get cleaned up, and we can talk. I do want to hear your plan. After all, I assume it affects my future and kingdom," Alexis said, wanting him to stay so she could attempt to pump him for more information.

"Why the change of heart, dear?" he snidely retorted.

"I do not plan to sit here with vomit and blood splattered all over me. I have enough self-respect to know I am better off allowing you to help me. So, can we please begin our conversation?"

"But of course, my dear," he said, summoning Korbin to ask him to help Alexis. Gardone instructed Korbin to locate clean clothes for Alexis and to allow her to get cleaned up. He wanted to ensure she was safe and clean. No matter what, he did not hate her. He just wanted her incapacitated while he worked on completing his master plan.

Korbin searched through the tall wardrobe in Alexis's big bedroom. He found some of her clothes and took them to the living area. He approached the couch, where she sat still tied up.

"Here you go, Alexis," he said as he shoved the clothes toward her. She looked at him and shook her head, unable to grab them. She extended her arms and showed him her wrists, still bound with thick Trimber rope. Korbin smiled as he cut her free. Alexis grabbed the articles of clothing and waited for further instructions.

"Gardone wants you to wash up. Change your clothes and come right back here. Don't even think about escaping, either. It is not possible. Gardone has cast a *Protection Spell Shield* over the entire top of Tullah Mountain. There is nowhere for you to go. Your Ceptre will not be of any help either," he continued as he saw her staring at her Ceptre.

"Gardone also cast a *Block Spell*, so…your Ceptre cannot aid you. You have zero power right now, Alexis." He smirked as he approached the fireplace, standing before her, waiting to see if she would follow the instructions.

"No problem. I shall do as Daddy asks," she said snippily. She crossed the room to head to her bedroom, wanting to change her nasty, stained outfit.

Korbin followed her and stood outside the ajar bedroom door. He could hear water running and assumed she was bathing. Alexis stood before the mirror as she stripped down to her undergarments. She let the dirty and vomit-stained cloak drop to the ground. Bending down, she removed her boots. Next, she removed her black flying pants and kicked them into the bathroom corner. She took a small hand towel and washed her face and body. She pulled out the small stool and sat down, wanting to cry.

*'When will Armbruster or Aerianna figure out something is wrong?'* She had been missing for several hours. *'Surely, they are worried by now?'* She grabbed the stack of clean clothes. Once dressed, she took the brush from the counter and ran it through her long hair. Though she had washed her hair, she still saw little chunks of dried blood in her hairbrush. Her head was sore, and she briefly worried about how deep the gash was on her skull. When she finished, she left the pile of dirty clothes on the floor and headed out of the room. Korbin met her at the door and escorted her back to the couch.

"Do you plan to be next to me this entire time?" she sarcastically asked.

"Yes, definitely. I will be your shadow until Gardone returns, whenever that may be."

"Perfect, I cannot wait," she said, trying to irritate Korbin.

"Do you want anything to eat or drink, Alexis? Gardone wants you to be comfortable." Korbin rolled his eyes, annoyed at having to babysit the Queen.

"Does he now? Well, I would be a hell of a lot more comfortable back in my room at the Palace. How about letting me go?"

"There is a zero chance of that happening. Good try, though. I already told you—you are stuck here until Gardone returns. I will make a meal for you. I am hungry as well. So, if you change your mind and wish to eat, let me know," Korbin walked toward the kitchen, leaving Alexis to sulk on the couch.

Pauto and his Torrin led the way to Tullah Mountain. Armbruster was right behind him, followed by the security forces. Armbruster steered his Torrin next to Pauto's and nodded.

"Sir, what is it?" asked Pauto, noticing Armbruster's scowl.

"See that dome?" he asked Pauto, pointing to the top of Tullah Mountain.

"Of course!"

"Well, we cannot get close to it. Let's land on the backside of the cabin, behind the wooded area. By Lake Blayden, there is a huge open field where we hold the Torrin Races every year. I think the dome does not extend that far. We should be okay to land there. We can tie up the Torrins at the Race Stables. Maybe we can find some supplies at the Grand Race Manor. We need to figure out our complete strategy."

"Sir, I was under the impression we were headed to the cave to find Aerianna?" asked Pauto, somewhat confused.

"I think we should proceed to the cabin. There is a reason a *Protection Spell Shield* is over it. Maybe Aerianna is there?" replied Armbruster.

"Understood. However, I still think we should check out the cave first," said Pauto, almost begging Armbruster.

Pauto was concerned and wanted to ensure Aerianna was safe. He would not share that information with Armbruster, but if he could convince him to visit the cave first, Aerianna might potentially be there.

"Alright, Pauto. You win. Let's head to the cave first and then Lake Blayden. I am sure there is a good reason for you pushing that destination. I know you are worried about Aerianna, but trust me...she will be okay."

The group steered their Torrins toward the cave. Halfway there, Pauto moved his head from left to right as if attempting to get a clear picture of something. Next, he turned around and looked at Armbruster.

Pauto pointed ahead so Armbruster could see what he saw. Off in the distance, they observed someone on a Torrin approaching rapidly. Pauto recognized her and sighed with relief.

Aerianna pulled up beside Pauto on her Torrin and said, "Hey stranger, what are you doing out here?"

"We were coming to the cave to look for you. Why are you out here?"

"I was at the cave for some time. I planned to head toward the cabin to relax and later return to the Palace. What's wrong? Why is Armbruster with you?" Aerianna asked Pauto, turning around and nodding at Armbruster. He reciprocated with an awkward grin.

"We were worried about you. Please follow. We are heading to Lake Blayden. Look!" he pointed to the top of Tullah Mountain so Aerianna would notice the glowing dome. Her eyes almost popped out of her head the second she saw it, and she gawked at Pauto in disbelief.

"What happened? Who did that?" she questioned, still fascinated by the dome.

"We do not know," Pauto replied, continuing to fly toward the mountaintop.

"Pauto, did you know Alexis also left for Tullah Mountain today? Did she inform you or Armbruster about her plan?"

"We talked with Essten. He informed us about Alexis's trip. We still do not know where she is on Tullah Mountain. However, we assume she is in the cabin. Since the dome has encapsulated the building, we have to figure out what we can do to get near it," declared Pauto, grimacing.

Aerianna nodded in agreement but remained silent for the rest of the flight, wondering if Alexis was safe. The group continued their flight toward the top of the mountain, veering off to the left side to move behind the wooded area and Lake Blayden.

Gardone appeared near the front of the hut on Earth. He demanded an update from his team and was eager to share the great news about Alexis. As he was about to open the door, Garlow, Yarlen's son, appeared.

"Hello, how did it go? Did they get her?" he inquired, hoping Alexis was now a prisoner.

"Yes, Garlow. She is inside the cabin with Korbin. Let's step inside to finish this conversation," replied Gardone.

The two quickly entered the hut. Garlow closed the door and allowed Gardone to lead the way to the Meeting Room. Once there, the others looked up excitedly from their chairs, eager to hear the news.

"Brothers, it has been done! Alexis is our prisoner. We will now start the next phase of our plan. I want you to know that she is safe. She is mad as hell, but okay. I have placed a *Protection Spell Shield* over the top of Tullah Mountain. She cannot escape. I will return to her shortly to discuss the next steps. I am sure she will be quite unhappy," explained Gardone. He felt tremendous pride, knowing he had control over Alexis. It was not an easy feat, but he had done it.

"Sir, that is wonderful news," said Cheeve, Gardone's assistant.

"Indeed, my friend. We are close to acquiring the kingdom. However, there is still much work to complete."

Inside the Palace, Carmin fed and changed Lilah's outfit. Once the baby was in her crib, Carmin left the chamber to locate a meal for herself. She asked Porti to keep an eye on the Princess. Carmin walked down the long corridor, still worried. She fretted about where everyone was and what had happened to Alexis. As time passed, she grew increasingly frantic.

The Queen would never have left her child alone for so long without seeing her. Carmin realized something awful had occurred. It was the only plausible explanation for the Queen's lengthy absence.

Yarlen remained alone in the hut on Earth. He ate a small meal in the living room. He wasn't in the mood to eat, but was starving. He wondered when Gardone would show up to update him on the plan's progress. It had been hours, and no one was outside except three security guards protecting him and the hut.

Yarlen picked at his food, legs crossed and tucked under his cloak, and a plate on his lap. He reached for a glass of Porting Wine on the table beside him. Somehow, he bumped the table, and the wine glass tipped over, spilling the Porting Wine on the floor.

Irritated, Yarlen placed the plate of food on the couch and got up to clean the mess. He walked into the kitchen to find a towel. Once there, he saw his Ceptre leaning against the counter. With a grin, he picked it up, returning to the living room. Yarlen stood over the spilled mess.

He aimed his Ceptre at the broken glass and wine. Instantaneously, the glass and spilled wine disappeared. A blue flash beamed from his Ceptre, and a new glass of Porting Wine appeared on the table, ready for consumption. Yarlen loved having his

Ceptre back and the ability to work his magic. It was the best time he had experienced in months. He sat back down, his Ceptre by his side, happily drinking and enjoying his Porting Wine. All of a sudden, he heard voices.

Alexis pouted, lounging on the couch. It made her insanely mad that she could not perform any magic, though she had tried repeatedly. She yearned for her Ceptre, though it refused to move. No matter what she tried, it stayed in its stand. She looked around the room, hoping to find a weapon. There was nothing in sight. Suddenly, she had an idea. She walked to the front door and opened it. Immediately, Korbin appeared.

"What do you want?" he bellowed, looking at her and speculating about why she was in the doorway.

"I need to go lie down on my bed. My head is killing me. Would it be okay if I stayed in my room for a while? As you stated earlier, it's not like I can escape."

"True. Yeah, sure, go lie down on the bed if that makes you feel better. I will come inside and sit in the living room and keep watch." He followed her inside the cabin.

Alexis headed to her room and slammed the door. She assumed he would follow her and open it. After waiting a few minutes to see what he would do, she figured he wasn't coming, so she approached the wardrobe to search for her weapon.

Alexis opened the heavy wardrobe doors. She reached up to the top shelf, feeling for her dagger. Slowly, she ran her hands along the ledge, hoping to find it. Finally, as she was about to give up, she felt a lump under her tunic. She got on her toes to get closer to the wardrobe and gain more height. The blade nicked her as she withdrew it from the upper shelf. She looked down at the shiny blade, licking the drop of blood off her finger. She admired the dagger with its twisted handle, braided and wrapped in leather. The blade was constructed from steel and was extremely sharp, with serrated edges.

Alexis slid the dagger into its holster, which had been on the shelf. The holster was leather, with a clip attached to secure it to pants or a belt. The dagger was a birthday gift from Shell. She had the weapon made on Earth to surprise Alexis at her birthday party. She knew Alexis would love it. Now, Alexis was grateful that she had kept it in the cabin, hidden in case she ever needed extra protection.

Alexis secured the dagger in the back of her undergarments and allowed her cloak to cover it. She figured that at least she had a means of defense. However, her Ceptre would be a better choice. She had not battled anyone in a long time.

There was a time when she actively participated in the Battle Rounds—a gaming event held yearly at the Battle Colosseum. She stopped participating once she became pregnant with Lilah. Alexis wished she had kept up with her training. However, she knew she still would be able to defend herself if she had to. *'Some things never change,'* she thought, laughing out loud.

# CHAPTER 9

Lorthana placed her feet on the couch and read the *Book of Discovery*. It was something she meant to do for a while. She wanted to find out more information on casting a *Discovery Spell*. She had not performed one in years and could not recall the necessary ingredients.

Lorthana loved her alone time, though she missed Zandorah and Alexis. She was still upset with Gardone and fumed over the fact that he had left her alone without an explanation. Lorthana listened to the soothing sound of the fire crackling in the fireplace. The room felt warm and comfortable.

"Hello, Mother," whispered Zandorah, sneaking up behind Lorthana. She stuck her head over the couch and looked down at her mom, who was reading. Lorthana jumped up, surprised by her daughter's visit.

"I did not hear you come in, dear. You are stealthy! How did you manage that?" she asked, smiling at her daughter, happy to see her.

"Mom, this is not a social visit. I came to update you on some news. I enlisted my security team to conduct a more thorough investigation to gather additional information. I discovered some rather disturbing things. I am glad you are sitting down, as you will be upset. Please try to remain calm. Promise me!"

"Zandi…that does not sound good. How can you expect me to remain calm? It seems as if something awful is happening. What is it, child? Please, tell me!" urged Lorthana, starting to shake. Lorthana wrung her hands nervously, waiting for Zandorah to fill her in on the news.

"Mom, my security team found out that Dad is attempting to remove Alexis as Queen of Alstromia. The rumor is that he wants Alexis dead to take over the kingdom with Yarlen. Supposedly, Dad helped Yarlen escape. Therefore, we need to locate him and determine the truth behind this matter. How can he think about killing his daughter? Mom, what can we do?" Zandorah began crying as she sat down next to her mother. Lorthana stared at Zandorah with an expressionless face, utterly shocked. Did she hear Zandorah correctly? Gardone, her husband, wanted to kill their daughter. There was no way!

"Zandi…your security team is wrong. I know Gardone and Alexis have not always gotten along, but there is no way he would kill his child. He would never do that to gain power. He is not that heartless. I do not believe it!"

"Mom, I warned you that you would be upset," replied Zandorah, still sobbing.

"I cannot understand it at all. Frankly, I am in shock. Alexis, his firstborn child! Has he gone insane?" yelled Lorthana, now standing up and attempting to remain stoic. She paced around the room, shaking her head. Tears dripped off her cheek.

"Listen, we used many resources to collect this information. I am telling you… My team is not wrong. They would never have shared this information with me if they believed for one second it could be fabricated. Mom, it is the truth. Please, believe me. It kills me to share this awful news. Nevertheless, you need to know!" Zandorah stood beside her mother, arm wrapped around her shoulder, attempting to make her feel better.

"Wow, I do not know what to say. Does Armbruster know? Did you tell Shawnatar?"

"I have not told anyone other than you, Mom. I wanted you to be the first to know. Let's find Armbruster and Shawnatar. I have no idea where they are, but we must locate them as soon as possible. Let us head to the Palace of Snipperdoom."

"I agree with you, Zandorah. We have to set off to find them. Let us leave right away."

Lorthana wiped the tears off her face and smiled at Zandorah. The two walked to the front of the fireplace, holding hands. Zandorah and Lorthana slammed down their Ceptres simultaneously.

They became enveloped in a swirling, green haze and disappeared. Instantly, the two Witches were transported to the Palace entrance on Alstromia. They stood before the elongated arch, eyeing the building, not ready to face Armbruster. Nervously, they held hands. Lorthana and Zandorah stared at the arch, finally ready to find Armbruster. Suddenly, three Security Commoners appeared.

"What is your business with the Palace?" asked the youngest guard member, Garrett. "State your business immediately," he continued. His Mesmer Ceptre aimed at the two Witches.

"Calm down, young man. Do you not recognize me? I am Lorthana, the Queen's mother. I am here to speak with my son-in-law, Armbruster. Where may we find him?"

"I would not have that information. I will lead you to the Security Command Center. Maybe Pauto will be there, and you can ask him," responded Garrett, now embarrassed he did not immediately recognize Lorthana.

Garrett and the two other Security Commoners led the Witches to the Security Command Center. They entered to find three security officers in the chamber, talking and looking at a map. Garrett announced Lorthana and Zandorah's presence and then quickly excused himself.

"Ladies, how may we assist you?" asked Andreh, Pauto's Second-in-Command. He wanted to come across as cordial and helpful.

"We are searching for Armbruster. Where may we find him? We must speak with him immediately to relay critical information," Lorthana impatiently replied.

"I am sorry to inform you that he is not here. He departed with Pauto and a few of our security team members to head to Tullah Mountain to respond to an urgent matter. Can I help you?"

"I am not sure. We have a pressing matter to discuss with Armbruster and Pauto. Why did they leave for Tullah Mountain? What is happening?" asked Lorthana, now getting worried.

"I cannot discuss Palace matters with you. I am sure you understand," Andreh asserted, nervously staring at Lorthana and Zandorah.

"You most certainly can and will," retorted Lorthana, getting mad. "Furthermore, you will tell me now. I will not accept your bullshit about the Palace policy. My daughter is the Queen, and her life could be in danger. I do not want to hear more of your nonsense," screamed Lorthana, standing before Andreh, her Ceptre in his face. They did not have time to waste or adhere to protocol. She needed immediate assistance.

"Okay, okay. What is this urgent matter regarding the Queen?" Andreh asked, figuring he better find out what was transpiring.

"Finally," said Lorthana, dropping her Ceptre down beside her. "Let me tell you what has happened."

Armbruster, Pauto, Aerianna, and the security team circled over the landing spot. Pauto was in the lead, followed by Aerianna and then Armbruster. One by one, they landed. Once safely on the ground, they expeditiously proceeded to the Race Stables.

Pauto jumped off his Torrin and tied her to the long and wide Rein Pole. He helped Aerianna off her Torrin, and they secured the beast. They observed Armbruster and his security team doing the same thing. Finally, they were ready to enter the Grand Race Manor.

The Manor was an elaborate building. It was long, tall, and dark blue. Its large walk-up featured wide stone stairs. Two giant statues graced the front sides of the walkway. The largest statue was of Alexis holding her trophy, and the other was of her Torrin. The Manor was primarily used to host celebrations and events, such as the annual Races.

The group neared the walkway, stopping to admire the surroundings. The Manor stood in the front, while the race track was in the back. The enormous Battle Colosseum was behind the Manor as well, which was used to host the annual Battle Rounds.

Once they stood before the entry, Armbruster advanced to unlock the doors with his Ceptre. The others followed him into the Manor. They looked around as Armbruster waved his Ceptre to light the chandeliers hanging from the ceiling, illuminating the room.

The grand entrance was bare. The entry area was empty now, but during the races, it would be filled with Witches, Wizzards, and Warlocks sitting or standing around tall tables, socializing. The shiny, smooth, gold-colored floors sparkled. Armbruster briskly walked toward the back of the Manor.

The group entered the Viewing Room. This room featured a long, tall, glass sliding wall that opened during races, allowing guests to walk out onto the back terrace. The terrace was U-shaped and lined with hundreds of seats surrounding the track.

Guests had a spectacular view of the racetrack. Off to the track's right was the Battle Colosseum, a tall, oval, glass-domed building. Inside the building was a center *'battle zone'* intended to give contestants the fight of their lives—the battle contestants trained for many years, eager to be chosen to participate.

The Battle Judges consisted of three Witches and three Warlocks from different Clans. Each year, they chose six participants from other Clans. Once they received their official notification of participation, the contestants had three months to prepare for battle. Being selected was a huge honor, and very few made the cut.

Alexis only missed the last year of battles since she was pregnant with Lilah. She was the strongest and most agile of all participants. She also never lost a battle. Pauto was honored to participate last year and placed second, losing to Gardone. He battled Alexis the year before her pregnancy and tried desperately to beat her, but ultimately, she won. She was able to overpower him in the last few seconds of the final battle. She had been gracious and extended an arm to help Pauto stand up after their match. He recalled feeling pretty good, considering she had beaten him up, and he was bruised and bleeding.

The yearly fights begin with one day of preliminary battles to establish the final three contestants. The second day consists of physical battles. The third day is the toughest. It allows contestants to use their weapons, wits, and magic. Pauto was a tremendous physical fighter, but could not match Alexis's magical abilities.

Pauto trained with Yarlen for many months, hoping to improve his magic. As Pauto stood on the terrace, staring at the Battle Colosseum, he smiled, eager for the next competition to begin.

Armbruster stood on the terrace, thinking. He turned around to see how far the green protective shield reached. The longer he thought about the fact that the force field was still active, the more nervous he became. Why was it in place? Pauto approached Armbruster, looking concerned.

"Sir, what are you thinking?" he asked, noticing Armbruster's face.

"I am curious as to why the shield is up in the first place. I would like to know what someone is keeping in or out. I hope Alexis is not inside the cabin, but I assume she must be. I still have no idea how we will get her out."

Aerianna overheard the conversation and advanced. "I want you to know I have an idea. I found a *Reversal Spell* that may work for the *Protection Spell Shield*. I am fairly certain I can reverse it."

"What? Are you sure, Aerianna?" asked Armbruster, getting excited. It would help them greatly to bypass the shield.

"Absolutely! First, we should look around, though. Let's try to ascertain how many others are guarding the cabin. Once the magic is reversed, we must act quickly. The enemy will try to recast the chant and ensure the cabin is secure," said Aerianna, glad she had the opportunity to help.

"I agree," added Pauto, surveying the area. "Let us head toward the cabin and see how far we can get before encountering the shield. Perhaps we will be lucky and locate the security personnel. It will be good to know what we are up against."

They headed back inside the Manor, followed by the security officers. Strolling down the walkway toward the cabin, Pauto stopped quickly. He pointed to the building off in the distance, noticing someone standing outside.

Sadly, it was not a great view since the shield's glow blurred his vision. The others looked to see why Pauto was pointing. They quickly realized that they had to do something about the security guards protecting the cabin.

Alexis snuck up to the bedroom door, hoping she could overpower Korbin swiftly. She wondered where the other Warlock was hiding, assuming he was outside the cabin, keeping watch. Cautiously, Alexis opened the door and entered the living area, pretending to be tired. She yawned and stretched, looking around.

Korbin sat on a stool at the other end of the living room. He ate a sandwich, observing her. He placed his plate on a long counter leading to a kitchen area and walked toward her. Alexis stood next to one of the couches, smiling.

"What is so funny?" he asked, watching her and noticing her odd facial expression.

"Nothing. Why do you ask?"

"Well, you look like you are up to something," he replied, standing on the couch's backside. Before he could say anything else, Alexis jumped on the couch, using it as a trampoline, bouncing high into the air, and landing quickly. She stood behind him, the dagger blade resting on his throat, whispering into his ear.

"How do you like this, Korbin?" she chuckled, feeling empowered.

Korbin swallowed hard, feeling the cold, sharp blade against his throat. He wanted to scream to alert the other sentinel, but he knew better. Alexis chuckled, knowing she had the advantage. Things were about to change, or so she hoped.

Gardone sat at the desk in his home, thinking. He stood up and grabbed his *Spells of Protection* book off the shelf, deciding to meet with Yarlen. He wanted to update him on everything that had occurred at the cabin with Alexis. He tucked the book inside his cloak and slammed down his heavy Ceptre, disappearing and transporting himself to the hut.

Yarlen waited in the building for Gardone. He was eager to learn about the Queen's fate. He had been spending a lot of time thinking about her lately, figuring Alexis was probably injured by now and violently mad. He smiled, but then his smirk quickly faded, thinking about how vicious she could be. It worried him greatly. Yarlen pondered how they could control her while she was in their custody. She was creative and resourceful.

Gardone arrived outside the hut. He opened the door, entering quickly to locate Yarlen. Gardone was eager to share the exciting news with him. Yarlen was in his room, reading a book, when Gardone showed up.

"There you are, Yarlen. How are you, my friend? I bring you exciting news," said Gardone, glowing with excitement. Yarlen looked up at him, smiling with approval.

"Well, what happened? I have been dying to find out how Alexis reacted to her imprisonment. How is she? I suppose she reacted with her usual manner, spewing threats."

"She is distraught. She was surprised to see me, but she tried to hide it. I believe she is in shock and denial. Korbin ensured her Ceptre was locked down. I cast a spell, so she has no magical powers. At this point, she is a meager little Witch lacking all magical abilities, just as I had planned," responded Gardone, feeling very proud of himself. He glared at Yarlen, seeking his support.

"Outstanding," said Yarlen, excitedly jumping off his bed and dropping the book onto the floor.

"Yes, we do not have to worry about her. She is safely tucked away in the cabin. I also conjured a *Protection Spell Shield*. The entire cabin is off-limits. No one can get close. All is well."

"You have truly planned out every little detail, Gardone. I am impressed," stated Yarlen, happy the plan was in play. He wanted Gardone to know he was his ally.

"Yarlen, we must discuss your participation. I will require you to perform magic, and I need your assistance. I expect you will be up for the job. I will return to the cabin, but I need you to join me later. I require your help with Alexis. Are you okay with that?"

"Of course, Gardone. I will be ready. Should I be researching any spells in particular?" asked Yarlen, eager to help with the rebellion and not wanting to fail Gardone.

"I will leave that in your capable hands to decide. In the meantime, I must return to the cabin. I have to speak with Alexis and get her to realize we are about to change history. I know it will be a battle with her, but I am ready." Gardone excused himself. He planned to head home first to speak with Lorthana and inform her he would be on a mission with his team for a few days. He did not want her to worry about his absence or get too nosy.

Gardone realized she would get Zandorah involved if she suspected anything, something he did not wish to happen.

Zandorah ran her kingdom well. She was a fair and kind leader who did not feel the need to run her empire in the same domineering manner as Alexis. Zandorah was not the Queen of Iriss but rather their Supreme Ruler. She followed in the footsteps of many well-respected Warlocks and Witches dating back hundreds of years.

Zandorah could be ruthless if necessary, but never felt the need to be so. She held monthly meetings to ensure her Clan was happy and productive. She allowed her followers to live peacefully without interference from her command staff. Everyone was allowed to speak up at her meetings, giving Clan members the ability to voice their concerns.

Lucky for her, the community ran smoothly without any problems or uprisings. Iriss was a peace-loving planet, and all members seemed to respect and admire Zandorah and her staff.

Gardone worried that if Zandorah were pushed too hard, she would make a stand against him, and he would not need that kind of confrontation. He preferred to keep her as an ally and not an enemy. Thus, he would keep his plans under wraps for as long as possible. He taught Zandorah well and was keenly aware of her capabilities.

At times, he became nervous that he had taught her too well. She displayed confidence in her abilities and seemed to handle her kingdom professionally, and he hoped it would stay that way.

If Zandorah had help from Lorthana, that would be even worse. Lorthana was a very talented Witch when she wanted to be. The problem was that she seemed to relinquish much of her control and powers to her girls. She taught and allowed them to shine while standing back and spending less and less time practicing her magic. Gardone figured she was pretty much useless at this point. Still, he knew he should never underestimate her either. She had proven to be quite clever and resourceful in the past when need be.

Alexis, on the other hand, was his problem child. She was always headstrong and a show-off. Alexis loved herself and made it clear from a young age that she would one day rule a kingdom. She possessed the ability to make people do what she wanted when she wanted. She was a leader and never a follower. Perhaps it was what gave her the chance to become Queen so quickly at the young age of 32.

Alexis rose to power swiftly without any difficulties. No one challenged her, knowing how well she handled every situation she faced. She was agile, not just physically, but mentally as well. Alexis knew how to think quickly and execute her plan without hesitation. She never felt remorseful about her choices. Once her mind was made up, she followed through with her idea. Those who disagreed with her were left behind without another thought.

Alexis could never be underestimated. Doing so would lead to a catastrophe. She would destroy anyone who got in her way. Alexis loved her family and friends and would fight for them no matter what. The Queen was formidable, but more than anything, she was loyal.

Gardone knew what he was up against, and it would be the fight of his life. Alexis would not allow him to get away with anything. She would make him pay for what he was doing. If things did not work out, he could be dead or banned from the Clans without the use of his magic. Gardone was getting concerned.

# CHAPTER 10

Alexis held the dagger against Korbin's neck, gently pushing it against his jugular just enough to cause him to bleed. Korbin felt the warm wetness running down his throat. He remained stiff, not wanting to move, scared she would slice his neck deeper, potentially killing him. He tried desperately not to shake, afraid of the consequences.

"So, Korbin, now what do we do? It seems like you are the one currently disabled. How does that make you feel?" Alexis asked, digging the dagger blade a little deeper into his neck. Korbin squirmed slightly from the blade's pressure. He was sweating, scared she would end his life.

"Alexis, you will not get away with this. Stop while you can," he said in a low tone, trying to sound intimidating but failing miserably.

"Oh, but you are mistaken. I will succeed. Now, tell me, are you willing to unlock my Ceptre, or would you prefer to face the consequences?" she inquired, casting an intense look at her Ceptre, which was securely fastened in its stand. She longed for her Star Ceptre more than anything else, recognizing its potential to rescue her.

"Ha, good luck. No matter what, your Ceptre is useless. Remember that Gardone cast the magic to stop. Why don't you just let me go before Gardone returns?" Korbin remained standing stiff, trying not to move. He felt his legs getting shaky, freaking him out.

"Yes, you would like that," replied Alexis, moving the dagger off his throat, now placing it on the base of his skull. She had every intention of killing him if it meant her freedom.

Unexpectedly, they heard voices outside. Alexis motioned for Korbin to walk toward her bedroom. He obliged. She kept the dagger on the base of his skull, applying pressure to show him she was in control. The two entered the bedroom, and Alexis kicked the door closed, waiting. She remained standing behind Korbin, the dagger firmly pressing against his head.

Gardone stood outside the cabin, talking with the security scout. He wanted to ensure all was going as planned. Once the young Warlock informed Gardone that everything was quiet and seemed okay, Gardone confidently entered the building, ready to face Alexis. He walked toward the couch inside the cabin, hoping to find Alexis sleeping.

Instantly, the Warlock noticed she was gone. He began to look around frantically, wondering what had happened to her. Korbin was absent, too.

Gardone realized something was wrong. He marched toward the bedroom, assuming Alexis would be in bed sleeping. He tried to open the door, but it was locked. So, he knocked loudly. After knocking twice, Gardone heard Korbin's shaky voice.

"Gardone, she has me at a disadvantage. Please help."

"Alexis, whatever you think you are doing, stop! You will not get away with it. I beg you to stop before you get hurt," yelled Gardone, now visibly upset. He placed his ear on the door, hoping to hear their conversation in the room.

"Let me go, Daddy," Alexis shrieked, "I am tired of your game. You are the one who will not get away with this. I will kill Korbin, and you cannot stop me." She sliced Korbin's throat more deeply this time. He bled more heavily, screaming out in pain.

Nervously, Korbin looked down and saw the blood running down his chest, watching it drip onto the floor, pooling in spots. He started to feel weak and dizzy. He braced himself on the doorframe so he would not fall over. Alexis watched him, not caring about his pain or the profound blood loss.

"Alexis, stop it. Korbin is not the problem. It is me you want." Gardone saw blood running out from under the door and assumed it was Korbin's.

"Let me in and allow Korbin to leave. We can talk reasonably about this," rationalized Gardone, now ready to do whatever it took to stop her.

Alexis remained silent and motioned for Korbin to sit on the bed while she walked to the bathroom to retrieve a washcloth and a towel.

She threw both on the bed, instructing him to use them to stop the bleeding. Korbin knew he could not use magic. He was too weak, and she would stop him. He took the towel, allowing it to soak up his blood, now gushing from his body. Korbin assumed he would die soon from the excessive blood loss. He tried desperately to hold back his tears.

Standing next to the bed, Alexis contemplated her options. She wished Armbruster were there to help, as she worried about her welfare and missed him.

The security guard came running through the cabin's front door, overhearing the yelling from outside. He stood by the front door, listening to Gardone's conversation with Alexis. He remained silent and out of the way, awaiting orders.

Gardone stood before the bedroom door, waiting for Alexis to make her next move. He was about to pound on the door again when it opened, and Alexis forcefully pushed Korbin out of the room. He stumbled into Gardone's arms, holding his throat, blood oozing out between his fingers as he attempted to stop the bleeding with the towel. The door slammed shut and locked. Alexis stood behind the closed door with the dagger in her right hand, ready to defend herself and kill Gardone.

In the Race Manor, Armbruster, Aerianna, Pauto, and the security team discussed their options for rescuing Alexis. They assumed she was inside the cabin, unsure who held her hostage.

Aerianna spoke up. "I read the list of items we need to remove the shield. I must return to the Palace and gather the necessary ingredients and a book."

"I will accompany you, Aerianna. I dislike the idea of you going alone," Pauto replied.

"Agreed," said Armbruster. "You two fly to the Palace, gather the ingredients, and return here. We will wait. I believe we need to cautiously assess the situation to determine if we can identify who is potentially holding Alexis hostage.

Aerianna and Pauto headed to the front of the Manor to retrieve their Torrins. They would be gone for a while, considering they needed to locate the necessary items in the Tower.

Armbruster walked onto the terrace and sat on one of the chairs overlooking the track. He was concerned about Alexis. He knew she was strong and would likely be okay, but he worried about who held her hostage. *'What is the purpose of kidnapping*

*Alexis? Would they harm or just threaten her?'* He watched as the other Security Commoners sat behind him, waiting for him to speak.

After a while, one of the security team members, Griffen, spoke up. "Sir, do you wish for us to get close to the shield and scout out the situation? I do not feel you should go with us in the event something happens."

"I believe it is best if you two go ahead without me. I will stay here and formulate a plan for later. Aerianna and Pauto should be at the Palace by now. They will return before too long. We must have a plan in place to rescue the Queen once the shield is down."

The Security Commoners acknowledged his orders and walked to the edge of the shield, attempting to get a better look at the cabin and the security detail outside. Armbruster stayed behind, seated, thinking about Alexis.

Aerianna and Pauto circled the Palace on their Torrins. Pauto pointed to a clearing off to the left side of the Tower. They proceeded to head in the direction to land. Once safely on the ground, Pauto tied up both Torrins onto a Rein Pole by the Tower's rear entrance. The two entered the Tower, hoping to find what they needed, knowing time was of the essence.

Within the cabin, Alexis stood quietly in the bedroom, shaking her head in frustration as she contemplated her next move. She wished to talk to Gardone, but suspected he would be deceitful. Alexis was acutely aware that he wouldn't tell the truth and would attempt to convince her of his concern for her.

Korbin stared at Gardone, uncertain that they could persuade Alexis to leave the room without putting her at risk. As if Gardone read his mind, he whispered to Korbin, "I want you to head outside and keep watch. Take the other guard with you. I will stay and attempt to lure her out." Before Korbin could leave, Gardone waved his Ceptre and cast a *Healing Spell*. Instantly, Korbin's wound stopped bleeding and began to close and heal. Unfortunately, he was still very weak from the blood loss. Gardone pointed to the front door, indicating he wanted Korbin to head outside.

Korbin winked at Gardone and left to join the other Security Commoner. He quietly relayed the information, and the two walked out the front door to keep guard.

Gardone stayed behind, standing in front of the bedroom door. He became more and more frustrated. He did not expect Alexis to have a weapon, wondering how the security team missed it during their security sweep.

During their initial search, the Security Commoners found numerous items, including knives and daggers. Someone must have failed to thoroughly check her room. Gardone was furious. Now, she had an advantage, something he did not want. "Alexis, open up. Let's talk. You are wasting time. We should discuss your future."

"Why would I trust you, Dad?" she replied sarcastically. She shook her head angrily, staring at the door, refusing to leave. Her hand's firm grip on the dagger was causing her pain, and she flinched.

"It is in your best interest, that's why. I will not harm you. You are my child, and I love you. I want to explain everything to you. Give me a chance. We can work it out," Gardone replied. He realized there was a slim chance she would believe him. However, he had to try to convince her to open the door. Gardone assumed curiosity would eventually lead her to come out of the room.

Alexis wanted to confront him. The bedroom door opened slightly. Gardone saw the long dagger, and then Alexis emerged from the room. She held the blade out in front of her, glaring at him. Gardone backed away. He turned and walked to one of the couches, leading the way. Alexis observed him and followed, leaving a considerable space between them for safety.

Back at the Palace, Pauto and Aerianna entered the Tower. They headed to the main vault in the basement, which contained the rarest of all magical items. Inside the storage room, they would find the StafflingBloom, a rare, teal-colored flower. It was a powerful plant used with various complex spells. It would work perfectly when combined with Zane's fur.

The Zane, a rare, dog-like animal, lived primarily on Hexxton Mountain, located on the other side of Alstromia, far from the Palace. Aerianna used her *Unlock Spell,* and the vault doors opened. It was a large, tube-shaped room. Inside, the walls were lined with shelves and boxes secured with locks.

Aerianna was one of the few who could remove the deadbolts. She cast the magic, and a purple haze enveloped the third box on the second shelf, causing it to pop open and reveal the flower.

Aerianna reached inside the box, withdrawing the delicate flower and handing Pauto the StafflingBloom. It was extremely delicate but beautiful. Its sweet and mesmerizing smell made Pauto nauseous as he held it.

Aerianna swiftly took it from his hands and placed it into a chant bag, realizing the effect on Pauto. She chuckled and said, "You understand, the StafflingBloom is quite exquisite. Its powers are superb. Did you notice how quickly it affected you?"

"Yes, the second I held it, I felt a warm, tingling sensation. All of a sudden, I started to feel dizzy and queasy. Why did that happen?" Pauto asked Aerianna, still feeling odd.

"You are not immune. However, I am. I can touch it, and it does not affect me. However, most are unprotected from its effects. Thus, it is a powerful, magical ingredient."

"Is that all we need for you to be able to cast the spell to remove the shield?"

"No, I still need Zane's fur and a book from my room. Can you help me reach the top shelf? See the purple box on the right? That is the one we need," Aerianna said, pointing to the shelf.

"Got it. Here you go." He handed the box to Aerianna.

Once Aerianna retrieved the necessary ingredients, she placed them into the chant bag. On the way out, she sealed up the vault. Pauto and Aerianna headed to her chamber to retrieve the book she required to complete the chant.

Marching down the corridor, several security guards stared at them, whispering to one another. Pauto became instantly upset, noticing everyone staring at them. He approached one of the security members and yelled, "What is going on here? Explain the secret whispering," he demanded. Aerianna stood next to him, confused, as well.

"Sir, we heard a rumor that you, Aerianna, Armbruster, and the Queen were taken hostage. Obviously, that is not the case," the Security Commoner informed Pauto. He bowed respectfully and kept his head low, awaiting Pauto's comment or orders.

"Get back to the Security Command Chamber. I will be there in ten minutes to brief everyone. Ensure all security command members are assembled. I will not tolerate the continued fabrication of lies. The Queen is fine."

Pauto fibbed about the Queen's current state but did not want anyone to know what was happening. He would meet with his team and ensure the Palace was secure during his extended absence. He would place Andreh in charge, one of the only Warlocks he trusted.

"Pauto, I will head back to the Manor while you speak with your team. We cannot waste time," said Aerianna, hoping he would agree.

"NO! You will wait for me. It will only take a few minutes. I do not want you flying back alone. Unfortunately, we must fly back since we cannot use our Ceptres to transport due to the *Blocking Spell* on the mountain. Please wait! If you head back without me, someone may still want more hostages. You would be a great find for them...Second-in-Command and all! Let's head to your room and collect what you need. Then, we will make a stop at the Security Command Chamber. After, we will depart the area." Pauto was adamant that they stay together. He did not want to risk anything happening to Aerianna. She was the only one currently capable of reversing the *Protection Spell Shield.* He had to keep her safe. The Queen's life depended on it.

Aerianna and Pauto entered her chamber. She quickly walked to her desk.

In a hurry, she riffled through papers, looking for something in particular. Pauto sat on her bed, watching. She picked up an old piece of paper and slipped it into the chant bag. She headed to the wardrobe closet, opening the large doors. On the top shelf, she found the book.

Excited she had everything in her possession, she nodded to Pauto, and together, they walked to the door. They expeditiously headed to the Security Command Chamber so Pauto could conduct his quick briefing. Aerianna and Pauto wanted to return to the Race Manor as soon as possible to help the Queen.

On Tullah Mountain, Armbruster sat in silence. He absentmindedly stared at the racetrack, continuing to think about his wife. Armbruster contemplated when Pauto and Aerianna would return. Just as he was about to walk inside the Manor, the two security members ran up to Armbruster, out of breath.

"Sir, we have news!" the excited Security Commoner began.

"Well, what is it? Tell me," responded Armbruster, impatiently waiting.

"There are two Security Commoners outside the cabin. One is Korbin. I recognize him. I have worked with him before. I do not know the other. They have Mesmer Ceptres. You know what that means..."

"Okay, we still do not know who is inside. Does anyone know if Alexis is in the cabin? Did either of you see anyone other than the two Security Commoners?" Armbruster was frustrated.

It was challenging to get a clear view of the cabin. The shield's green glow distorted the view. The tall, outspoken Security Commoner responded, "No, we did not. We could not get a good look. Did you want us to go back and try again?"

"No, let's wait until Aerianna and Pauto return," said Armbruster, frowning. The three sat on the terrace, waiting with impatience. Armbruster played with his beard. He rubbed his chin, frustrated, hoping the two would arrive quickly. Waiting was not one of his favorite things, and he scowled.

★*.★*.★*.★*.★

Gardone poured himself a glass of Porting Wine. He held the bottle out, wondering if Alexis would like to drink wine with him. She looked away, rolling her eyes. Gardone sat on a stool facing Alexis. He sipped the Porting Wine slowly from his tall, clear glass. He smirked as he swallowed it, teasing Alexis.

However, Alexis remained calm, not letting on that she wanted to strangle him. She glared at her father, eyebrows raised, hoping to annoy him.

Gardone slammed the glass down, causing the stem to shatter. The glass crumbled and splintered under his hand. The Porting Wine dripped onto the floor. Gardone frowned. He felt the blood on his hand, realizing he was deeply cut. He brought the hand up to his face and sucked on the wound, licking the blood.

Alexis shook her head. *'He is revolting,'* she felt repugnance.

"Are you happy? Now, I am bleeding. It is your fault, Alexis. You have a way of always pissing me off. I think you enjoy making me angry. Why?" he asked, now wiping the blood on his cloak.

"Daddy, do not flatter yourself. I am not intentionally trying to upset you. You are a jerk all on your own. You are the most ruthless person I know. I really thought Yarlen was more evil. I am mistaken. You are, by far, the biggest ass I have ever met. You make me sick," she hissed, squinting her eyes, standing before him.

"Clearly, you are upset. Do not worry. In the end, all will work out. I will rule

Alstromia with Yarlen by my side. Speaking of Yarlen, where is he?" said Gardone, attempting to infuriate Alexis even more. Then, with perfect timing, Korbin entered the cabin.

"Sir, you must remove the shield long enough for Yarlen to be able to enter the protected area. He is standing outside the shield, waiting. I will retrieve him. Please, take down the shield."

"Great, go ahead. I will do it now." Gardone walked outside and stood near the cabin's door. He waved his Ceptre and cast the magic. The green dome flickered for a second, then completely disappeared. Yarlen strutted toward the cabin. He stood beside Korbin. Within seconds, the green dome reappeared, securing the cabin's perimeter.

Gardone reentered the cabin and found Alexis sprawled on one of the couches with her feet up, attempting to appear calm. He approached and tried to sit next to her. But before he could, she kicked him hard, causing him to fall onto the ground. She evilly smirked as he looked up at her, grinding his teeth in anger.

Gardone jumped up and walked to the fireplace, bracing himself on the right side of the mantle. He remained standing, glaring at Alexis, awaiting Yarlen's arrival.

Yarlen approached the cabin door. His chant bag was flung over his left shoulder, with his Ceptre tightly held in his right hand. He entered the building and was greeted by Gardone.

Yarlen proceeded to walk toward the couch, where Alexis waited. She played with her straight, black hair, pretending she was okay with no care in the world. However, her facial expression said otherwise.

"Well, well, look what the cat dragged in," said Alexis, glaring at Yarlen spitefully. "You know, that was one of Shell's favorite sayings on Earth. It seems appropriate right now. You look very smug, Yarlen. Enjoy the moment. I promise you... It will not last." She stood up, reached Yarlen, and slapped his face as hard as possible. He dropped the chant bag and his Ceptre. She watched as he bent down to pick them up, appearing embarrassed in front of her and Gardone.

Yarlen shook his head as his face pulsed in pain. He observed Alexis as she bared her teeth and returned to the couch. She plopped down and stared at the fireplace. She had more in store for him. Hopefully, he was ready.

Yarlen felt highly uncomfortable with Gardone and Alexis at the cabin. He could only assume Armbruster would be there soon. The King had a way of knowing things before anyone else. Yarlen knew they had minimal time to get Alexis to relinquish her title and kingdom.

If Armbruster appeared, everything would change. He would destroy Gardone quickly and protect his wife, the Queen.

"So, how long do you think you can last up here, Gardone?" asked Alexis, still seated on the couch.

"Whatever do you mean, Alexis? The shield is back in place. It makes no difference if anyone tries to rescue you. The dome is secure. You are locked down with zero abilities. I am in total control," Gardone replied, laughing. His self-righteous grin made Alexis want to puke.

"Really, Daddy? What about when Mom, Zandorah, Armbruster, and everyone else show up? You know it is just a matter of time. They are probably already working on my rescue. I believe you and Yarlen would be better off rethinking this idea. You have failed!" Alexis announced, feeling upbeat.

"Sir, she has a point. They will come for all of us. They will rescue her. What shall we do? How long do we try to keep this thing going?" asked a nervous Yarlen. He regretted his decision to side with Gardone. At this point, he hoped to get into good graces with Alexis.

Yarlen refused to face off against her or the rest of the Clan. It would end badly. He felt ready to pledge his undying allegiance to Alexis and all of Alstromia.

Yarlen wasn't sure how he would do it without upsetting her father. Gardone would kill him if he believed for one second he was siding with Alexis. Yarlen would have to find a way to earn Alexis' trust.

Gardone observed Yarlen and mentally gathered facts about what he had said. He realized it was all true. They would come for Alexis. Yarlen had not yet helped in any capacity. Gardone demanded that he create a spell to block all communication between the shield and the outside.

"Yarlen, I assume you are ready to prove your worth," started Gardone, "I expect you to devise a chant to stop all communication between our shielded dome and the outside. I also want to ensure no one can cast a *Reversal Spell*. It is your responsibility to make it happen."

"I assumed as much. I have a few spells. There are no guarantees they will work with the magic in place. However, I will try!" responded Yarlen. He was not excited about the prospect of returning to his prison cell. He figured that in time, the others would overpower Gardone.

Yarlen was ready to give up. He was tired of fighting against Alexis and Armbruster. He wanted his old life back, as well as his job. Working for Gardone was a nightmare. He was more demanding than Alexis and much more ruthless. Gardone was also very condescending. Yarlen regretted ever becoming involved with Gardone and his group of delinquents. He was ready to sever the ties and end his relationship with Gardone. Unfortunately, now was not the right time. He would have to find the perfect moment.

# CHAPTER 11

Lorthana stood with Zandorah inside Armbruster's chamber, wondering about his whereabouts. They wanted to speak with him and worried that he was unavailable. No one had seen him in a while. Andreh stood by the fireplace and set eyes on Lorthana and Zandorah. He insisted on accompanying them to the King's chamber, hoping to protect them.

Andreh also ordered increased security and a sweep of the entire planet. He worried something awful was happening. Frustrated and confused, Andreh sat on Armbruster's chair beside the desk. He assumed the Witches would want to wait and see if Armbruster would return shortly.

Once seated, he observed the two Witches. They remained by the window, whispering to each other. After a few minutes, they chose to sit on the bed, eyeing Andreh. He was about to ask them what they were discussing when the chamber door opened.

"Sir, Pauto and Aerianna were spotted leaving her chamber. We have asked them to come here to speak to you. They claim to know where Armbruster is located," a Security Commoner stated, addressing Andreh.

"Great, where are they?"

"They will be here momentarily. Should I tell them to enter once they arrive?" the commoner asked.

"Yes, inform them that I am waiting in Armbruster's chamber. I must see them immediately."

The Security Commoner departed quickly on his new mission. Andreh glanced at Lorthana and Zandorah. He hoped to figure out what they were talking about behind his back.

The door opened, and Aerianna and Pauto appeared. She held a bag and her Ceptre. Pauto stood behind her, watching.

"What is it you want, Andreh?" Aerianna demanded, looking into the room. She noticed Lorthana and Zandorah sitting on the edge of Armbruster's bed, wondering why they were congregated in Armbruster's chamber.

"I'm glad you're here. There seems to be a problem. What do you know about Armbruster's absence? Please share all you know."

Pauto moved from behind Aerianna and raised his hand. "Andreh, you are excused. Return to the Security Command Chamber and inform the others that I will be there briefly. First, I must speak with Lorthana and Zandorah alone. I will explain everything in a bit." Andreh excused himself and followed Pauto's orders, heading to the Security Command Chamber.

Lorthana and Zandorah listened intently to Pauto, bracing themselves for disappointing news. Aerianna also showed signs of anxiety. Lorthana leaped off the bed and approached Pauto and Aerianna, swiftly positioning herself beside them.

"What has happened? I know it is bad news. You both look frightened and are very evasive. Please, tell us," begged Lorthana, holding Zandorah's hand for comfort.

"There is no easy way to tell you, Lorthana," began Aerianna, walking up to her. She reached out and gently grabbed her hand. "We believe that Alexis has been kidnapped and is possibly being held as a hostage inside the cabin on Tullah Mountain. We surmise your husband, Gardone, is to blame. We heard from a few other security members that they had spotted him near the structure a while ago, though we had not seen him. Someone, we assume Gardone, has cast a *Protection Spell Shield* over the entire area's top. Armbruster is at the Grand Race Manor. We left him there with security to ensure his safety. We are attempting to remove the shield to gain access to the cabin. We believe at least two Security Commoners are protecting the outside of the building. We do not know how many are inside." Aerianna released Lorthana's hand.

Zandorah stared at her, shaking her head. "Are you sure?" she asked, furious with Gardone and scared for her sister's safety. "My security did inform me they heard Gardone was responsible for breaking

Yarlen out of his prison chamber. Everything makes sense now. He must be behind Alexis' kidnapping and Yarlen's prison break." Zandorah felt ill.

"Yes, we are quite sure," replied Pauto. "That makes things more difficult—if Yarlen is involved!"

"Well, what can we do? What is your plan to bring down the shield? Do you have a spell? How will you accomplish this? Who is casting the magic?" asked Lorthana, ready to rescue her child, Alexis.

"I will be the one," answered Aerianna. "I found all the necessary ingredients inside the Tower, which is why Pauto and I came back from the mountain. Armbruster wanted us to gather ingredients and a Spellbook to potentially remove the shield. Do you have any ideas, Lorthana? I found the *Vaporizing Spell*. It is the only thing I believe will work. What do you think?" Aerianna opened her chant bag and removed a book. She flipped open a page and handed the paper from her chant bag to Lorthana.

Lorthana read the notes written on the piece of old parchment. She glanced at the instructions on how to cast a *Vaporizing Spell*. She showed Zandorah the notes and book. Zandorah nodded.

"Yes, I concur. The *Vaporizing Spell* is probably the best choice for removing the shield. It is the only *Reversal Spell* that will work. As far as I know, it takes two Witches to cast such a powerful chant. We should try it together. We must remove it right away. When are we heading to Tullah Mountain?" asked Lorthana, ready to leave.

Pauto intervened, "First, I must speak with Andreh and leave orders to secure the Palace. I do not want the village commoners to know about the Queen's abduction. It would cause unrest and possibly other issues."

"Yes, Pauto. Please instruct your team. I will remain here with Lorthana and Zandorah. When you are ready to return to Tullah Mountain, please come and retrieve us," added Aerianna. She wanted more time to review the complex spell with the other two and show them the ingredients in her chant bag.

Pauto left the three Witches alone in the room. He hurried to the Security Command Chamber, prepared to instruct Andreh on securing the Palace. He was nervous about how Andreh would take the news. He knew Andreh cared deeply for Alexis and had been on her special detail service for many years. The two shared a special bond.

Andreh would not be happy once he heard that Alexis was in trouble.

Lorthana walked to the bed and sat down. Zandorah sat on her right side and supportively placed her arm around her.

"Mom, Alexis will be okay. You know she can handle herself."

"Child, it is not Alexis I am concerned about right now. I fear for Gardone. He will either die or be placed in the High Tower for treason, no matter what happens. I am worried about all the consequences. How could he betray our family like this?" Lorthana exhaled deeply and began to sob. She placed her head into her hands, her whole body shaking. Zandorah remained by her side, her arm firmly wrapped around her mother, feeling awful.

Aerianna neared the mother and daughter. She plopped down on the floor in front of Lorthana. She smiled at her reassuringly, "We will work with Alexis to ensure Gardone gets a fair trial. I am so sorry you must endure such a horrific situation. I was shocked to hear that Gardone might have been implicated in the situation. Let's wait until we know whether or not he truly is involved in such a vile act against his child. What do you say?"

Aerianna's goal was to keep things positive for Lorthana. She realized Lorthana already suspected Gardone. It was evident by the look on her face. Aerianna felt sad for her and Zandorah.

Pauto plowed through the door of the Security Command Chamber with his head held high. Confidently, he approached the large conference table and took a seat. Andreh stood by the window and observed Pauto.

Pauto addressed him, "Andreh, please join me. I must speak with you alone. Everyone, please step outside for a few minutes while I talk with Andreh." The crowd of Security Commoners left quickly, closing the door to the chamber.

"What is going on, Pauto?" asked Andreh, now more concerned than before.

"The Queen is in trouble. I need to tell you everything. Please sit down and allow me to fill you in quickly. I do not have much time. I must return to Tullah Mountain."

Pauto proceeded to share the information with Warlock. The news petrified Andreh, and he stared at Pauto in disbelief. Pauto noticed a small tear trickling down Andreh's right cheek. He knew Andreh was frightened for Alexis. However, he was a bit shocked to see Andreh cry.

Andreh jumped up and pounded his fists against the wall, causing him to cry out in pain. "I am going with you!" he boldly declared, looking down at Pauto, who was still seated.

"No, you are not. I need you here to protect the planet and the Palace. I am leaving you in charge. I need you to ensure the village commoners do not hear about any of this until the Queen is safe and back in the Palace. Do you understand?"

"Sir, I beg you to reconsider. The Queen needs me. I have always been there for her. You know this."

"Andreh, I am afraid you must remain here. I insist. You can better serve the Queen by staying behind and doing your job. Please, do not argue with me!" responded Pauto, irritated with Andreh. *'Why is he so adamant about going to Tullah Mountain?'* Was there something going on between Alexis and Andreh? Pauto did not like the feeling he received from the young Warlock.

"I am leaving. I will retrieve Lorthana, Aerianna, and Zandorah. We are flying back to Tullah Mountain immediately. Get the job done, Andreh." Pauto stormed off, not allowing Andreh another word. He hoped he would do his job and keep his mind where it was needed.

The three Witches gathered in Armbruster's chamber to discuss the *Vaporizing Spell.* They also considered the consequences of bringing down the shield and how much time they would have to access the cabin. Lorthana was confident that they could quickly execute the spell and eliminate the protective barrier.

Zandorah felt less optimistic. She had used the *Vaporizing Spell* before on something less grand than this shield, which failed miserably! Zandorah assumed there was a better and more potent spell.

Aerianna walked to the window and looked out. She frowned, staring at the mountain, the faint, green glow almost taunting her. She hoped Alexis would be rescued shortly and all would be well again.

Pauto entered the chamber, grimacing. He stood before the others, his nose flaring, eyebrows arched. Aerianna noticed right away that something was amiss. She approached him and asked, "What is wrong? Are you okay?" She touched his hand.

Irritated and still mad about his conversation with Andreh, Pauto pushed her away. "Let's go. We must return to the mountain. Armbruster is probably impatient and getting deeply upset. We are taking too long." He sprinted from the chamber, hoping the others would follow.

Aerianna gave a slight shrug to Lorthana and Zandorah, who shook their heads before following Pauto. Aerianna hurriedly stuffed her chant bag with the collected items from the Tower, along with the book. Then, she dashed out of the chamber to catch up with the other three as they made their way to the back of the Tower, where the Torrins awaited.

Pauto informed the others that he would retrieve two more Torrins for Lorthana and Zandorah. Zandorah stopped him quickly.

"Don't bother. Mom and I will transport ourselves using our Ceptres. We don't want to fly." Zandorah hated to fly. She was not very good at it and had no intention of doing it now.

"I must insist. I think we should all go together. Plus, the spell currently cast may not allow you to get close enough. Something could go wrong," replied Pauto, looking at Lorthana for approval and help.

Lorthana got the message. "We will fly back with you. Please retrieve the Torrins. We will wait here," she agreed, winking at Pauto.

Pauto left but returned quickly. He handed Lorthana and Zandorah the Torrins.

Pauto aided Aerianna and gave her the bag. Once everyone was ready, Pauto mounted his Torrin. He led the way back to Tullah Mountain, hopeful they would finally rescue Alexis.

★*.★*.★*.★*.★

In the Security Command Chamber, Andreh stood by the window, pouting. He saw Pauto, Aerianna, Lorthana, and Zandorah fly off toward Tullah Mountain. He wiped away his last tears and walked to the door to allow the rest of the security personnel back inside the chamber. He planned to brief them. Much work needed to be done to ensure the safety of Alstromia and the Palace. Andreh would complete his mission no matter how much he worried about Alexis.

In the cabin, Alexis lounged on the couch. She surveyed the surroundings, questioning when someone would come to rescue her. She felt Armbruster was near, though she could not see or hear him. Alexis wondered, *'Where is Aerianna?'*

Gardone sat down next to Alexis. This time, he hoped she would not kick him off the couch. She didn't. Instead, she blatantly batted her eyelashes to aggravate him.

"What is it, Daddy? You look upset," she said, still trying to annoy him. "Are you waiting for something? Do you think Yarlen will save the day? HA! You are crazy. That worthless Warlock will not save shit, let alone the day. He is washed up. I hope you have another plan."

"Stop it, Alexis. I am tired of your mouth and your attitude."

"Really. And I care, why? This is all you, Daddy! I hope you are proud of yourself. When this is all said and done, you will be dead. I will see to it personally. At the end of the day, there is only one victor – ME!"

"Alexis, stop this, all of it. Yes, Yarlen is helping me. I broke him out of his prison chamber. You should never have thrown him into prison. You know it. His actions were not treasonous but rather a huge misunderstanding. You always make assumptions. Yarlen did not deserve what you did to him. You were ruthless and went too far."

Gardone shook his head in disgust. He could not tolerate another minute in the same room with her. He stood up, leaving her to think about what he had said before she could respond.

Alexis jumped off the couch and ran to her bedroom, flopping onto the bed. Angry, she pounded her fists, screaming. She acted like a spoiled teenager, and she did not care. She was violently angry with Gardone. *'How dare he talk to me like that?'* she said to herself. Furious, she rolled onto her back and stared at the ceiling. She wanted to kill him for betraying her family and all of Alstromia. Alexis tried to calm down. She was angrier than she had been in a long time. Feeling abandoned and lonely, she hopped off the bed and made her way to the window.

Outside, she noticed Gardone and Yarlen engaged in an intense discussion. Both were quite expressive, and Yarlen appeared noticeably troubled. Alexis also observed that the two security guards were missing, assuming they were monitoring the situation from a nearby location. Irritated, she walked to the bathroom, picked up a clean washcloth, and washed her face. Seconds later, she briefly looked at the floor in the bedroom and saw Korbin's blood still existed. The sight of it made her feel queasy. It was nasty.

Realizing she had no magical abilities, she returned to the bathroom and grabbed the towel and wet washcloth off the floor. Disgusted with the blood stains, she scrubbed the filth off the floor.

As she cleaned, she reminisced about Yarlen, wondering if he truly was Gardone's ally. She'd observed Yarlen taking orders from Gardone without much argument. That was unlike Yarlen. Alexis frowned. She threw the towel and washcloth back on the bathroom floor when she finished cleaning. '*At least the blood is gone,*' she thought, still mad that her magic did not work. She headed to the front door, ready to confront Gardone and Yarlen.

Mid-flight, Pauto turned around to ensure the three Witches safely followed him to Tullah Mountain. He noticed Lorthana and Zandorah flying closely together. Aerianna was far behind. He assumed she was pouting since he had dismissed her earlier when she wanted to be affectionate. '*Oh, well,*' he thought.

Aerianna would get over it. He turned his head around and continued to fly toward the mountain.

The dome was now straight ahead, glowing a bright neon green color. Pauto veered off to the back, hoping to land by the Grand Race Manor. The three Witches followed him. Lorthana looked at Zandorah when they neared the shield. Lorthana assumed Zandorah was scared by the look on her face, worried about having to land the Torrin, something her daughter hated to do.

Aerianna was furious with Pauto. She knew he was upset about something. Why did he push her away? It was not like him to do so. Something must have happened when he talked with Andreh. She would ask him about that once they landed.

Pauto landed first. He walked toward the Rein Pole by the entrance of the Grand Manor to secure his Torrin. He waited for Lorthana to land. Once she was safely on the ground, she proceeded to join him. Zandorah circled above. Pauto looked up.

"Why is Zandorah still up there?" he asked Lorthana, pointing to the sky.

"Zandorah has never been very good at flying. She is extremely nervous about landing the Torrin. I am sure she will figure it out. She'll be okay. Stop watching her, or she will never land," said Lorthana, finding it funny that her daughter was so scared to land.

Aerianna approached the large area, allowing the Torrin to touch down. She saw Zandorah circling, holding on tightly to the reins. *'What is she doing?'* Then it hit her. She remembered a conversation a long time ago with Alexis telling her about how much Zandorah hated to fly. Flying was not her strong suit, and she tried to avoid it whenever possible. Aerianna pulled back on the Torrin's reins, headed back into the sky, and approached Zandorah.

"Listen, come with me down to the ground. Just follow my lead, and you will be alright. Just mimic my actions. You are capable of doing this, Zandi."

"Okay…" replied Zandorah, shaking, her hands turning purple from her tight grip on the reins. She was terrified of landing. She wondered why her mother had left her alone in the sky. Lorthana knew how much she despised flying.

Aerianna headed for the landing area. It was a wide strip of open land. She touched down quickly and perfectly with her Torrin. She headed off to the side to allow Zandorah to land. Unfortunately, she came in too high. She risked crashing.

*'Her Torrin should be lower,'* thought Aerianna. She yelled, "Lower, Zandorah, get the Torrin lower, hurry!!" Zandorah panicked and pulled hard on the reins, causing the Torrin to dive quickly. Instinctively, the Torrin took over. It landed safely and rapidly. Zandorah sat on the back of the beast, holding the reins so tightly that her hands ached and throbbed. She was furious, never wanting to fly again, and this incident reminded her how much she loathed it. Aerianna clapped and approached her.

"You did great, Zandorah. See, it was nothing to worry about." Aerianna grabbed the Torrin's reins and helped Zandorah jump off the beast.

Once she was on the ground, Zandorah snidely remarked, "Right, no problem." She walked off to join the others while Aerianna secured the Torrin.

The four entered the Manor and headed to the back terrace. Armbruster heard them approach and met them halfway. He appeared pleased to see Pauto and Aerianna, but confused when he spotted Lorthana and Zandorah.

"Why are you two here?" Armbruster interrogated.

He approached Lorthana, and she replied, "That is a long story, Armbruster. Zandorah and I came to the Palace to speak with you about Gardone. Zandorah's security discovered he was behind Yarlen's escape and possibly the one holding Alexis hostage. When we arrived at the Palace, we spoke with Pauto and Aerianna. Long story short, here we are. We are ready to help. What have you been able to discover so far?"

Armbruster frowned. "We have not discovered much. It seems two Security Commoners are standing outside, keeping watch. We still have no idea how many are inside. I am not sure there is anyone else.

Gardone probably assumes the shield will keep him safe and others out. He probably has not considered securing the entire cabin and surrounding areas," responded Armbruster. He looked distraught and tired. Lorthana could see it in his eyes. She hugged him.

"Listen, Armbruster. I know you. You are powerful. We are here to support you. Nothing will happen to Alexis or anyone else. We have a plan," Lorthana said reassuringly.

Aerianna stood next to Armbruster and showed him the chant bag. She opened it, allowing him to peek inside. He nodded approvingly at Aerianna. "Are you ready to begin the spell?"

"Yes, Lorthana and I will chant together. Let's get close to the shield. However, before we remove the shield, what happens after it is down?"

Pauto responded, "We will rush inside, use the Ceptres if possible, and incapacitate the security guards. If our magic does not work, we will use force if a *Magic Stop Spell* is in play. I have been practicing for the Battle Rounds and am prepared to destroy them." He smirked as he said it. Aerianna looked away, ignoring him. His previous actions toward her still hurt.

"Once the shield is down, we can enter the cabin. However, we should assume that Gardone will recast the spell right away. Time will be of the essence once we're inside, as we'll need to rescue Alexis quickly. To ensure efficiency, let's split up. I'll take care of Gardone while the rest of you can go after everyone else," Armbruster directed, glancing at the others, who all nodded in agreement. He was ready to rescue his wife.

Aerianna and Lorthana stood before the shield. The Spellbook was open, and the necessary ingredients had been combined. Both Witches twirled their Ceptres over the book and items, chanting. The glow of the dome seemed to intensify. They assumed it would vanish. It flickered on and off several times. Lorthana and Aerianna increased their chant, louder and more boldly, declaring the *Vaporizing Spell*. The dome remained in place, the shield glowing a green hue. The two halted the magic. The others looked on.

"Why did it not work?" yelled Armbruster. He was visibly angry, glaring at the two Witches. He glanced at the dome, still intact, shaking his head.

"I don't understand," said Aerianna, confused, staring at the green, glowing shield.

"I was worried about this," added Lorthana. "I believe we need something else. I have an idea. This failed attempt leads me to believe that we must involve Florenzzah Lovecraft. If she cannot dissolve the shield, no one can."

"Then, we must visit her immediately and ask for her assistance," replied Pauto. "Who will accompany me?"

Aerianna stepped forward and approached Pauto. "I will. I have dealt with her before when Alexis required a *Reversal Spell*. Let's travel to Florenzzah's hut, negotiate with her, and rescue Alexis once and for all."

# CHAPTER 12

Aerianna leaned against a wide pillar on the terrace. She waited for Pauto to retrieve their Torrins for the flight to visit Florenzzah. Aerianna recalled her last conversation with Florenzzah quite a while ago. It did not go well. Aerianna had flown to Tullah Mountain to retrieve Florenzzah and deliver her to the Palace, hoping to reverse Alexis' unfortunate ghostly condition.

Yarlen had turned Alexis into a spectral figure with a spell, attempting to leverage Armbruster over Alexis.

Regrettably, the plan backfired. Yarlen was blamed for the fiasco and sent to the High Tower for treason. Florenzzah demanded a position on the Royal Staff in return for the reversal. Alexis disagreed with the terms and tricked Florenzzah into believing she would reward her with a prestigious job. That never happened. Florenzzah was livid, telling Alexis she would never agree to help her again.

As Aerianna continued waiting for Pauto, she contemplated what she could offer Florenzzah to entice her enough to agree to help with the *Shield Removal Spell*.

Perhaps Aerianna would have to enlist Armbruster's help, who held greater authority to grant Florenzzah her demands. Surely, Florenzzah would be much more demanding this time, especially since Alexis had not followed through with any of her previous promises. Aerianna was nervous about seeing Florenzzah. She was glad Pauto agreed to accompany her.

Hopefully, Florenzzah will see the value in helping out during this crisis and agree to reverse the *Shield Spell*. Aerianna decided to speak with Armbruster before her departure to obtain a reward to offer to Florenzzah. She hurried to locate him.

On the opposite side of Tullah Mountain, in a dilapidated hut, Florenzzah Lovecraft relaxed in her favorite chair when she suddenly experienced a peculiar tingling in her right hand. This sensation typically indicated that an unexpected visitor was about to arrive.

She stood up and made her way to the Chant Room. Hurriedly, she opened her *Book of Insight.* She placed her right hand on the book, which flipped open to page 649. She stared at the words, *"Betrayal is never the end. Respect and power can change the outcome. Be the one to set the standard. It will set you free."* She closed the book and nodded, assuming someone needed her for a unique project.

Florenzzah returned to the furry, brown chair by the window. She closed her eyes and let the words speak clearly to her: *"Betrayal is never the end."* Florenzzah knew precisely what the book was telling her. It involved Alexis, the only one who had ever deceived her.

So, it was up to Florenzzah to set things right this time. She would wait to see who visited her and what they wanted.

Meanwhile, she decided to revisit the *Book of Insight* and seek additional information, anticipating further revelations.

Armbruster, Lorthana, and Zandorah sat on the terrace, conversing. Everyone was quite upset that the *Reversal Spell* failed, keeping the shield in force. Aerianna approached the others, looking somber. Armbruster noticed she had been crying.

"What is it, Aerianna? You look awful. You know it is not your fault that the shield did not disappear."

"Armbruster, we need to talk. Privately, please," Aerianna insisted. She did not want Lorthana or Zandorah involved.

"Of course, let's walk together." Armbruster stood up and grabbed her hand. He walked beside her and released her hand once they were away from the others. Armbruster stopped walking and laid eyes on her. He realized something was amiss. Aerianna looked pale and was breathing rapidly.

"Aerianna, what is wrong? How can I help?" he asked, concerned. His eyes were large, and he was paying attention to her every move.

Aerianna swallowed hard, attempting to smile at him. "Armbruster, do you remember when Yarlen turned Alexis into a ghostly figure? Well, I convinced Florenzzah to help reverse the spell cast by Yarlen, and she agreed to help. However, Alexis pledged things to Florenzzah and never followed through on her promises. I believe Florenzzah will want a lot more this time during our negotiation. She will still be upset at Alexis. Once she finds out we need her help, her demands will be ridiculously high. I know it. So, what are you willing to promise her to ensure the Queen's safety and the removal of the shield?"

Aerianna scrutinized his face, trying to read the expression. Armbruster looked up at the sky, remaining silent. Aerianna began worrying. It had been at least 5 minutes, and he still refused to talk. Armbruster stood beside her, his hands on his hips, tapping his right foot.

"Sir, I need your response. The longer we wait to visit Florenzzah, the longer the shield will remain in place. Please, say something," she begged, getting desperate.

Armbruster spun around and faced Aerianna. Finally, he took her hands into his, maintaining eye contact with her as well. "Aerianna, we must promise and follow through this time. I do not care what we offer Florenzzah. I must ensure the safety of the Queen. Nothing else matters. What is it you believe Florenzzah wants?"

"She demanded a Royal Staff position last time. I believe we can negotiate if we offer her the same this time. Alexis will not be thrilled, but at this point, who cares?"

"Do it. Give Florenzzah what she desires. I want the shield down so I can rescue Alexis. Florenzzah is very talented. We would be stupid not to want her on our Royal Staff. I will leave it to you and Pauto to convince her. You have dealt with her before. I am sure you know more about her than I do," replied Armbruster. It did not matter to him what they promised Florenzzah.

"Okay. I will do as you ask, Armbruster. Thank you for your help and insight. Pauto and I will head to the other side of the mountain and speak with Florenzzah. Please, wish us luck."

She released Armbruster's hands and turned to walk back inside Grand Race Manor, heading to the entrance where Pauto waited with the Torrins. She was ready to negotiate with Florenzzah.

The cabin was eerily quiet, and Alexis rolled onto her side, feeling uncomfortable on the hard bed. She wondered what

Gardone was doing in the living area. Alexis chose to return to bed, experiencing another debilitating headache and being unwilling to listen to him or Yarlen for another second. The two Warlocks sat on the couch, discussing the next step in their plan. She did not care, assuming their plot would be foiled. Armbruster would come to her rescue. She stretched and decided it was time to face them again.

Feeling exhausted, she strolled to the bathroom and rewashed her face. She sat on the short stool by the sink and brushed her hair, staring at the reflection in the mirror. She quickly realized how exhausted she felt. Her eyes were puffy and swollen. The dark rings under her eyes looked as if someone had punched her.

Disgusted, she got up and walked to her wardrobe. She removed her dirty cloak and reached for a clean one on the back of the shelf. She pulled the black cloak over her head, wishing she were at home, wearing something else. Finally dressed and wearing something clean, she exited the room and entered the living area. Gardone immediately greeted her.

"Well, I guess you finished pouting? Is your head feeling any better?" he asked, acting snippy and rude toward her. It did not go unnoticed by Alexis.

"Why can't you ever be kind, Daddy? You used to be a decent being. What happened to you? Did Yarlen poison you with his vision of grandeur?" she responded, hating him and his presence around her. She wanted to scratch his eyes out. Just looking at him turned her stomach.

"Don't be like that, Alexis. You know I am just kidding. I love you. I am not here to harm you. As I previously mentioned, I am asking you to voluntarily relinquish your title and power and transfer them to me. I do not want to cause an outright war on Alstromia to gain control. I want what I feel is rightfully mine. You are not capable of running the planet effectively. You are too one-sided, and your vision for the planet is poorly thought out and unorganized. You have upset 90% of all Clan members by changing the environment. They loved the planet the way it was before. No one wanted the gloomy and doomy atmosphere you created. Your Clan members miss Earth and prefer you keep things the same. Why did you start changing everything? Unfortunately, you are too vain and self-absorbed to see any of it. It makes me sick."

"Wow, Dad, why don't you tell me how you really feel?" she retorted, pissed off and defensive.

"I am clearly a much better option as a leader. Even Armbruster would be a better choice than you, dear. Don't worry. In time, I will replace you and make Alstromia a much happier place. Yarlen and I will take care of it. If you behave, I may allow you to keep some sort of a position on my Command Staff." Gardone laughed. He knew she was ready to kill him, but he did not care. He would take over soon, and she would give him the power voluntarily, or he would take it forcefully.

"Daddy, you assume a lot. You think others will believe your lies. You can fool some, but not all are naïve enough to believe the falsehoods you are trying to sell them. You will not get away with this. And as far as you *'allowing'* me a position on your Command Staff…you can kiss my royal ass! You will NEVER, EVER, be the leader of Alstromia. Dream on…" Alexis screamed at him, getting angrier the more she thought about it. She approached Gardone and stood before him, waiting for him to say another word.

Gardone locked eyes with Alexis. He knew she was furious. In a way, he felt nervous, aware of her powers. When they worked, she was quite powerful. She also had many loyal followers. It would not be an easy feat to take the kingdom from her.

He would need more substantial support. Gardone knew he would have to gain Armbruster as an ally to remove Alexis from power. With Yarlen and Armbruster's help, he was confident that Alexis could be removed.

The main question of the day was how he could persuade Armbruster that it would be in his best interest to oppose his wife and assist him. This could prove to be a challenging endeavor. Gardone understood that he would need to devise a more strategic plan, and he also wished to seek Yarlen's advice.

Alexis turned away from Gardone and flopped down on the couch. She propped her feet up and stretched out, yawning as she felt both bored and exhausted. She longed to go back to her Palace. This whole adventure was starting to wear on her. '*What the hell is going on? Is Armbruster working on a plan to rescue me? Is Aerianna helping? Where is Andreh?*' Alexis wondered.

Aerianna strolled down the walkway to meet Pauto. He stood by the Rein Poles, holding onto the restless Torrins. He was happy to see her approach. Without a word, Pauto helped her onto her beast. Once she was seated, he mounted his Torrin, and they headed to the field to take off for their flight to the other side of Tullah Mountain to speak with Florenzzah.

During the short flight, Pauto flew closely to Aerianna. He watched her intently as she focused ahead, unaware of what she intended to say to Florenzzah. Pauto shifted his gaze downward and noticed the hut, with smoke rising from the tall, stone chimney. He gestured toward a small clearing to the west. Aerianna nodded in understanding, and together they made their way in that direction.

Landing safely, they allowed the Torrins to trot toward the hut. Before they could dismount, the short, wooden door opened, and Florenzzah appeared. Her wild and curly white hair flapped in front of her face from the warm breeze. She brushed the stray hairs away from her wrinkled face to get a better look at the two. She grinned, exposing her dark yellow, stained teeth, and recognized Aerianna.

"What brings you to my humble hut, Aerianna?" she asked gruffly, leaning on her twisted, wooden cane.

"I must speak to you. I am here to discuss an urgent matter. May we dismount and come inside?" asked Aerianna, watching Florenzzah staring at them.

"Who is that with you?" she asked Aerianna, pointing to Pauto and refusing to speak to him directly.

"This is Pauto. He is our Chief of Security of the Command Security Team at the Palace. He accompanied me to ensure my safety."

"Oh, alright, then. Why don't you tie up the Torrins over there?" The old Witch pointed to one of the tall Trimbers next to the hut.

Pauto dismounted from his Torrin and helped Aerianna down. After she was safely on the ground, he grabbed both Torrins by their reins and led them to the Trimber, securing them carefully. He quickly followed the two Witches into the hut, prepared to start the negotiation process.

On the terrace behind the Grand Race Manor, Lorthana and Zandorah were deep in conversation. Armbruster sat away from them. He was uptight, wondering how things were progressing with Florenzzah in the hut. He hoped Aerianna would convince her to help them.

It had been almost 24 hours since they first spotted the *Protective Shield Spell* stretched over the cabin. Armbruster fretted about Alexis's safety, still curious if she had tried to escape her captors.

"Mom, we should head back to the Palace and care for Lilah. With Armbruster and Alexis gone, Carmin is all alone with her. I do not feel comfortable leaving my niece in the hands of a stranger during such a tumultuous time," announced Zandorah, seeking Lorthana's approval.

"I agree, Zandi. Let's inform Armbruster that we are returning to the Palace to care for Lilah. I am sure he will understand and agree. Have you spoken with Shawnatar at all since the situation arose? Is he aware of the developments? Maybe you should head to Iriss and see if he is there. I could head to the Palace, and you can join me later. What do you think?"

"No, I have not spoken with him. I have not seen him in over a week. He left to visit friends on Earth and has not returned. I am confused about what is happening between us. We haven't been getting along, so I haven't been in touch with him. I figured he would come home when he was ready. I will accompany you to the Palace. Lilah is my priority, not Shawnatar!"

The two Witches headed across the terrace to speak with Armbruster. He stood by one covered area, staring at the sky. Lorthana gently tapped him on the shoulder. He spun around and faced Lorthana. She quickly shared her ideas about flying back to the Palace with Zandorah and caring for Lilah. Armbruster nodded in agreement.

"Sounds like a great plan, Lorthana. It would be good to have you and Zandorah watching over Lilah. I wouldn't say I like the idea of Carmin and the security team being the only ones watching her. I prefer the family to take care of my child. Thank you both. Safe travels."

He headed back inside the Grand Race Manor, leading the way. Lorthana and Zandorah followed. Once on the front patio of the Manor, Armbruster pointed to the Rein Pole and the Torrins.

The Witches acknowledged the suggestion and headed toward the Torrins. Once standing by the majestic beings, Zandorah looked at Lorthana with a crooked smile on her face. She was not ready to fly again. Lorthana assumed as much and said, "Would you prefer we transport using our Ceptres, dear? I can see the apprehension on your face. I know how much you hate to fly."

"Can we? I mean, it would be so much easier," replied Zandorah, eager to return to the Palace without flying.

"We can try. I am not sure if the spell on the mountain will allow it. Here, take my hand. Let's do it together." The two held hands and slammed down their Ceptres, hoping to be transported to the Palace. Nothing happened. They remained in the same position. Lorthana realized what transpired. There was definitely still magic covering the entire area, keeping others from transporting to or from the location. No one could use magic. This was not good!

"Zandorah, I hate to tell you this, but we must fly. There is still a *Block Spell* in place. We cannot use our spells or Ceptres," said Lorthana, shaking her head. Armbruster witnessed the lack of teleportation. He quickly approached the two Witches.

"Is it a *Block Spell,* Lorthana?" he asked, assuming it was. It was the only reasonable conclusion about why they were still standing there.

"Yes, I believe so. Zandorah and I will fly back using the Torrins. I do not believe the *Block Spell* will keep us from flying. Aerianna and Pauto were able to take off. They were not blocked from leaving. This situation is ridiculous."

Lorthana helped her reluctant daughter mount her Torrin, knowing how uncomfortable she was with the beast. Once Zandorah was steady on her Torrin,

Lorthana mounted hers. They pulled back on the reins to walk the Torrins to the open field for take-off. Lorthana led the way, zooming off into the darkening sky, looking behind her, waiting for Zandorah to follow.

Quickly, Zandorah followed with a smooth take-off. She flew right up to Lorthana, laughing. Her hair whipped behind her. Zandorah looked like she was actually enjoying the flight.

Lorthana figured that in time, Zandorah would come to love flying as much as Alexis, or so she hoped. The two bolted off toward the Palace, ready to care for Lilah.

Florenzzah's hut was bright and cozy. Numerous baskets lined the entry. They were filled to the top with herbs and other items. Aerianna knew they were ingredients used for potions and other magical objects. She looked down to see if she could identify any items in the basket, but Florenzzah turned around and said, "Let's sit in my living area, shall we? Come on, hurry up."

She pointed to the couch and two oversized, fluffy chairs in the middle of the room. The wall ahead was a large stone fireplace. It held a large, round, black cauldron filled with a mysterious potion. It bubbled over the edge, dripping onto the roaring fire and producing hissing noises. The steam swirled over the top of the pot in a light purple color. The smell from the kettle was sweet and overpowering, making Aerianna woozy.

"I constantly experiment with new potions to stay prepared," Florenzzah remarked, gesturing toward a shelf on the opposite side of the room that was lined with hundreds of vials in different sizes and shapes.

Aerianna was impressed. Florenzzah was an amazing and talented Witch. She was also quite resourceful.

"So, why are you here, Aerianna? Did the Queen send you again? What does she want now?" Florenzzah was unwilling to aid them unless it would benefit her. She was denied her wishes the last time. This time, there would be a reward worthy of her talent.

"We need your help. Yes, the Queen is in trouble. However, she does not know we are here. I am sure you have seen the protective shield over the cabin on the other side of the mountain, no?" asked Aerianna.

"No, I have not left my hut in days. I have been busy working on my potions and making custom orders for friends. Why is there a shield? Are you talking about Alexis's cabin? I am confused. Please elaborate," replied Florenzzah, highly curious as to what was happening. It had to be serious if they would come to her for help. Florenzzah smiled. Maybe this would be her chance to get what she wanted.

"We believe Alexis has been taken hostage. We assume it is Gardone, her father. It is a long story, Florenzzah, and we do not have time for all the details. The bottom line is this: We need your help to remove the shield—a *Reversal Spell* of some sort. We require time to get inside the cabin and rescue the Queen. I have spoken with Armbruster. He has permitted me to offer you a Royal Staff position in exchange for your assistance. It is his promise, not an agreement by Alexis. He will keep his pledge to you. I am a witness and will attest to it. If you help us, I will ensure that you receive the position you desire. However, you must, in return, help us now. We cannot waste time. What do you say? Are you willing to do this for us?" asked Aerianna, begging and hoping Florenzzah would agree.

Florenzzah rolled her eyes, staring at the two sitting in the chairs facing her. She sat on the old, patched couch with a blanket covering her lap. "How do I know you will not lie again? You can tell me whatever you want and still not follow through. I have been betrayed before. You know this, Aerianna." She mindlessly played with the blanket on her lap, staring at Pauto and Aerianna.

"I told you—you will get what you want. We need your help. Armbruster is backing this offer and reward. He will ensure your position at the Palace and will not allow Alexis to renege on anything, I promise. Please, do this for us."

Florenzzah thought about it for a minute and stood up, making her way toward Aerianna and giving her a strange look. "Fine, I will do it. However, I require your assistance. You need to help me concoct the potion. It will take time. It is not an easy spell. Are you ready to begin the process? Please ask your friend to leave and ensure he speaks with Armbruster. Tell him we will join them once we have the completed potion. I expect to receive my payment at that time. I want Armbruster to present me with a written decree stating my position, name, and title. Only then will I give up the potion. Do you understand?" Florenzzah cackled. She realized she had finally won. Armbruster would grant her the dream job, and Alexis would be unable to stop her. The victorious moment thrilled her!

"Fine. Pauto will return to speak with Armbruster, share the newly formulated plan, and relay your request. I will remain here with you while we concoct the potion to use with the spell."

Pauto leaned over the chair and whispered to Aerianna, "I truly dislike the idea of you staying with Florenzzah. I think it is unwise. I do not believe we can trust her."

Aerianna stood up and helped Pauto out of the chair. "Go on. Please inform Armbruster about the new game plan. I will be fine. Florenzzah and I will complete the assignment. Do not worry." She escorted Pauto to the hut's main entrance door, firmly pushing him out. She knew he would not leave unless he were forced to go. She closed the door behind him before he could object or try to stay.

Aerianna joined Florenzzah in the potion-making room, which was brightly illuminated by the roaring fire. She read a book standing by the fireplace, giving Aerianna a slight grin, stirring the fowl-smelling concoction in the pot, which sizzled over the flames.

Aerianna hoped the magic would be strong enough to bring down the force field so the others could try to rescue the Queen. She continued worrying about Alexis as she stood beside Florenzzah and the bubbling cauldron.

# CHAPTER 13

Lorthana and Zandorah arrived at the Palace quickly. They landed near the stables and handed the Torrins to Essten. Together, they strolled leisurely down the path toward the Palace, talking the entire way. It was a beautiful day on Alstromia. It was bright and warm, with a gentle breeze, though the night was almost upon them.

Small children played by the riverbank, watching their parents fish in the Miccay River. For some miraculous reason, there wasn't a thundercloud in the sky.

Lorthana reached the arch and entrance, waiting for the young security sentry to allow her to pass. Just as he had last time, he denied her admission. Lorthana remained calm and asked the young guard to check with the head of security. Contacting Andreh, he was told to let her pass and enter the Palace immediately.

Furthermore, Andreh reprimanded the young security personnel for not checking the *'special VIP list'* posted inside the large security checkpoint shack. It identified Lorthana Snipperdoom-Stainnard as a VIP, granting her unlimited access to all areas of the Palace, as ordered by Pauto and Armbruster.

The embarrassed commoner led Lorthana and Zandorah to the Palace's main entrance, allowing them immediate access. He excused himself and ran back to the security checkpoint shack to continue patrolling the area.

Lorthana felt it was ridiculous that there was a permanent *Block Spell,* so only certain Witches or Warlocks could be transported directly into the Palace. She complained to Alexis several times about this and was informed it was a security measure to ensure only specific individuals had instant access to the Palace.

Those not granted direct access were required to pass through one of the three security checkpoints located around the Palace. One was on the north side of the Palace, and the others were situated to the east and west.

Since the south entrance also served as the Security Training Center, there was no need for a security checkpoint. Armed guards and security personnel regularly monitored the gateway, which was considered an *'off-limits area'* to most.

Still, Lorthana felt upset and hurt when Alexis explained the reasoning behind the *Block Spell,* basically informing Lorthana she was not granted instant access to the Palace.

Lorthana and Alexis argued over the situation for a long time. Lorthana figured that, as her mother and grandmother to Lilah, she should be given unconditional access. However, Alexis disagreed and told her, *'No.'* Eventually, Lorthana gave up and felt it was better to stop arguing over something that would only cause conflict within the family. Luckily, Armbruster ordered Lorthana permanent access to any place on Alstromia, including the Palace.

After arriving at the Palace, Lorthana and Zandorah made their way toward Lilah's chambers in search of Carmin. They intended to let her know that they would take care of Lilah's needs until the Queen returned. They were apprehensive about anyone getting close to the child, fearing that someone might harm her or take her hostage, just like her mother.

The door to Lilah's chamber stood slightly ajar. They could hear Carmin talking to Lilah in a loving, soothing voice. She held the child in her arms, standing before the large window, looking out over the valley below. Startled by the noise of them entering the room, Carmin turned around quickly. She still held Lilah firmly in her arms, pressed tightly against her body. She recognized Lorthana and Zandorah and nodded, acknowledging them.

"You startled me. I was not expecting anyone. Why are you here? Is everything okay?" asked Carmin, perplexed by their unexpected visit.

"Carmin, we are here to watch over Lilah during the Queen's temporary absence. Armbruster ordered it so. We will be taking care of Lilah. You may return to your chamber and relax. We will send a security guard to summon you if we require your assistance. Thank you, and good night,"

Lorthana announced as she roughly pulled the child from Carmin's arms.

Carmin looked at her, squinting, wondering what was happening. Carmin bowed her head and left the room without saying another word. She quickly entered her room, still upset at the abrupt dismissal by Lorthana.

"Mom, you were not very nice to Carmin. She is a kind Witch, and she loves Lilah. What is wrong with you?" Zandorah chastised her mother, glaring at her.

"I wanted to make a point—no need to be all lovey-dovey. We do not need her. I am here to take care of my grandchild. She should understand how important that is to me. Carmin is a caretaker, nothing more," retorted Lorthana, displeased at Zandorah's tone toward her.

"Whatever you say, Mom." Zandorah walked to the bed in the corner of the room and lay down. She was tired. Lorthana cradled Lilah in her arms as the sleepy child drifted off to sleep.

*'She is getting so big,'* thought Lorthana, smiling. She placed Lilah in her bed and joined Zandorah, who was fast asleep, loudly snoring. Both Witches were exhausted. Lorthana plopped down on the bed beside her daughter. She pulled the light cover over her body, feeling warm and

secure. Lorthana felt relieved they were there with Lilah.

Carmin was restless, trying to sleep. She was appalled at how Lorthana treated her, especially since she loved Lilah as if she were her own child. She was stunned that Lorthana and Zandorah had arrived to watch over Lilah at the Palace. Was there more to the story? Where was the Queen? Carmin assumed something horrible had happened to Alexis. She got up and headed to the Security Command Chamber to find out what was happening.

Andreh instructed his team on the security measures he wanted in place in the Security Command Chamber. Carmin entered in a huff, instantly stopping next to one of the security members. Not seeing Pauto, she continued walking around the room, searching for him.

"Excuse me, what do you think you are doing?" asked the security member.

"I am here to speak with Pauto. Where is he?" responded Carmin.

Andreh overheard the conversation and intercepted Carmin. "I am in charge. What do you require, Carmin? Is everything okay with the Princess?" he asked, worried.

"Everything is just fine. The Queen's mother and sister are taking care of her. I want to know where I can find the Queen. She has been away for a while, and I have been feeling uneasy about her absence. Something is not right—I know it!"

"Don't worry, and return to your chamber. The Queen is at her cabin, taking some time to relax, and Armbruster is there as well. There's nothing to be concerned about!" Andreh hoped he sounded persuasive. He didn't want Carmin to be aware of the situation. He had promised Pauto to stay discreet, so he tried to assure Carmin that everything was fine—just business as usual.

Carmin observed Andreh with her head tilted to one side. She did not believe him. He had refused to look into her eyes when he told her about the Queen's whereabouts. Carmin suspected there was much more to his tale of lies. He was hiding something. She assumed it was something significant and noticed Pauto was also absent. It made her even more curious.

Ultimately, she decided it was in her best interest to head back to her chamber as requested. On the way out of the room, she thanked Andreh, giving him a fake smile.

In the Witch's hut, Florenzzah instructed Aerianna on how to help her combine ingredients for the completion of the complex potion. She opened the *Book of Insight,* her most-used Spellbook. Afterward, she placed her hand over the top, allowing the book to show her the appropriate page and spell. The thick book flipped open to page 918—the *Reversal Spell* page.

Florenzzah was familiar with this spell but knew she needed something more. She waved her hand over the book a second time. This time, it flipped open to page 333 - the *Blocking Spell.* Florenzzah understood what the book was telling her to do. The two spells had to be combined to remove the shield and block anyone from recasting the original hex. She smiled at Aerianna, ready to concoct the special potions required. The two read the list of ingredients requirements. Florenzzah strolled to the entryway and riffled through the baskets filled with herbs and other ingredients. Aerianna watched and stayed out of her way, awaiting instructions.

Armbruster stared at the glowing shield. He became more nervous as time passed, desperately wanting to rescue Alexis. She was probably getting irritated and angry because no one had come to save her yet. Alexis lacked all forms of patience. Armbruster could only imagine what was going on inside the cabin. She would be giving them hell. There was no way she would accept being held hostage without trying to do something to gain her freedom. Alexis was not stupid. He was convinced she had a plan.

Alexis was comfortable, stretched out on the couch, making huffing noises. Bored, she picked at her long fingernails, hoping to escape the cabin. Irritated, she stood up and paced around the room like a prowling lioness. Gardone watched her, saying nothing. He instantly wondered about Yarlen. *'Did he return to the hut on Earth to work on spells?'*

"I want to go outside. I feel like I am dying in here, Daddy. Could I sit outside for a while, please? You can accompany me and keep watch. I don't care. I need to get out of the stuffy building," she begged.

"Sure, we can head out for a while. It is almost time to eat, though. Let's make it quick," Gardone responded. He opened the door and talked with Korbin, instructing him to keep an eye on Alexis.

Alexis exited the cabin, plopping down on one of the stone benches on the front porch. She closed her eyes and tried to slow her breathing, listening to her heart beating in her ears. She inhaled deeply, trying to meditate and relax.

Armbruster observed the shield. He saw several figures outside the building. He could barely see, though he was fairly certain one of the figures was Alexis. He noticed her long, black hair.

Seeing Alexis and knowing she was there alone without help scared him. *'Where is Aerianna? Did she convince Florenzzah to help?'* Armbruster felt a tap on his right shoulder, and he turned around. It was Pauto smiling at him.

"Well, what happened?" asked Armbruster, anxiously awaiting the news.

"Florenzzah has agreed to help us with a spell. Aerianna stayed behind to help her concoct the potions. They will arrive as soon as it is done. It should not take too long. Hopefully, they will be successful," Pauto explained.

"Fantastic. Look over there," Armbruster pointed toward the cabin. "Does that look like Alexis sitting in front of the cabin?"

"Hard to tell, Sir. It does look like someone with long hair. I would say it has to be."

"That is what I thought, too," replied Armbruster.

The two walked back to the terrace, preparing for the rescue. Neither felt too confident. They worried Florenzzah would not be able to cast the magical chant correctly. So much had already gone wrong. They could only hope it would go as planned.

★*.★*.★*.★*.★

It was chilly as Alexis sat quietly on the cold, hard, stone bench. She remained seated with her eyes closed. Her legs were crossed, and her arms were firmly placed on her legs as she leaned against the wall.

She continued to breathe deeply, hoping to stay relaxed. It was getting late. The daytime teal-colored moons changed to bright white, welcoming the night.

The evening was windy, and Alexis shivered, feeling miserable. Attempting to stay warm, she recalled the beautiful day on Earth when Shell taught her to meditate.

It had been a glorious, sunshiny day. Shell met Alexis in the enormous field behind her house. The grass in the field was very tall. Butterflies and dragonflies zoomed all around them. Suddenly, Shell dropped down in the middle of the area, sitting upright. She pulled Alexis down beside her.

"Here, sit like me. Cross your legs and sit up straight. Place your palms up on your legs and close your eyes," instructed Shell.

"Umm, why would I do that?" retorted Alexis. She felt it was a stupid thing to do in the middle of a field.

"Do you trust me?" asked Shell. "If you do, just do it. You need to learn to relax, Alexis. This will help! I promise." Shell watched as Alexis followed her instructions.

"Now what?" Alexis asked, irritated.

"Now, breathe deeply. Clear your mind. Continue to breathe in and out. Listen to the sounds all around you. Breath in, breath out," Shell continued.

The two mediated for ten minutes. Shell stood up and helped Alexis stand. "Well, do you feel better?" Shell inquired.

"You know…I do! Thanks for showing me how to relax and meditate. I will do this daily. Clearing the mind and forgetting about stress is good. You are the best, Shell." Alexis hugged her best friend, feeling refreshed.

Alexis jumped as her thoughts were interrupted by Gardone. He appeared outside with two lanterns in his hands, one of which was handed to Korbin. He hung it by the front door and stood near Alexis, watching her. Gardone turned around, heading back inside.

Gardone shook, disliking the brisk night. He added a few pieces of Trimber logs to the fireplace, making a roaring, warm fire.

The room lit up a bright yellow and orange from the flames. Then the fire turned purple and green, darkening the room. Trimbers always burned yellow and orange, but the hotter the fire, the darker the flames became until they turned a purple and green color.

Gardone sat on the couch, warming up. He waved his Ceptre and lit up the big, drop-down chandelier hanging in the living area. His magical abilities were the only ones working in the entire cabin. He smiled, knowing this would piss Alexis off even more if she understood he could still perform sorcery.

Alexis continued to sit quietly outside, thinking and meditating. She was aware Korbin was nearby. She could hear him breathing loudly, assuming he was angry, as he had to guard her.

After a few more minutes, Alexis opened her eyes and stood up. She entered the cabin, turning around for a moment to look toward the Manor. She felt someone was watching her, ever hopeful it was Armbruster and her security team.

Inside the cabin, Gardone sat on one of the couches, eating a bowl of Golden Fin Stew. He loved the sweet and sour meal. Yarlen had not returned from the hut on Earth, making Gardone wonder what he was doing. He saw Alexis walk through the door and approach the couch. He moved to one side, allowing her some space to sit down. She chose to walk to the other couch and sit down, staring at him. Obviously, she was not prepared to engage in a civil conversation.

"Are you hungry, dear?" he asked, holding the green bowl filled with the warm meal.

Alexis could smell the Golden Fin Stew. Her stomach rumbled with hunger, but she shook her head *'no.'* She would not allow him to act kindly or caring toward her. Alexis was done with his games.

"Daddy, why don't you just let me go? We can work out an agreement. I am even willing to allow for an election. We can let the commoners of Alstromia decide if they wish to replace me," Alexis suggested. She knew her words would upset him and that he was not interested in allowing an election to take place. He wanted to take her power away from her by force.

"Absolutely not! We are not holding any elections. I already told you that I am taking over Alstromia. This is not up for negotiations. I am informing you of what will happen. As previously stated, I am willing to give you a position on my staff. That is all, nothing more. Just accept it. We are done talking about this. You will be able to return to the Palace in time. Then, you can pack your things and move back here to the cabin, for all I care."

"You really think it will be so easy? What makes you believe that, Daddy? You are greatly mistaken. You continue to believe my people will let this happen. I took care of Loggane. I can do the same with you. Just remember that." Alexis was no longer interested in his threats. She was done with his crazy visions for Alstromia.

Now, Alexis knew it would come down to her family. If they failed to rescue her, she would have to do what she needed, including taking care of Gardone once and for all. She hoped it did not come to that.

Andreh paced around the room, getting impatient. *'Is Alexis safe? What is happening to her?'* His stomach was upset, and he felt awful. His neck ached from the stress, and his temples throbbed, forcing him to rub them, hoping the pain would subside. All he wanted was to talk with her. He missed her and worried about her welfare. *'What if something awful happened to her? What if Armbruster fails to bring her back safely to the Palace? Is Pauto on his way back to the Palace to brief me?'*

Andreh left the Security Command Chamber and made his way to the basement. He was eager to explore the laboratory, a place he had nearly exclusive access to. Alexis had granted him entry to this hidden location, where they often met to discuss matters away from the prying eyes of Alstromia. Andreh was determined to figure out a way to bring Alexis back, unwilling to rely on Pauto, Aerianna, or Armbruster for her rescue. She was far too important to him.

Andreh waved his left hand over the large, oval stone embedded in the wall in the basement. It looked like an ordinary stone, but it was not. It was the access panel to the secret room and laboratory. He turned around to ensure he was alone while waiting for the wall to separate and open. Once it did, he stepped through the opening and entered the room.

The wall closed quickly behind him, illuminating the room. He walked to the long, black velvet couch by one of the shelves and admired the candles flickering on the wall in the large metal sconces.

He felt it was clever. Alexis thought about everything. She cast the chant perfectly. Once someone entered the room, it lit up brightly.

The hanging metal chandelier, with its twenty candles, illuminated the entire room. Andreh stood before the tallest shelf in the room and pulled down a few books. He wanted to see if he could find a spell to help rescue Alexis. Though he was not the best or most gifted Warlock, Alexis taught him well. They worked together frequently. She wanted him to perfect his craft.

Andreh smiled, thinking about her. Alexis usually laughed and grinned whenever he miscalculated a spell and something awful happened. She never became upset with him. She would touch his hand lightly and show him how to perform the magic correctly. He missed her so much that his heart ached. The thoughts of her gave him the courage to seek out new magic to help rescue his beloved Alexis.

Inside the warm cabin, Alexis watched Gardone devour his dinner. She thought he looked like a pig, snarfing his food, which made her sick. She considered eating something, but decided against it. It would only appease Gardone to see her eat. She wanted him to worry that she had not consumed food in a long time. Maybe he would eventually come around and give her what she wanted—her freedom.

Gardone ate the last of his Golden Fin Stew. He stood up and placed the bowl on the table next to the couch. He walked to the fireplace and stood before it, facing Alexis.

"What do you want to do, Alexis? I am tired. I need to return home to your mother. I do not want to stay here for another second. Will you please agree to give me Alstromia and the Palace?"

"Drop dead, Dad. I already told you, NO! What part of *'no'* did you not understand? I cannot be any clearer. I will NEVER relinquish my position as Queen nor surrender to you. Get that through your thick skull. I will kill you before I allow you to take Alstromia away from me," she hissed. She stood up and approached him.

Forcefully, she punched him, and he stumbled, falling backward. He landed in the large fireplace on the hot flames, screaming in pain. He jumped out as quickly as he could, rolling on the ground, his cloak on fire.

Alexis cackled in delight and did nothing, watching him frantically trying to extinguish the flames scorching his clothing.

He stood up, still smacking the side of his cloak, little puffs of smoke billowing from it. Korbin came rushing in through the front door. He heard Gardone scream and was horrified to discover what had happened.

"That's it, Alexis. I am done with you. I am returning to Earth. I will do whatever I need to in order to take Alstromia from you. I wanted to be kind, but after this last stunt, all bets are off."

He walked to the entryway, grabbed his Ceptre, slammed it down, producing a loud thud, and disappeared into a green fog. Alexis laughed, not worried about the consequences of her actions. Though she became distraught, realizing Gardone's magic seemed to work just fine. She thought about what she could do to reinstate her abilities.

On Earth, Gardone appeared in the kitchen of his home. He looked around, smelling the burnt odor still on his cloak. He was curious about where Lorthana was hiding, so he called out her name. However, there was no response. He walked around each room, looking for clues, and wondered where she might have gone. Immediately, he noticed her Ceptre was missing.

Instantly, he worried about what that meant. *'Where is Lorthana?'* Since Lorthana was not home, he planned to visit Yarlen. Before heading out to see him, he would change his cloak and dress in a new one. He did not want to show up in a burnt cape that would evoke a multitude of questions from Yarlen. He was not in the mood to deal with inquiries.

Yarlen sat on a stool in the kitchen in the hut on Earth. He figured he should be working on something to help Gardone, but he did not want to do so. He was more worried about the consequences he would face from Alexis.

Yarlen decided it was best to make her his ally. He had no idea how to accomplish this, but Yarlen figured he would do his best to convince Alexis he was loyal to her. Yarlen knew the only way to save his own life was to ensure he saved hers. *'Now, how to do that?'* he contemplated.

Outside, the weather turned horrible, with blustery winds producing strange howling and whistling noises inside the hut. Rain poured out of the sky while lightning flashed in white and purple colors in the darkness, illuminating the building.

The Trimbers swayed in the wind, making cracking noises. The rickety structure shook violently as branches fell onto the roof, producing loud thud sounds.

Nervously, Florenzzah looked up at the ceiling, hoping her hut would withstand such awful weather. She stood in the doorway, peering outside to watch the pouring rain, though it was difficult to see anything else. The rain was coming down fast and hard. She smiled while listening to the thunder roaring outside, loving the weather.

Even so, she was nervous they would have to fly through the dreadful weather since they could not use their Ceptres to transport themselves onto the other side of the mountain. *'At least it will be a short flight,'* she thought, still feeling apprehensive.

Aerianna and Florenzzah smiled at each other, feeling a sense of accomplishment. They knew now the real test would begin. Did they concoct the potions correctly? Would the mixtures work correctly with the spell? Aerianna carefully placed the two potions, which were red, round bottles, into the chant bag. Florenzzah added a few other items. One was the *Book of Magical Reveals*, a book she wanted to take with them for backup, just in case any of the other spells did not work.

"Do you think we have gathered everything?" asked Aerianna, worried. She did not want to forget any items, as they had no time to waste.

"I believe we do. We have both potions, two books, and two different spells handy to try. I think it is the best we can do. Now, let's hope all works out. We have done a great job. We have been very thorough and careful working on the magical items. Let's see how it goes. Are we ready to head to the Manor?"

"Of course, I am ready! I hope we can get this done to rescue Alexis. She is the priority right now. We have to make this happen." Aerianna replied, feeling hopeful. She looked outside, noticing the relentless rain pouring out of the sky with no end in sight.

Aerianna speculated how their flight would go. Torrins were not fond of water and performed poorly on flights when it rained. Aerianna hoped her Torrin would be okay and not too anxious.

Most Torrins disliked thunder and lightning and were usually restless and unwilling to fly. They were timid creatures. Although Torrins were known to be loyal to their owners, they had a propensity to misbehave if they did not like the flying conditions. Some would even refuse to take off for flight, standing adamantly still, clearly indicating they were unhappy.

"Shall we head outside and prepare the Torrins? I know that making our way to the other side of the mountain with them will be a challenge, but it's a quick flight. I believe we will be okay. What do you think, Aerianna?" Florenzzah asked Aerianna optimistically. They both knew the Torrins would be agitated.

Florenzzah walked outside and headed to the small stable off to the right of her hut. Aerianna followed her with the two bags. She attached the gear to her Torrin and mounted her quickly. Both Torrins seemed restless and not interested in leaving the stable. Aerianna pulled back on the reins, forcing her Torrin to exit the stable.

Once outside, the Torrin immediately started bucking and acting up. Aerianna leaned forward and whispered into her Torrin's right ear, *'It's okay, girl. We can do this. It is a short flight, I promise.'* She ran her hand over the Torrin's head. Instantly, the majestic creature turned to look at Aerianna as if she was giving her the approval to fly.

Quickly, Aerianna seized the moment. She gently tapped her Torrin on the side of her stomach with her feet and pulled back on the reins. They headed toward the empty field for take-off through the torrential downpours. Florenzzah followed on her Torrin, which seemed less upset by the weather conditions.

Within seconds, the two Witches were airborne on their beasts, flying toward the Manor on the other side of the mountain. It wasn't easy to see, but the lightning illuminated the sky enough for them to know the way. The rain drenched the two Witches, making them cold and wet. Aerianna leaned forward on her Torrin, shivering. She tried to stay warm, leaning up against the warm-blooded creature.

Florenzzah sat straight up on her Torrin with her head tilted to the sky. She loved the feeling of the rain on her face, her hair soaked and clinging to her. The old Witch smiled, feeling happy and excited about the new adventure about to start. Florenzzah could not wait to help rescue Alexis and rightfully begin her new royal position at the Palace.

Armbruster remained quiet, wringing his hands nervously. He stared at the cabin, waiting impatiently for Aerianna and Florenzzah. The wind picked up, and it was raining, which added to his glum mood. He looked around, realizing he would have to enter the Manor to stay dry. Hopefully, the two Witches had successfully made the necessary potions to complete the magic. Somewhere in the back of his mind, he assumed it would not work but tried to dismiss the thought. Florenzzah was undoubtedly very talented. He figured she would be the only one to complete such a complicated spell other than Yarlen.

Suddenly, Armbruster felt an overwhelming stabbing pain in his stomach. He bent over quickly, trying to catch his breath. Then it hit him—Yarlen was probably the one responsible for producing the Protection Shield. *'Why would Yarlen do that?'* Armbruster said aloud.

The King strongly believed it was a terrible choice for Yarlen to rally against Alexis a second time. *'Where is Yarlen?'* Armbruster was getting worried, waiting for the Witches to appear. He walked inside the Manor, still not feeling too optimistic about rescuing Alexis. He found a chair in the back of the main hall and sat down.

Armbruster's patience was practically non-existent at the moment. He called out Pauto's name, hoping he would join him in the main hall to discuss the possible next step in trying to rescue Alexis.

Pauto stood outside the Manor by the main doors. He paced around, feeling restless and worried about Aerianna, hoping she would return soon. He heard Armbruster calling his name. Part of him wanted to head inside to speak with Armbruster, but he also wanted to stay outside and wait for Aerianna. Ultimately, Pauto decided it was best to keep Armbruster happy.

Before entering the Manor, he looked off toward the River of Miccay. He noticed that the rain was pouring heavily from the sky. The flashes of lightning were more frequent than before. He knew Aerianna and Florenzzah would have to fly through the treacherous weather to get to the Manor. Pauto also realized Torrins hated rain and lightning. He hoped all would turn out okay for the Witches during their flight.

Feeling on edge, Pauto entered the Manor searching for Armbruster. It did not take long. He found the King in the back of the main hall, his hand on his lap. He looked tired, raising his head when he heard Pauto approach.

"Sir, you wanted me?" asked Pauto with a smile.

"Yes, I was hoping you had news about Aerianna and Florenzzah?"

"No, I do not. I have not seen them. The weather is also quite challenging at this time. It is raining heavily, and the wind is blowing strongly. It will be a difficult flight on the

Torrins. I hope they are safe," responded Pauto. He began to suspect that something was amiss. He nervously glanced at the backroom window and noticed the weather was getting worse. The water pooled outside the door, and it looked like hurricane weather, with water gushing down the windows and doors.

The Trimbers swayed violently back and forth, branches crashing to the ground. The lights flickered inside the Manor, and Armbruster looked up at the chandelier, which swung lightly. Pauto deliberated about what was happening as he heard noises on the roof. *'Did a Trimber hit the roof?'* He appeared edgy as he looked outside, standing before the glass door. Pauto wondered why Armbruster did not try to cast a spell to stop the horrific weather. Perhaps he believed it would not work.

Alexis curled up on the couch, falling asleep. She heard the booming thunder getting closer to the building. The cracking and snapping noises were noticeably louder as well. She assumed it was the Trimber branches breaking and hitting the cabin. Korbin stood before the fireplace, adding more Trimber logs to keep the fire going. The house was warm and comfortable.

Once in a while, the room became bright from the flashes of lightning. The rain produced a clicking noise on the metal roof.

Alexis pulled the blanket over her head and closed her eyes. All she wanted to do was sleep, feeling physically drained. The weather conditions made her even more tired. Alexis missed Lilah and was ready to return to the Palace. She hated feeling trapped in the cabin. *'Where is Gardone?'* she wondered. *'Is he on his way back to the cabin?'* She snuggled more deeply into the couch, finally succumbing to much-needed sleep.

Andreh scoured over the books on his lap. He sat comfortably on the black, velvet couch in the secret room. He wasn't able to find anything that gave him hope. Everything he read in the books was useless.

He slammed the big, red book shut on his lap, staring down at it. Andreh sighed, wondering what Alexis was doing. He pushed the book off his lap and onto the couch.

Frustrated, Andreh stood up and paced around in a circle, talking to himself. Abruptly, he stopped. He stared at the large shelf in front of him. Then he saw it—*Protections & Safety*.

He knew it was the book he had been looking for. Quickly, he pulled it off the shelf and took it back to the couch, hoping to find something that would help him rescue his beloved Alexis.

Andreh touched the dark-blue cover. The book was fragile and old. The printed title, *"Protections & Safety,"* was challenging to read since *the* gold letters were dull and faded.

Excited to have found the book, he waved his hands over it with his eyes closed, chanting softly. The book flipped open to page 288. He opened his eyes. He ran his right index finger down the page and stopped on the second paragraph: *"Invisible, you shall appear. Not an ear shall hear. Protection is near, do not fear."* He smiled and read on.

*"Frumble Potion, greater notion, these spells are great and fine, breaking the protection line."* The instructions followed: *"Use this spell while pouring half of the Frumble Potion onto the dome, barrier, or shield you are attempting to infiltrate. Once the dome, barrier, or shield flickers, you will be invisible, allowing you to penetrate the shield, but you must move quickly, as it does not last. Once you wish to leave the protective dome barrier or shield, you must use the Frumble potion's remainder to exit.* ***NOTE:*** *This spell does NOT permanently remove the*

*dome, barrier, or shield. It only allows you to enter and exit safely."*

Andreh saw the dome glowing, gazing at the mountain earlier. He was well aware it was the biggest hurdle keeping him from Alexis. He smirked, realizing what he had to do. Now, how would he be able to carry it out? He couldn't just arrive at the cabin hoping to free Alexis. Armbruster would be there with Aerianna and Pauto. But he would be invisible, so maybe they would never find out.

Andreh made a list of ingredients necessary for the Frumble Potion. He knew the items were available in the Tower. He closed the book gently, tucked it under his arm, and walked toward the door to exit the secret room. He planned to head to the Tower to retrieve the potion-making items and hopefully concoct the Frumble Potion correctly. He wished Alexis were around to help. He had never completed such a complicated task on his own.

Minutes later, Andreh entered the Tower alone. He was glad he had memorized the chant to open the vault's main door, where all the items were stored. Alexis had shared it with him a while back. He searched the shelves trying to locate the items: *8 Frumble Berries (dark purple and sour), two drops of Cuvvey (spider-like creature) venom, 3*

*Snipperly feathers (bird-like creature), 1 Snout of Rue (similar to a pig on Earth), and 4 Hunddeh hairs (dog-like creature).*

He read the potion concoction instructions:

*"Combine the Frumble Berries with the two drops of Cuvvey venom. Stir carefully over the hot flames in a medium-sized, hot cauldron. Slowly add one Snipperly feather at a time until it is dissolved. Gently add the Snout of Rue. If done correctly, it will cause a slight explosion noise, and a green vapor will appear. Last, add the Hunddeh hairs one at a time. This will cause the potion to become thick and blue. Stir until it smells sweet, and a teal haze floats over the top of the cauldron. Pour the completed potion carefully into a tall, thick potion bottle (#3 Capacity).*

*The bottle must be sealed immediately with a black stopper to ensure the freshness of the potion. It is not necessary to keep the brew warm. DO NOT open the bottle until ready to use. If you use part of the potion, reseal the bottle immediately to keep the remaining liquid fresh. The potion's power will only last 24 hours."*

Andreh walked to the end of the large table and pulled a medium-sized cauldron off it, placing it on the fireplace stand. He waved his hands over the Trimber logs, igniting the fire. Next, he expeditiously assembled the missing ingredients one by one, finding some in baskets on shelves while others were stored in small vials.

The Cuvvey venom was in a black bottle with a neon-green X on it. Cuvvey poison was green and smelled foul, like rotten eggs.

Once the fire burned steadily, Andreh stood before the fireplace with all the ingredients lined up on the table. He began adding the items to the cauldron, as instructed in the book. The Frumble Berries made a loud, hissing noise as they hit the bottom of the hot pot. Instantly, they melted.

Andreh carefully removed the stopper from the bottle containing the Cuvvey venom. He carefully added two drops of the venom, which instantly produced a wretched scent. It made him want to puke.

Next, he dropped the Snipperly feathers into the cauldron's goo, one at a time, stirring the potion in a circular motion. As he added the Snout of Rue, a big banging noise filled the chamber, causing him to jump. He smiled. The potion was coming along correctly. The green vapor appeared over the top of the cauldron, glowing an iridescent color.

He finished by adding the Hunddeh hairs. They smelled odd and immediately caused the cauldron to bubble furiously, hot steam pouring out of the pot with an almost disgustingly sweet scent. To Andreh, it smelled like cotton candy. The smell made him gag. He was happy to see the potion turn a dark blue color. The signature teal haze hovered over the cauldron, indicating the brew was complete and done correctly. He felt pleased, imagining what Alexis would say and how happy she would be witnessing him independently complete such a complex potion.

Andreh could not wait to tell her all about the process. Happily, he grabbed a size #3 Capacity Potion Bottle and placed it next to the cauldron.

Slowly and cautiously, Andreh poured the steaming liquid into the bottle using a long ladle, feeling the container getting heavy in his hand. He quickly sealed the potion bottle with a black stopper to keep the brew fresh.

Finally, he was ready to clean the room, leave, and head to the Security Command Chamber to inform his staff he would be gone for a while. Andreh was prepared to rescue Alexis, and no one would stop him.

Alexis stirred from sleep, her head pounding, her ears buzzing, and a gnawing hunger in her stomach. Feeling annoyed, she glanced around the living room to check for anyone else. As she sat up carefully, feeling unwell, she caught the sound of voices outside, guessing it was Korbin along with the other Security Commoner. She could not help but wonder when her father would return to the cabin to start more drama. She managed to stand up and sauntered to the kitchen area, looking for something to eat.

She found an apple in a blue glass bowl on the counter. Famished, she grabbed it and bit into it. It tasted so good. It was crisp, and its juices ran down the side of her mouth. She wiped the mess off her face, thinking it was the best apple she had ever had. Alexis assumed Gardone brought it with him from Earth. She had not eaten an apple in a long time. She devoured it and placed the apple core and stem on the counter beside the bowl.

Feeling satisfied, Alexis went back to the bedroom and chose to freshen up. She tossed her shoes onto the floor and took off her clothes while sitting on the stool. Despite her lingering headache, she successfully navigated to the shower stall without stumbling from the discomfort.

Alexis appreciated that a shower had been installed when the cabin was constructed. It was one of her favorite comforts from Earth. As she turned the shower faucet, hot water cascaded over her head and down her body. The sensation was incredible. She felt herself warming up, experiencing happiness and relaxation for the first time since arriving at the cabin. Alexis leaned against the shower wall, enjoying the warmth of the water. After she washed her hair and rinsed her body, she stepped out of the shower and grabbed her thick, white robe off the hook hanging on the wall. Reluctantly, she returned to the living room to sit in front of the fireplace to help dry her hair.

Alexis thought about Gardone and hoped he would return soon. She wanted to end this ridiculous game they were playing. He would lose this battle between them. She was sick of it and not amused. He crossed the line and had to pay the price. Gardone would be sorry he tried to take Alstromia, the kingdom, and her title from her.

Exhausted and frustrated, Armbruster slumped in the chair, resting his elbows on his knees with his hands covering his face. He was barely awake, his eyes shut tight. Pauto watched him, wondering if he was trying to stay composed. Moments later, a noise from outside caught Pauto's attention. He hurried over to the glass door to investigate what was going on.

Aerianna saw the field below where they planned to land. She pulled back on her

Torrin's reins, directing her toward the field by the Manor. She turned around to ensure Florenzzah was still behind her, following closely. The two landed their Torrins safely on the slippery and wet ground and quickly headed to the stable to tie up the beasts. Once the Torrins were secured and warm, the two Witches made their way to the back of the Manor.

Aerianna climbed the terrace steps and approached the back door, drenched and chilled from the pouring rain. Florenzzah was beside her, holding her hand to steady her on the slippery steps.

Pauto noticed Aerianna by the door and swung it open, allowing water to rush into the room. The Witches hurried inside, and Pauto quickly shut the door behind them. He wrapped his arms around Aerianna, who returned the embrace, relieved to see him. Meanwhile, Florenzzah remained quiet, scanning the surroundings.

Armbruster heard the voices and woke up from his nap. He stood up and approached Florenzzah and Aerianna, eager to find out if they had brought the necessary items.

Aerianna let go of Pauto and smiled, aware that he wanted to kiss her. However, she quickly stepped back to avoid drawing Armbruster's attention. She stood beside

Florenzzah as Armbruster approached, yawning and raking his fingers through his hair. His bright blue eyes appeared lackluster, and the whites were tinged with red—he looked worn out.

"Welcome! I am so glad you both made it. What dreadful weather we are having. Thank goodness you were able to maneuver through the rain. How was your flight? Did the Torrins hold up okay for you?" he asked.

Aerianna spoke up, "It was okay. The Torrins behaved. Yes, they were not happy about flying in the dark and rain. However, they handled it well. We hurried, knowing you were waiting and anxious. Sir, Florenzzah did an amazing job with the potion. She worked hard and fast. We have brought it along with a variety of spells. We are ready when you are."

"Excellent! I am so happy to hear that. Though, I believe we may have to wait until the rain subsides. The weather is still too bad for us to venture outside. There are dry clothing items in the Clothes Storage room. Why don't you get something dry to wear for you and Florenzzah while I speak with her?" Armbruster explained as he looked at the old Witch. He wanted the opportunity to speak with her alone. "Take Pauto with you!"

"Oh, of course. We will be back shortly," replied Aerianna. Pauto followed her as they walked to the Clothes Storage room near the kitchen, searching for dry articles of clothing to wear.

Pauto walked behind her, hoping to get a chance to kiss her. He was glad she was safe. They reached the room, and Aerianna opened the door. Pauto held the door open as she turned around and embraced him. She took the opportunity to kiss him since they were alone in the dark room. He did not resist.

Pauto held Aerianna tightly in his arms. He wanted so badly never to let her go. Unfortunately, he knew it was time to return to the others before they became suspicious of their long absence. Aerianna pushed herself away from Pauto and gathered two cloaks from inside the closet. She grabbed two dresses neatly folded on a shelf. She smiled as she turned to walk out of the closet, heading to the room to speak with Armbruster. Pauto allowed her to walk ahead, wishing he could take her back to the Palace.

Armbruster observed Florenzzah as she stood holding both bags in her hands. The chant bag was in her right hand, and she gently placed it on the ground. She held the other sack in her left hand, waiting for Armbruster to speak.

"Florenzzah, first, I'd like to thank you for coming. It means a lot to Alexis and me. We are in your debt. Second, as Aerianna explained, I will grant you the new position on my staff in exchange for your help. You have my promise. This job is guaranteed, regardless of the outcome. I know you do not trust Alexis. However, I am not Alexis. I always keep my word. So, do you have any questions for me?"

"Your Majesty, it is my pleasure to be of service to you and the Queen. There are no hard feelings. What happened in the past is in the past. We shall move forward. I trust you and am grateful for the position you have offered me. Thank you!"

Florenzzah handed Armbruster the chant bag. He took it from her and opened it. He glanced inside and nodded approvingly.

Andreh entered the Security Command Chamber in the Palace of Snipperdoom. He informed Harshim, Armbruster's assistant, that he would be gone for a while, placing him in charge of security during his temporary absence. He also asked him to find Porti, one of the head Security Commoners, and ensure the Palace was protected. Harshim accepted the responsibility and did not ask any other questions. Andreh left the chamber and headed outside to the stables to inform Essten to prepare his Torrin for flying.

The rain seemed relentless, steadily pounding the ground, occasionally turning to hail. The wind was strong and chilly. Andreh felt cold even though he wore his riding cloak and long pants. He held a Mesmer Ceptre in one hand and a small chant bag in another, which contained his precious potion. The Spellbook, *Protections & Safety*, was safely tucked into a large, inside pocket of his cloak. Andreh found Essten grooming a Torrin as he approached.

"Good evening, Essten. Could you please prepare my Torrin? I must depart for Tullah Mountain immediately. Please hurry. It is imperative that I take off right away. The Queen needs me."

"Hello, Andreh! Of course, I will get him ready for you now. I'll be right back and promise to hurry." Essten disappeared down the corridor as he walked toward one of the back stalls, ready to retrieve Fangoh, Andreh's Torrin.

Within minutes, Essten reappeared with Fangoh. He handed Andreh the reins. "Be careful out there, Andreh. The weather keeps getting worse. I am not sure how long the weather will be like this."

"Thanks, Essten, I will. Have a good night, my friend," he replied, mounting the spooked beast. Essten tied the chant bag to the back of the Torrin and handed Andreh the Mesmer Ceptre. Andreh bowed his head, thanking him, and trotted out of the stable on his Torrin, heading to the field for a challenging take-off.

Essten watched Andreh head to the field, wondering what was happening and why everyone's destination was Tullah Mountain. It seemed very suspicious and more than just a coincidence. Something did not seem right. He shook his head and decided to let it go.

The evening was uneventful for Lorthana as she rocked Lilah in her arms. The child was getting so big, growing up fast. Her hair was dark brown, curly, and long. The child was now a toddler but still liked being rocked to sleep.

Zandorah slept in the bed on the other side of the room, lightly snoring. Lorthana questioned if Alexis was okay. She also reminisced about Gardone and what he was up to, assuming it was something horrible. She stood up from the rocking chair, walked to the small bed in the corner of the room, and lay Lilah on the bed, covering her up. Lilah rolled onto her side, still sleeping. Lorthana approached the big bed where Zandorah slept.

"Zandorah…," she said, shaking her gently, trying to wake her.

"What? What is it, Mom? I'm tired. I want to sleep," Zandorah responded, yawning and looking at her mom, perturbed that she had woken her.

"I need to go home for a bit. Can you watch over Lilah? I have to find out what your father is involved with… Will you be okay if I leave?" Lorthana asked.

"Sure, no worries, I will take care of my niece. She is in good hands. Carmin is here, too. Go find out what Daddy is doing. Hurry back and be safe. I am going back to sleep. Bye, Mom." Zandorah lay back down and pulled the blanket over her head.

Lorthana walked to Lilah's bed and bent down to kiss her on the cheek. She left the chamber, quietly closing the door, and sprinted down the corridor to the Security Command Chamber on a mission to locate Andreh or Pauto. She wanted to inform them that she planned to leave the Palace.

Gardone made his way toward the hut on Earth, eager to find out if Yarlen was ready to share new magic that could help him combat Alexis. He burst into the old structure, calling out Yarlen's name, but received no reply. Assuming Yarlen might be having dinner, Gardone headed into the kitchen only to find it empty.

"Yarlen, where are you?" he yelled, now getting angry. Still, there was no response from Yarlen. Gardone walked to the living room to see if he had missed him sleeping on the couch. He was not there either. Gardone decided the only other place Yarlen could be was in his room. So, he opened the door, expecting to see Yarlen sleeping. The bedroom was empty.

Enraged, Gardone left the hut and walked outside to locate the security detail that was supposed to be watching Yarlen. Weston, a security guard, sat on a stool leaning up against the back door, asleep. Gardone hit him in the leg with his Ceptre, waking him.

"Where the hell is Yarlen? Why are you sleeping, and where is Adoren? Someone is supposed to be protecting Yarlen at all times. He is gone!" Gardone stood in front of Weston, screaming.

Weston struggled to stand, his body trembling as he looked Gardone directly in the eye. "Sir, he was in the hut less than an hour ago. I conducted my hourly check, and he was resting on the couch in the living room. Adoren was in the living room, too. He was sitting in a chair by the fireplace, keeping watch over Yarlen," he responded nervously.

"Well, neither of them is around now, so you better start looking for them. I expect you to find them and bring them back to the hut! Get going, you idiot!" Gardone screamed as he slammed down his Ceptre and disappeared.

Weston tried to reply, but Gardone was already gone. He decided to head back inside the building to figure out where to look for Yarlen and Adoren. Sitting on a chair in the kitchen, he assumed they had either gone to Alstromia or Iriss. Knowing his life depended on locating Yarlen quickly, he decided to find some reinforcements. Yarlen was crafty and would not be easily captured.

Regardless, Weston knew he had to return Yarlen to Gardone or face dire consequences. He secretly hoped Yarlen would appear on his own, solving the problem for him.

However, he felt there was a minimal chance of that happening. Yarlen was not one to surrender easily. Yarlen would probably stay far away from Gardone, hoping to evade trouble. He was brilliant and not one to gamble with his life. Weston sighed, desperate to locate Yarlen. He did not want to face Gardone and tell him he had no idea what had happened to the old Wizzard and Warlock. The thought made him feel queasy. He closed his eyes and chanted, leaving Earth.

Lorthana returned home to Earth, scanning her surroundings for any sign of Gardone. Finding no trace of him and noticing his Ceptre was missing, she chose to prepare dinner and wait to see if, and when, he would return. In the meantime, she decided to focus on refining some of her spells.

Minutes after Lorthana arrived home, Gardone appeared outside. He stepped inside the house, calling out her name. In the kitchen, Lorthana was busy preparing dinner when she heard his voice echoing through the rooms.

"I'm in here, dear," she yelled, glad he was home. Now, she would have the chance to interrogate him about his absence and get to the bottom of what he was doing when he was not home.

"Hello, Hana. What are you making?" he asked, walking up behind her and hugging her.

"I see you are busy cleaning vegetables. Is there anything I can do to help?" Gardone asked.

"No, but I did want to speak with you. Can you sit down at the table for a minute?" she asked him, ready to find out where he had been.

"Sure." He sat down reluctantly, wondering what she wanted to talk to him about, assuming it concerned his constant absence. She was growing increasingly suspicious. He would have to convince her it was routine Warlock and Clan business keeping him away. Her meddling in his affairs needed to come to an end. If she interfered, he would have to stop her. It was something he was hoping he would not have to do.

Lorthana removed her apron and hung it over a stool. She pulled out a chair and sat down, directing her gaze toward Gardone. She offered a brief smile before quickly looking away. Preparing to confront him, she folded her hands and rested them on the table, waiting for him to say something.

"What is it, Lorthana? You look upset. Is everything alright?" He knew nothing was okay. He assumed she was mad at him and wanted to know the answers.

"Gardone, I am agitated. I have heard some bizarre rumors, and I need you to be honest with me. I have always been by your side, standing up for you and your beliefs. However, I need to know what's happening. You are not being honest with me at the moment. I am tired of the lies and deceit. I beg you to tell me what you are doing."

"Lorthana, I am not exactly sure what rumors you are talking about. I am working a lot with the Clan. It is all Warlock business. You know this. What is it you want me to say?" He tried to grab her hand, but she swatted his hand away, giving him a dirty look. She squinted her eyes, glaring at him. He could tell she was pissed off and ready to fight.

The two stared at each other for a few minutes, though it seemed like an eternity to Lorthana. She started tapping her right foot, impatiently waiting for Gardone to tell her something. "Gardone, you are lying! I heard our daughter, Alexis, is being kept a prisoner on Tullah Mountain. You wouldn't know anything about that, would you?" she asked him directly, hoping he would flinch or do something to give a sign he was guilty. He stared at her, saying nothing, remaining cool and calm with his hands in his lap.

"What do you expect me to say, Lorthana? That I kidnapped my child? Have you lost your damn mind?" He stood up, leaning on the back of the chair, glaring at her with his eyebrows arched. He did not expect her to accuse him of kidnapping Alexis. He had no idea how to convince her he was not involved.

"Gardone, I am warning you, if you had anything to do with Alexis' kidnapping, you would be held responsible. I promise you! I am sick over this. I sure hope Zandorah's sources are wrong about the information they uncovered. I cannot believe you would want to harm our daughter. Why the hell would you do that?" she screamed, walking toward him. She pushed him hard. He fell backward slightly, then managed to stand straight with his head tilted, trying to figure out what she thought she would accomplish by hurting him.

"Get out of the house. DO NOT come back until you are ready to tell me the truth. Do you hear me?" Lorthana turned her back to leave the kitchen, and as she did, Gardone hit her as hard as he could on the back of her head with a pan he picked up from the counter. She fell to the ground, face down onto the hard, concrete floor.

He looked down at her. "See what you made me do? Why couldn't you just leave it alone, Lorthana? Damn, it. Now I have to deal with Zandorah and Alexis." He bent down to make sure she was still breathing. Quickly, he picked her up from the floor and walked to the bedroom, her head dangling over his right arm, blood running down the side of her body.

She felt light, and her body was completely limp. Gardone tied her hands to the bedposts, securing her. Feeling bad, he walked to the bathroom and picked up a washcloth. He sat on the edge of the bed, bent over her body, and gently wiped the blood off her forehead. She had a large, dark-red lump on her face from hitting the concrete floor. Her eyes were still closed, but she was breathing steadily and shallowly.

He felt terrible as he did not intend to hurt her, but he needed her out of the way for a bit longer. He walked out of the room and headed back to the kitchen.

Lorthana's Ceptre leaned up against one of the walls. Gardone grabbed it and locked it up in its stand, securing it. Then, he cast a *Block Spell* so she could not use the Ceptre if she regained consciousness before he returned.

Gardone felt irritated that he was forced to hurt Lorthana to ensure she was out of the way. He hated hurting her, and it was not something he planned on doing. She forced him into it, though, by pushing him and accusing him of the kidnapping. He did not know how to respond or what to do. It seemed like the only solution—to get her temporarily out of the way!

Gardone knew he had to find Yarlen. The plan to replace Alexis was getting complicated, and he needed his help. Too many others became involved in the plot, ruining the well-thought-out plan. Gardone snatched his Ceptre and decided to head to Iriss to search for Yarlen. He hoped Zandorah would not be there because he felt unable to face her. She would not understand his actions. He needed time to gently break the news to her and let her become comfortable with the idea of Alexis losing Alstromia. He chanted quietly and slammed down his Ceptre, transporting himself to the planet Iriss.

Yarlen inspected his chamber. It looked just like he had left it a long time ago. His bed was still unmade—the top sheet pulled back, the blanket hanging halfway off the bed. The big window was closed, and the heavy, dark gray velvet curtains pulled back.

Yarlen considered the reasons why no one had been in the chamber since his imprisonment. He was glad to be back in the Palace. It felt like home. Tired, he sat on the chair by the fireplace and looked around. He desperately wished to stay, though he knew that was impossible for now.

Somehow, he managed to evade all security when he entered the Palace and planned to remain quiet and out of sight while searching through the bookshelves in his chamber for a specific book. Yarlen assumed a spell would help him get the job done. He was on a mission to aid Alexis and hopefully regain her respect and trust. He wanted nothing more than to be back in the Palace, working as Head Seeier. It was the only thing on his mind.

The rain finally stopped. Once in a while, a few flashes of lightning still lit up the sky, followed by loud, rolling thunder. The twin moons tried to peek through the clouds, now finally clearing. The River of Miccay sparkled under the twin moons' reflections, looking like sparkling diamonds dancing on the gray water. The night was lovely. The wind slowly calmed down, lightly rustling the Trimbers, causing the old, dry leaves to fall to the ground.

It was the Third-Season (*Fall*) on Alstromia. Alexis reluctantly agreed to bring back the multiple seasons after a lengthy fight with Armbruster and Aerianna.

They did not share her love for one season, and the Clan also wanted multiple seasons. Feeling the pressure to comply, Alexis decided to make the Clan happy by changing everything back to how it had been when they first arrived on Alstromia, with four changing seasons. She cast a *Reversal Spell,* and instantly, the planet reverted to how it had been. However, she still wanted to add things not originally part of Alstromia, such as specific regions and climates.

She quickly changed the northern part of Alstromia to become a winter wonderland of ice and snow by casting a *Colding Spell.*

This northern region, Cortonniah, was popular with Witches, Wizzards, and Warlocks, especially those who loved to ski and ice skate—something they learned on Earth. There were five main cities in the area. The most populous city, Amaranteh, was famous for its intricate ice castles, in which the more elite members of Alexis' staff resided during the Fourth-Season (*Winter*).

The southern part of Alstromia had the most extensive water feature on the planet—a Gorshann, similar to an ocean on Earth. This southern region was hot and tropical, known as Troficcah. Alexis thought a lot about how she wanted to change the planet and seasons, insisting they turn out perfectly. She figured if she had to give in and comply with others' wishes, she might as well make it fun for herself, too.

She loved the wintery and tropical locations she had visited and experienced on Earth. It took a considerable amount of research to find the perfect spells to alter the environment and regions of Alstromia. However, once the changes were complete and the last spell was cast, she was happy with the results, as were most Clan members. They now experienced the weather and climate of Earth but did not have to worry about human interference.

The far eastern region was a wasteland of nothing, called Draffenite. It was hot, dry, and sandy, resembling a desert on Earth. This is where most Witches and Warlocks ended up if they were banished from Grandullah, stripped of their magic, and not returned to Earth.

They learned to survive in the heat by building clay huts on tall sand dunes and digging for water in valleys or dry river beds. Food was scarce and difficult to grow. Most banished to Draffenite perished quickly, appropriately known as the Last Resort. No one ever wanted to go there!

The western region was tropical and humid, similar to the jungles of Earth. Some of the Clans lived in this area along the end of the River of Miccay. It was a small area of the planet but well-populated. Farmers in this region cultivated tropical fruits and vegetables, some of which were native to the area, while others were imported from Distant Lands. The biggest city in this zone, Stainnah, named after the Great Prince Stainnard, was also the birthplace of Gardone Stainnard, the Prince's son.

The middle region of the planet, known as Grandullah, was where Alexis erected her Palace of Snipperdoom, high on a mountaintop. It stood majestically surrounded by numerous mountains, the tallest and most well-known of which was Tullah Mountain.

Below the mountains, the Valley of Grandu served as the perfect place for most commoners to build their homes along the winding River of Miccay. The valley was also lush with vegetation, lined with many Bloommitz, similar to flowers on Earth.

During the First-Season (*Spring*), Bloommitz turned bright colors of pink, purple, yellow, and blue, lining the riverbank in the Valley of Grandu. Bloommitz ranged in size, color, and species, some large and spectacular, though Alexis still preferred flowers from Earth. She had brought and transplanted many varieties of flowers from Earth, hoping they would acclimate on Alstromia.

After the Second-Season (*Summer*), she realized the flowers had to be planted in specific regions to survive. Some did not perform well in colder climates, while others thrived in the cold. She quickly determined which plants needed to be relocated to the region where they would thrive.

In the Third- Season (*Fall*), she figured out she could grow and harvest pumpkins, which were also transplanted from Earth. She was delighted to share them with the Clan. Many members build enormous growing fields to accommodate pumpkins and other Earthly fruits and vegetables. Clan members quickly adopted many Earthly customs and celebrated holidays such as Halloween and Christmas. They enjoyed living a *'normal life'* on Alstromia as they had previously lived on Earth.

By far, the Fourth-Season (*Winter*) was a favorite among Clan members and commoners. The Valley of Grandu became frosty and white with snow and ice. Trimbers covered in snow glistened and sparkled. The River of Miccay became frozen, allowing the children of Witches, Wizzards, and Warlocks to ice skate. Alexis decked out the Palace with decorations similar to Earth's.

The Palace lit up in bright colors, and all the windows were glorified with garlands. Alexis loved the Fourth-Season the most. She planned a massive holiday event and celebrated Christmas on Alstromia yearly, so Clan members would not miss Earth as much. She always thought about her best friend, Shell, especially during the Fourth-Season.

Alexis became more restless. She felt like a caged animal, unable to roam around freely. She could leave the cabin, restricted to the front porch. She was allowed to sit in her bedroom or stay in the living area. It was difficult for Alexis to be confined to such small spaces. She was used to going where she wanted, when she wanted. Frustrated, she opened the front door and found Korbin on the stone bench by the entry. He looked at her and gave her a crooked smile, which she wanted to slap right off his face. She had no more patience for any of his bullshit.

"I want to get out of here. You can either retrieve Gardone or let me go. I am NOT going to sit here forever. How can you sit there like that? Aren't you bored? The weather is finally clearing. Let's go for a walk. I do not want to be stuck here," she complained, her arms crossed.

"You know damn well I cannot let you go. Even if I wanted to, I could not remove the Protection Shield. Only Gardone can do that. So, deal with it. You are stuck here with the rest of us. If you wish to go for a walk, by all means, go for a walk. It is muddy outside, and it is still pretty chilly," replied Korbin, tired of her constant whining.

Alexis rolled her big, green eyes at him, shaking her head in disgust. She turned around and returned to the cabin, slamming the door shut. Infuriated, she leaned against a nearby wall and slumped down on the ground, crying. She wanted to go home, missing Lilah. Alexis wanted to be free. *'Where is Andreh? I hope he is trying to free me!'* Alexis placed her hands on her forehead and sobbed, tired of her imprisonment.

Andreh landed in the field on the backside of the Manor. He knew Armbruster and Aerianna would be there. He assumed Pauto was, too, and instantly worried that Pauto would be furious with him for showing up.

Nonetheless, Andreh figured everyone would be happy to see him once he told them about his specialty potion and spell. He decided against using the invisibility potion. He felt it was merely too dishonest. Andreh would approach the others and inform them of his reason for being there. He was ready to rescue Alexis, and he did not care if they liked it or not. He would not allow her to be a prisoner another minute if he could help it.

Lorthana regained consciousness and instantly felt dizzy. She opened her eyes and looked ahead. She saw herself in the mirror across from the bed and squinted her eyes, trying to make out the picture forming. She was tied up! What had Gardone done to her? She looked to the left and right and saw her hands tied to the bed's posts.

*'That bastard,'* she thought. *'How could he do this to me?'* She tried to wiggle around, hoping the ropes would loosen, but they didn't. If anything, the squirming around hurt her wrists more, causing the rough ropes to cut into her flesh. How long would she be stuck like this, tied up? She looked around for her Ceptre. It was not in the room. Gardone must have hidden it from her.

Lorthana closed her eyes and chanted, casting a spell to will her Ceptre to come to her. She waited, yet nothing happened. *'What is going on?'* she contemplated. Lorthana closed her eyes and chanted again, this time using a *Release Spell.* It should have untied the ropes on her hands, but it did not. Lorthana realized Gardone must have cast a *Block Spell* to keep her from performing magic. This was bad!

The moons shifted to a vivid teal hue, signaling the arrival of daytime. The sky brightened, revealing fluffy purple clouds floating above the Palace. Zandorah stretched out in bed, pulling back the covers. She could hear Lilah chatting to herself in her crib, though her toddler speech was a bit hard to make out.

Zandorah jumped off the bed and walked to Lilah's bed. The Princess sat up and hugged her, calling her Zana. Zandorah smiled and picked her up. They walked to the bathroom to get clean. Once they were done, Zandorah summoned Carmin. She arrived quickly, eager to be of assistance.

"Good morning, Zandorah and Lilah," she announced, entering the chamber. She was wide awake. Her hair was pulled into a tight bun high on the back of her head. She had on a dark pink cloak with matching slippers. The small white apron was tied around her stomach. A Spellbook and a small wand peeked out of the pocket in the front of the apron.

Most Witches used Ceptres, but a few still liked smaller wands. Carmin was one of them. She liked the simplicity and compact size of the wand, which was much easier to tote around than a Ceptre, which was usually heavy and awkward.

"Good morning to you! Can you feed Lilah and watch her for a bit? I'd like to head to Earth for a while to discover what is taking Mom so long. I hope she is okay."

"Of course! I will take care of Lilah. Go ahead and do what you must. I will be here. Do not worry about anything," replied

Carmin, picking up Lilah. She held her in her arms as Zandorah approached and kissed Lilah on her cheek.

"Thank you, Carmin. You are amazing, and I am grateful. I should be back by this evening."

She exited the chamber and headed to the Security Command Chamber to inform Andreh or whoever was in charge that she would leave. She also wanted him to know Carmin was responsible for caring for Lilah. She planned to request extra security for Lilah and Carmin.

Zandorah entered the Security Command Chamber to find that Andreh was gone. Harshim informed her he was temporarily in charge. She explained her need for extra security for Lilah and Carmin. Finally, she told Harshim she planned to depart for Earth to locate her mother, Lorthana. She reiterated, hoping to return by the evening. He acknowledged her requests and wished her safe travels. Zandorah smiled and slammed down her Ceptre, disappearing.

Zandorah appeared outside her parents' house on Earth. She walked up to the door and knocked. After waiting a minute without a response, she turned the handle and stepped inside. It was quiet. She looked around, hoping her mother would be up and in the kitchen cooking. Unfortunately, she was not there. The room was empty.

Zandorah disliked the feeling in her stomach. Something felt off. She roamed around the living room, inspecting the house. She spotted Lorthana's Ceptre in its stand, locked down. So, Lorthana had to be around. *'She would not have left without her Ceptre,'* she thought as she continued her search, heading toward her parents' bedroom. The door was closed. She stood in front of it and listened, hearing strange noises coming from the other side.

"Mom? Are you in there?" she yelled.

"Zandorah, oh my goodness! Yes, child, get in here, quickly," replied Lorthana, excited that her daughter had arrived to rescue her.

Zandorah opened the door and stopped. She saw her mother tied up on the bed. Instantly, she ran to her mother, untying her as quickly as possible. "Mom, who did this to you? Was it Dad?" She felt sick. She knew the answer before Lorthana said anything. "Oh my gosh, look at your wrists, Mom. They are bloody. Are you okay? And what happened to your forehead?"

"Calm down, child. It is okay. Yes, I am pretty sure it was Gardone. He was the only one in the kitchen with me earlier. There was no one else around. I cannot believe he would do this to me," she yelled. She was sad and angry, realizing her husband had betrayed her.

"Why would he do this to you, Mom? Is he insane? How could he do such a thing?"

"Zandorah, I confronted him about Alexis and her kidnapping. I asked him if he had anything to do with it. He became belligerent. Next thing I knew, I woke up in this bed tied up."

"Do you have any idea where he might be? We need to find him. Are you okay to stand up?" She helped Lorthana to her feet.

Lorthana walked to the bathroom. She spun around and said, "I would like to take a quick shower and bandage up my hands, then we can leave. Give me five or ten minutes. Why don't you make us something to eat in the meantime? Will you love?"

"I will do that, Mom. I am so sorry. Yes, get cleaned up. I will make a great breakfast, and then we can sit down to figure out where to look for Daddy."

Lorthana entered the bathroom and took off her clothes. She walked into the steamy shower and rinsed off. The cuts on her wrists stung, and she gently placed the washcloth over them, cleaning the wounds.

After she finished, she turned off the water and stepped out of the shower. She sat on a stool by the toilet, drying off.

Everything hurt. Her head throbbed, and her wrists ached.

In the kitchen, Zandorah decided to make her favorite Earthly breakfast—Pancakes. She loved them with miniature chocolate chips and thick, gooey maple syrup. Lorthana kept a stash of ingredients in her pantry, and Zandorah knew where to look.

She quickly prepared the pancakes, eager to eat. As the food cooked, she sniffed the air, approving of the delicious smell. It caused her stomach to growl loudly. Zandorah laughed, flipping the pancakes. She poured the syrup on her pancakes when Lorthana appeared in the kitchen, fully dressed. Her hair was pulled back into a ponytail, still damp.

Zandorah handed Lorthana her plate, allowing her to eat first. Lorthana took it gratefully and sat down to eat. Zandorah made her plate and joined her mother at the table. They ate and began a lengthy discussion about Gardone.

Armbruster observed Florenzzah as she sat quietly on a chair across from him. She looked around the room, not talking. Pauto and Aerianna entered, holding the clothes. Aerianna handed Florenzzah a clean cloak and dress. The two walked off to find a secluded spot to change. Pauto stayed behind, sitting in a chair by Armbruster.

"Well, what do you think, Sir?" Pauto inquired, pointing to the chant bag.

"What do I think about what, Pauto?"

"Do you believe the spell and potion Florenzzah concocted will work? I assume it is our only hope at this point." He wanted to sound optimistic, but did not feel it.

Armbruster shrugged his broad shoulders and shook his head. "I have no idea if it will work. It is all we can do. I can feel Alexis and her presence…she is in the cabin. I just know it. I need to get her out of there."

Armbruster's patience was officially gone. He no longer wanted to wait. As soon as the Witches changed out of their wet clothes, they would head to the end of the Protective Shield and attempt to penetrate the barrier.

Pauto agreed with Armbruster. "Sir, they are spells and potions ...who knows if they will work. Some do, some don't. Let's hope for the Queen's sake these do."

# CHAPTER 16

Alexis stood in front of the pantry, searching for something to eat. She was starving. She figured eating something would at least make her feel a bit better. How long had she been stuck at the cabin now? She believed this was her third day, but she lost count.

She felt better after eating a bowl of Grained Suhffle with wild mushrooms and vines, one of her favorites. The Suhffle, a tiny, pig-like animal native to Alstromia, was tender when simmered over a hot stove or cauldron. This one had been cooked and canned. So, it was good, but not as delicious as it would be if it were fresh.

Alexis was hungry and did not care either way. It was something to stop her stomach from growling and aching. She looked around for something to wash it down with and found a few bottles of Porting Wine on the top shelf of the pantry. She searched for a glass. Unable to find one, she popped the purple, short cork out of a bottle and took a swig. She felt the tingling, tart, and sweet wine run down the back of her throat. She loved it. Porting Wine was her favorite drink. She preferred Porting Wine from the western region of Alstromia. It was a bit tangy, which was precisely what she liked.

After she finished eating and drinking, she returned to the bedroom. She felt restless and tired. She stood in front of the window looking out, wondering about Lilah, hoping she was okay in her absence. She also briefly thought about Armbruster and her mother, Lorthana. *'Where is everyone? They should have been here by now!'*

Alexis returned to her bed, plopped down, and curled up in a ball. She closed her eyes and hoped she could fall asleep, wishing she would wake up at home. She was quickly losing hope and figured there was a chance she would die at the cabin.

Andreh dismounted from his Torrin, Fangoh, and tied him to a Rein Pole. After that, he made his way to the back of the Manor to check if anyone was in the building. Noticing the warm glow of light emanating from within, he guessed that someone was inside. He hoped it was Armbruster, Aerianna, and Pauto.

He pulled open the door and entered the Manor. Andreh proceeded to walk into the front area of the building and quickly spotted Armbruster, Aerianna, and Pauto talking with someone else. They heard him approaching and turned around.

"What are you doing here?" shouted Pauto, angry to see Andreh. He shook his head with disapproval.

"Sir, I came bearing a great gift. I have a potion to help." Andreh quickly explained.

"What are you talking about, Andreh? You are supposed to be at the Palace, taking care of the Princess and ensuring her safety.

Why are you here? I placed you in charge to ensure everything runs smoothly while I am away. Who is taking care of the Palace and planet while you are here?" interrogated Pauto, approaching Andreh. Pauto was confused as to why Andreh had left his position. He had never disobeyed an order before.

Andreh stood before Pauto. Armbruster stood next to Pauto, and Aerianna was right behind him. They looked at Andreh, expecting an answer. Florenzzah walked away and sat on a chair, watching the interactions with an evil grin.

"Sir," Andreh started, looking Pauto in the eyes. "I made a potion and found a spell to temporarily reverse the shield so we can rescue our Queen. I am 99% sure it will work. I brought it as quickly as I could."

Armbruster pushed Pauto out of the way and gawked at Andreh. "Why would you do this? I do not understand. You are security! You are not supposed to be here. Why would you think you can get involved in this?" Armbruster was confused and frustrated. He continued to keep his eyes focused on Andreh, expecting a rapid and logical response.

"Sir, the Queen has been teaching me how to make potions. It is a long story, but I have perfected many of them. I would appreciate it if you could allow me to help. That is why I came. I just want to be of assistance." He backed away and walked toward a chair next to Florenzzah. He sat down, still holding his chant bag, waiting to see what Pauto or Armbruster would say or do.

Florenzzah smirked. She thought it was funny that a security guard from the Palace believed he was some sort of exemplary Warlock. It took her many years to perfect her craft and become a powerful Witch. *'Who is this idiot?'* Florenzzah said to herself, looking him over.

Armbruster turned around and walked to the front of the room. He realized something was wrong. *'Why would Andreh appear out of nowhere with a potion and spell? Why had Alexis been teaching him how to perfect potions?'* This seemed odd. Pauto followed Armbruster and tapped him on the shoulder.

"Your Majesty, I need a moment with you. Please allow me to apologize for Andreh. I did not allow him to do this. I had no idea he would appear with a potion. I ordered him to stay at the Palace and protect the Princess. I will ensure he is properly reprimanded when we get back. Please accept my apology." Pauto bowed before Armbruster, hoping to accept his explanation and not kill Andreh.

"Pauto, you do not need to apologize. You are not responsible for other people's actions. You gave an order, and he chose to disobey it. I do not understand why. Time will tell. You handle Andreh. I will leave that to you. For now, let's escort Florenzzah to the shield so she can cast her magic and get this job done. I want to rescue my wife. Andreh can stay here and keep watch. He is NOT accompanying us," Armbruster announced adamantly.

"Understood, Sir!" Pauto returned to speak with Andreh. He sat in the chair, looking down at his chant bag, realizing he was in deep trouble.

However, it did not faze him much. All that mattered to him was that Alexis would be back at the Palace shortly. He saw Pauto approach and stood up.

"Andreh, I will deal with you later. For now, you will stay here and keep watch. We will head to the shield and attempt to bring it down to rescue the Queen. I better not see you anywhere near the cabin or shield. Am I making myself clear? Keep your ass here, at the Manor."

"Pauto, I will do as you ask. Please get me if you cannot reverse the magic, and the shield stays in place. I have something that will work. I promise."

"Sure…stay put and out of sight. That is the last time I will tell you this, Andreh. I am so disappointed in you. I cannot even tell you." Pauto turned and walked outside to meet up with Armbruster, Aerianna, and Florenzzah.

Florenzzah reviewed the plan and explained how the magic was supposed to work. She informed the others that there was just a tiny window of time to enter the protective barrier.

Once inside, they would rescue the Queen and return to the area from which they had entered. She would then cast the chant again, hopefully allowing for a speedy and safe exit from the shield. After several minutes of discussing every single detail, the group of four headed to the shield to see if the potion and spell would work.

Gardone arrived on Iriss feeling optimistic. He hoped to find Yarlen waiting for him. He assumed he would be in the Castle of Zandor – named after the Supreme Ruler, Zandorah, his daughter. The Castle was majestic and enormous, erected on a tall, green hill on the northern side of Dorleenah, the capital of Iriss.

The Castle was built using an off-white stone, causing it to shine in the sunlight. At night, when the sun dimmed and the moon shone, the castle glowed pink and purple, depending on the color of the sky.

It was a beautiful sight. Zandorah cast a *Reflection Spell,* intending to make the Castle shine during the night, to serve as a beacon of hope on her planet. The planet of Iriss was much different from Alstromia. It was cheerful, bright, and light most of the time. Zandorah did not like the gloomy weather that her sister, Alexis, enjoyed.

Iriss was a smaller planet than Alstromia. Its population size, however, was about the same as Alstromia. Residents of Iriss lived in one of three regions—the Northern Region, the Southern Region, and the Western Region. Very few wanted to live in the Eastern region as it was hot, dry, and desert-like.

Most chose to live in the Northern and Western Regions of the planet. The farming Witches, Wizzards, and Warlocks decided to live in the Southern Region, where the climate was conducive to growing almost any type of food or herb.

The Western Region was the greenest and most lush, renowned for its stunning scenery. The Castle stood next to a waterfall, flowing into the River of Dorleenah, which ran along the Valley of Zandor. The water was bright and clear, reflecting the brilliant blue sky. The sun and moon were always out, though one was more luminous, depending on the time of day.

Gardone entered the Castle and was immediately stopped by a young security guard who asked him about his business with the Supreme Ruler. Gardone was upset that the young guard did not recognize him and reprimanded him, demanding access to the Castle. A supervisor of the young, uninformed security guard apologized and allowed Gardone to enter quickly.

Gardone strolled down the bright and white corridor toward Zandorah's private room. Once standing in front of the door, he knocked loudly. Since there was no answer, he entered and began looking around. He hoped to find Yarlen there. However, he was not in the room.

Disappointed, Gardone walked to the security chamber to ask the Head of Security Officer, Carhlston, if he had seen Zandorah or Yarlen. He hoped Carhlston would provide him with information about his daughter's whereabouts. Carhlston was a wise Warlock who was highly aware of all the happenings on Iriss.

Yarlen sat behind his desk in the chamber on Alstromia. He loved being back at the

Palace and wished it were a permanent circumstance. Four books were stacked on the desk, one of which was open. He flipped through the book, looking for a specific spell. After hours of reading, he closed the book of *Hidden Meanings*, an old Spellbook given to him by the Great Vizzork, the greatest Warlock and Wizzard ever to live.

Once in Vizzork's private collection, the book was given to Yarlen during his Magical Greatness Ceremony back on Earth. Vizzork knew his days were numbered. He had been ill for quite some time.

Though he was well over 250 Earthly years old, he knew it was time to disappear into the *Eternal World of Guidance*. Vizzork tried many spells and potions to regain his energy, but after two long years of pain and suffering, he closed his eyes and entered the *Eternal World of Guidance*, happy.

Now, he would be a Guiding Force for Witches, Wizzards, and Warlocks seeking knowledge through the *Books of Truth*. The *Hidden Meanings* book was one of those books, and he gladly passed it on to Yarlen when he graduated from Magical Greatness, an intensive Warlock & Wizzarding Schooling course taught by Vizzork himself. Vizzork knew Yarlen would become a great Warlock and wanted to guide and mentor him as long as he was alive.

Once Vizzork knew he would die, he ensured his legacy lived on through Yarlen by giving him all his books and potions. Vizzork taught Yarlen all he needed to know to become the next great Elite Wizzard—a prestigious title held by very few.

Yarlen looked at the *Transparent Spell* and felt confident it would be a great choice given the circumstances. He could make himself transparent, allowing his body to slip through the barricade. Once inside the barrier, he would use the *Recovery Spell* to change his body back to normal.

He needed to get inside the Tower to retrieve certain magical items to concoct his potion. It seemed like a good idea for him to use his Ceptre to transport himself directly there, continuing to avoid all security.

Before leaving for the Tower, Yarlen packed a large chant bag with two books and two potion bottles. Since he planned on making a Transparent Potion, which needed to be used in conjunction with the *Transparent Spell,* a large potion bottle was required. He grabbed two #5 Potion Bottles off the tall, black shelf in the corner of his room.

One bottle would be used for the Transparent Potion, the other for the Recovery Potion. He looked around his room, wishing he could stay, but knew it was best to leave for the Tower to make the elixirs. He grinned, slamming down his Ceptre with his right hand and holding the chant bag with his left, disappearing in a purple cloud of fog.

Yarlen entered the Tower cautiously, hoping no one saw him. He found all the necessary items to concoct his potions. It took him less than an hour to complete both items. He poured them, one at a time, into the #5 Potion Bottles and sealed them with the short, black stoppers. He gently placed them in the chant bag, wrapped in a cloth he found lying around on one of the chamber tables. Finally, he was ready to head to the cabin on Tullah Mountain, hopefully rescuing Alexis and becoming a hero.

Standing in front of the *Protection Spell Shield,* Armbruster felt small. The shield looked tall and wide. He feared the newly concocted brews would not work, but he refused to think about that.

Florenzzah approached the shield. She turned around and grabbed the chant bag from Aerianna, who was standing next to her and holding it patiently. Florenzzah opened the bag and removed the Spellbook and potion. She handed the chant bag back to Aerianna. Pauto, Aerianna, and

Armbruster stood behind Florenzzah, waiting to see what would happen.

The old Witch turned around and asked Aerianna to stand next to her. "I need you to hold the Spellbook. I have to be able to read the words while I pour the liquid onto the shield. Are you ready? Everyone, as soon as the shield is down, we must enter the barrier quickly. It does not last long. Here we go…"

She handed the book to Aerianna, with the page flipped open to the spell they needed. Florenzzah cautiously popped the stopper out of the potion bottle. She held the bottle high above her head and leaned down to read the words aloud. She chanted, swaying back and forth.

Quickly, she poured the potion over an area of the shield while chanting. The shield flickered green but remained stable and in place. It did not open or disappear. Florenzzah continued to chant, hoping the magic would work. After a few minutes, she realized they had failed. Either the potion was not concocted correctly, or the charm and potion did not work together. It made no difference. The *Protection Spell Shield* remained in place.

Armbruster touched Florenzzah's shoulder. "It is okay. Do not worry about it.

You tried. We must figure out something else."

Pauto met Aerianna's gaze, troubled by the thought that the shield might remain up indefinitely, preventing them from rescuing the Queen.

Armbruster turned back and made his way solemnly to the Manor. With his head bowed, he dragged his heavy Ceptre along the ground, sending red sparks swirling around him.

Reluctantly, the others followed, feeling like failures, frustrated and disappointed, not knowing what to do next.

Andreh waited for the group to return. He witnessed the unsuccessful shield removal. He noticed the flickering shield, but it never entirely disappeared. He hoped they would come to ask him for his potion and spell, though he doubted Armbruster would want to ask him for help. The King's pride would get in the way.

Earlier, Armbruster had acted rudely toward him, making him feel like just one of his minions, a nobody. Andreh hoped he would have the opportunity to prove himself to Armbruster, but most of all, to Alexis.

The four quickly emerged at the rear of the Manor. Armbruster lifted his Ceptre, which he had been dragging along the ground throughout his journey back. He paid it no mind. All that occupied his thoughts was Alexis. He longed for her safe return and felt utterly powerless for not being able to dispel the shield. He imagined her frustration, likely questioning why her rescue was taking so long. Patience was not one of Alexis's virtues, especially when it came to handling incompetence.

Andreh opened the sliding glass door, allowing them to enter. He could tell they were all distraught. Aerianna looked like she had been crying. Her eyes were red and puffy. Pauto held her hand, looking subdued. Florenzzah walked in, holding her Ceptre and chant bag with a noticeable scowl.

"What happened?" Andreh asked Pauto.

"You see it, nothing. It did not work." Pauto walked to the back room to join Aerianna. She sat in a chair with her elbows resting on her knees.

Armbruster left the building, wishing to sit on the terrace, feeling confined. He also did not want to talk with anyone, so he closed his eyes and tried to clear his head. How could he get Alexis out of the cabin? He continued to meditate silently on the terrace. Then it hit him. He recalled Andreh bragging about a potion and spell he believed would work.

Armbruster opened his eyes. He stood up and ran back inside the Manor, ready to confront Andreh.

Yarlen was ready to head to Tullah Mountain. He closed his eyes and slammed down his Ceptre, hoping he would be transported close to the cabin. He opened his eyes in pain. Luckily, he managed to get close. He looked around—he was outside the house on Tullah Mountain, facing a green shield. By some miracle, he had been able to get close to the shield but was hurt by the scorching, hot barrier. Yarlen assumed he would have ended up at the Manor, farther away from the shield. He wasn't even sure if he could transport himself using his Ceptre. Yarlen figured it would not work, and he would have to fly on a Torrin.

Thus, he was pleasantly surprised that he could get so close to the mountaintop's shield. He stared at the barrier, feeling optimistic about penetrating it. He approached it cautiously, looking around to see if he could locate any security forces inside the shield. Fortunately, there were no security guards at the front of the cabin.

Yarlen placed his chant bag on the ground and put his Ceptre next to it. He withdrew the first potion, the Transparent

Potion, to initiate the *Transparent Spell.* He flipped open the Spellbook to the page entitled: *Transparency.* He memorized the words quickly.

*"Hide behind the sheet of clear, grab the potion, and pour it near. Make the way, but do it quickly, otherwise, you will feel sickly."*

Yarlen poured the potion onto the shield, facing the cabin. He chanted the words repeatedly. The shield flickered green, then turned a bright white. Suddenly, there was a slight popping noise. The shield retracted and disappeared. Yarlen grabbed his chant bag and threw the book into it. Excited, he picked up his Ceptre and ran full force toward the cabin.

Pauto stood on the terrace, observing the cabin and shield. All of a sudden, he saw the shield flicker and disappear. He looked again, shaking his head, thinking he was dreaming. Quickly, he realized the shield was down. He turned around and sprinted inside the Manor to inform the others.

Andreh tried not to smile. He could not believe his good fortune. Armbruster came to grovel and beg him for his potion. He wanted his help.

"Of course. I will happily use the potion and chant to remove the shield. I am grateful to serve you and the Queen," replied Andreh, still gloating.

"Very well, let us head toward the shield to try again. We must make it work this time," retorted Armbruster. He was getting tired of failing. They had to be successful this time.

Just as they were about to walk out onto the terrace, Pauto came plowing through the door, out of breath. "You are not going to believe it… the shield is down! Hurry!" The others followed him out onto the terrace. Armbruster stopped to stare at the glowing, green shield.

"What are you talking about, Pauto? It is very clearly still in place!" Armbruster pointed to the dome, active and glowing. He shook his head, wondering why Pauto would lie.

"Sir, it was not! I swear, I saw it flicker and then disappear. I came to retrieve you right away. It was not there…I promise you!" Pauto was just as confused as the others. He knew he saw the shield disappear, but he did not imagine it. The question was, how did it disappear in the first place? How and why did it reappear?

"Well, I suppose it makes no difference now," said Armbruster. "Let's head closer to the shield and see if Andreh's magical concoction can do anything to bring it down."

The King felt zero confidence and shook his head. The group walked expeditiously toward the glowing zone, Andreh leading the way.

# CHAPTER 17

Yarlen made his way to the cabin, acting stealthily and dodging behind large Trimbers, hoping to evade the security patrolling the perimeter. He walked to the back of the cabin and tried to open the door. It was unlocked. He held his Ceptre, ready to use it as a weapon, as he opened the door partially, peering through the small opening to see if anyone was around.

Hearing nothing and seeing no one, he gently pushed the door open further, now standing in the back room, which also served as a storage area. Quietly, he closed the door and walked toward the cabin's main living area. He heard Alexis speaking with someone. She sounded livid, her voice elevated.

"I do not care if you do not want to let me go. I am telling you, I am not staying inside this damn cabin. Do you get it, you freaking moron?" Her voice was loud and powerful.

"I told you to calm down. Gardone will be back soon, and the plan to take over the Palace will have already been initiated. Sit down and shut your mouth," Korbin demanded.

Yarlen stood behind a wall, peering around the corner to look into the living area. Alexis sat on one of the couches. A security guard talked with her, holding a Mesmer Ceptre. She looked angry, throwing something into the fireplace. There didn't seem to be anyone else around.

"When is Daddy going to make his grand appearance? Huh? Speak up, Korbin. I demand answers. You just have no clue how much trouble you are in now. Wait until they come to rescue me. I promise you… I will KILL YOU!" she screamed, standing before him.

"Whatever you say, My Queen!" Korbin responded snidely. He was sick of her unruly mouth and comments. He knew Gardone would handle her once he returned.

Korbin wished Gardone would hurry up. He was tired of dealing with Alexis and her feelings of superiority. She was powerless with her Ceptre locked down. She could yell, scream, and threaten all she wanted to. It would do her no good. Korbin found this funny, and he started to laugh.

Alexis glared at Korbin with pure hatred, wanting to kill him. He was a disgusting little, fat blob. She wondered how he managed to waddle around, considering he was extremely overweight, always huffing and puffing as he walked. She could not wait to end his worthless life.

Alexis longed to head to the kitchen, thinking about drinking a glass of Porting Wine. Looking in the kitchen's direction, she saw Yarlen's head peek out from behind the wall. She looked at him in disbelief. *'What is Yarlen doing there? Is he here to rescue me?'* She pretended not to notice him.

Instead, she taunted Korbin some more by aggravating him with her idle chatter and threats. It allowed Yarlen to sneak into the room. Korbin had his back turned to Yarlen and did not hear him.

Yarlen nodded to Alexis, and she smiled. Yarlen spun his Ceptre in a circle and whacked Korbin on the back of his head. It was all he could do. He could not cast any spells. He had already tried to do that when he entered the cabin. Yarlen worried if he could get the *Transparent Spell* to work to escape. Korbin crashed down onto the floor. Alexis clapped with excitement. She looked stunned at Yarlen.

"What are you doing here, Yarlen? How did you get here?"

"I came to rescue you, My Queen," he responded, bowing before her.

"I must confess, I am shocked. You are the LAST one I figured would come to free me. How did you manage it?"

"It is a long story, Your Majesty. I will tell you in time, but I am unsure how we will get out of here. I cannot perform magic. Believe me. I have already tried. We can try again once we get closer to the barrier. Hopefully, the magic will work once we are closer to where we want to exit. Are you ready to get out of here, My Queen?"

"What do you think, Yarlen?" She followed him to the back of the building, hoping to leave the cabin. They opened the back door. Yarlen looked out to ensure no one else was around. Alexis tapped him on the shoulder. She pointed to a figure off in the distance, whispering into his ear, "That is the other Security Commoner. I think we can take him. Let's try to stay to the left of the cabin and head to the front. We will have a better chance of escaping going in that direction." Yarlen nodded.

They opened the door the rest of the way and snuck out, Yarlen leading the way. The two turned left and ran to the front of the cabin. Yarlen walked briskly toward the shield. That was when they saw the others.

"Yarlen, look!" screamed Alexis, pointing to Andreh, Armbruster, Aerianna, Pauto, and Florenzzah.

"I see them. Hurry, let's see if we can get out," responded Yarlen, dropping his chant bag onto the ground.

On the other side of the *Protection Spell Shield,* Andreh smiled at Alexis. He knew he was about to get her out. He opened his chant bag and removed the potion. The Spellbook was in front of him, and he began chanting. Andreh poured the potion onto the shield, causing it to flash a bright, blinding white color. It produced a zapping noise and disappeared. Andreh dropped the bottle and sprinted toward Alexis. She ran into his arms, happy to be free.

Armbruster and the others stood still, watching. Yarlen approached Armbruster proudly, declaring, "Well, I got in there to rescue her. Does that count?" Yarlen laughed, winking at Armbruster.

Alexis turned toward Armbruster, smiling. "Thanks for coming to get me," she said, holding his hand in hers.

"I am confused. Why did you run into Andreh's arms? Is there something you want to tell me, Alexis?" Armbruster pulled his hand out of hers. He looked at her sternly. His feelings were hurt.

"What are you talking about, Armbruster? I was excited to be free. It could have been anyone. I just ran toward the first one headed toward me, and that was Andreh. Why are you making this into such a big deal?"

"Oh, never mind. Let's get out of here. I do not want to stay here talking. Let's head back to the Manor. I think we will be much safer there."

Andreh gazed at the cabin. The shield reappeared and secured the cabin. This also meant that the two Security Commoners would be inside the shield, unable to pursue them. This made Andreh smile. He looked at Pauto and gave him a thumbs-up, approving his actions.

The group walked leisurely toward the Manor. Outside, on the terrace, Pauto took Aerianna by the arm.

"Come with me. I want to talk with you in private." She obliged. The two sauntered toward the Battledome to find a quiet place to talk alone.

Armbruster and Alexis walked into the Manor, not talking. Florenzzah, Yarlen, and Andreh followed behind, talking with each other, excited about rescuing Alexis. The five stood in the Manor's main hall. Alexis observed Armbruster. He bit his bottom lip, holding his Ceptre. She knew Armbruster was upset, but was unsure what she could say to make him feel better. She looked at Andreh and saw he was chatting with Florenzzah.

Alexis instantly felt a bit jealous. She wanted to speak with Andreh, but realized right now was not the right time to do so. She walked toward a table with four chairs and sat down, glad to be safely away from Gardone and his goons.

"When can we get out of here? I do not want to be around when Gardone gets back."

"I agree. As soon as Aerianna and Pauto join us, we should head out. I do not want more trouble today. We need to get you back to the Palace," Armbruster announced, looking at Alexis.

On the terrace, on stone benches holding hands, Aerianna stared at Pauto lovingly.

She realized she loved him. He smiled and squeezed her hands. "Aerianna, there is something I need to say to you. I need to say it now before I lose my nerve. You already know how I feel about you. I love you. I have always loved you!" He stood, facing her.

Aerianna remained seated. Pauto bent down in front of her, getting on his knees. He continued to hold her hands in his. "Marry me! Let's hold our Ceremonial Exchange. I want to be with you forever!" He looked deeply into her eyes, awaiting a response.

Aerianna felt a tear trickle down her cheek. She beamed with excitement. "YES! Of course, I will marry you. I want to hold a Ceremonial Exchange with you as soon as possible." She jumped up, looking down at him. He stood up, happy she agreed to marry him. They embraced, and he grabbed her waist, pulling her against his body. His soft, warm lips kissed her gently. She melted in his arms, feeling nothing but love.

Alexis stood up and walked to the large, sliding glass door at the back of the Manor. She saw Pauto and Aerianna approach. "They are here!" Alexis yelled, opening the door.

"Come on, you two love birds, get in here." Alexis saw they were holding hands. She was elated for Aerianna and Pauto. They looked happy and in love, something she envied.

"Alright, let's head to the stable and the Rein Poles. Let's retrieve the Torrins," announced Armbruster, grabbing Alexis's hand.

The group walked to the stable to retrieve the flying beasts. Alexis jumped on the back of Armbruster's Torrin. She wrapped her arms around him, holding on tightly. Pauto mounted his Torrin and reached down to grab Aerianna's arm, helping her up. Aerianna managed to get on the Torrin and placed her hands on Pauto's hips, excited to return to the Palace.

Florenzzah expeditiously mounted her Torrin and was ready for take-off while Andreh walked to the Rein Pole, untying Fangoh, his Torrin. Yarlen stood by the stable, prepared to use his Ceptre to transport himself back to the Palace.

Armbruster shook his head and pointed to Aerianna's Torrin. "Yarlen, be so kind as to bring Aerianna's Torrin back to the Palace, will you?"

"Of course, Your Majesty. I will be happy to do so." He quickly jumped on the Torrin and joined the others in the field, ready for take-off. They soared into the sky one by one, leaving the cabin and the nightmare kidnapping experience behind.

Korbin opened his eyes. The back of his head hurt badly. He glanced around, hoping to see Alexis. Unfortunately, she was not in the room. He stood up and instantly felt his right eye burn, with a sharp, stabbing pain that radiated to the back of his head. Korbin swallowed hard, trying to remain conscious. The pain was unbearable. He felt the back of his head and noticed the warm wetness on his hand. He knew it was blood even before he pulled his hand back to look at it.

Korbin walked to the bathroom to find a towel to put on his head. Once he placed the towel on his skull, he applied firm pressure. It seemed to help with the pulsing pain he felt. He sat on the couch by the fireplace, wondering what had happened. He assumed Alexis had been rescued and worried about what Gardone would do once he reappeared. Korbin did not have to wait long to find out. Gardone appeared in a bright cloud holding his Ceptre in his right hand.

"Why are you sitting on the couch with a towel on your head?" Gardone interrogated him, wondering what had happened.

"Sir, I was hit over the head. I believe it was someone who came to rescue the Queen. She is gone!" He pressed the towel down on his skull, hearing a weird squishing noise coming from underneath. He worried he was losing too much blood.

"What? How did you let this happen? Where is the other Security Commoner? WHO came to rescue her? Tell me!" Gardone stood before Korbin, tapping his Ceptre on the ground, demanding an answer. He watched the blood drip off Korbin's head onto the shiny floor.

"Sir, I do not know. Someone hit my head from behind. I was unable to see them. They must have come in through the back, by the storage room. I did not hear anyone. I am sorry." He held the towel to his head while Gardone glared at him. His head was hurting badly, and he was starting to feel nauseous.

"Well, shit! How did they manage to penetrate the barrier? I cast a *Protection Spell* and enabled a shield when I left."

Gardone sat down beside Korbin, attempting to calm down. He could hear his blood pressure pulsing in his ears. His head was spinning with anger. "She could not have just gotten out. Someone cast a spell. It is the only way," he continued, thinking and talking aloud, trying to make sense of her escape. He watched Korbin and noticed he looked tired. He assumed from the blood loss.

"I do not know. I am sorry, Sir." Korbin sat quietly, allowing Gardone to vent more, trying to stay awake. He was getting dizzy and very sleepy.

"Damn it. This ruins everything. I will not be able to return to my home. I will become a fugitive. What the hell am I supposed to do now?" complained Gardone, only thinking of his needs.

"Sir, the shield is still up, no? Why don't you remove it? It is a moot point now, anyway. Where am I supposed to go now? I cannot go back to the Palace either." The other security guard entered the cabin. He stood by the door, listening to their conversation.

"I do not know what to tell you, Korbin. We will all be fugitives now. We cannot go back. I will return to my secret hut, and I suggest you and your friend join me. It's not like you have any other option right now."

"Thank you, Sir, we will."

Gardone slammed down his Ceptre, chanting. Within a minute, the *Protection Spell Shield* disappeared. He looked around the cabin one last time. He walked back to the couch and held his hand out to Korbin. "Come on. Grab my hand. I'll transport you back with me. I need to help you stop the bleeding, too. You do not look so good." He noticed the other security sentinel, thinking he would join them. He shook his head *'no.'*

"Sir, I will not be going with you. I will try to return to the Palace and take my chance. My family is back in the Valley of Grandu. I cannot just abandon them."

"Understood, good luck with that," responded Gardone. He held Korbin's hand and slammed down his Ceptre, and they both disappeared.

The young commoner left the cabin, planning to head back down the mountain's steep path toward the Palace. He wanted to turn himself into security and take his chances with Pauto and Andreh. They would ultimately decide his fate. He was okay with that. He did not want to be involved with Korbin or Gardone. They would be captured eventually and probably tried in the courts for treason and kidnapping. He did not want any part of that. He strolled down the path whistling, not worried about his future.

The group of seven landed safely outside the stables near the Palace. Armbruster helped Alexis slide down from the beast. Essten approached, taking the reins from his hands. "Sir, I will take the Torrin. Go tend to the Queen," he replied, directing the Torrin toward the stable.

He heard the others talking outside and knew he would have his hands full, putting the Torrins away safely into their stalls. He wished Collan were around to help. It was on days like this that he missed his son. It was still a horrible loss.

Pauto and Aerianna dismounted the Torrin and secured it on the Rein Pole outside the building. They waited as Florenzzah and Yarlen did the same. Once all the Torrins were secure, the group headed toward the Palace.

Pauto and Aerianna held hands as they headed toward the Palace, blissfully in love and not afraid for others to witness their affection. Alexis and Armbruster walked side-by-side in silence. Yarlen trailed behind Florenzzah, wondering what would happen to him once he returned to the Palace. He had no idea if he would be granted immunity for his help or if he would be sent back to his prison chamber, having escaped in the first place.

Entering the Palace, Alexis spoke with Armbruster before heading to her chamber. "I am so grateful you came to rescue me. I need to get to my chamber and see Lilah. You do understand, right?" She squeezed his hand, hoping he would be okay with her, not wanting to talk too much.

"I understand. You have been through a great deal over the last few days. Do not worry about me or us. Everything is okay. I will head to the Security Command Chamber and speak with Yarlen, Andreh, and Pauto. I will come to check on you and Lilah later. Get your rest, dear." He gently kissed her on the forehead, then walked away. He wanted to speak with Andreh and get to the bottom of why he seemed so close to the Queen. Something about that nagged at him.

Zandorah held Lilah. She contemplated when Alexis would return. She listened to the chamber door open, spinning around to see who was in the room. Alexis approached, looking disheveled and tired. She smiled when she saw Lilah holding out her arms, wanting Zandorah to hand the toddler to her mother.

"Alexis…Oh my goodness! I am so glad you are okay." She approached Alexis, handed her the child, and hugged her sister in the process.

"Hi, Zandorah, thank you! I'm okay, but I'm exhausted. All I could think about was coming home and seeing my daughter. I did not know you were here. Where is Mom?"

"She will be back shortly. She returned home to Earth. What happened at the cabin?" Zandorah looked worried, wanting to hear all the details.

"It is a long story. Let me spend some time with Lilah. After I get cleaned up, I will come to find you, and we can talk." Alexis turned her back to Zandorah and walked to the window with Lilah in her arms. The young princess snuggled against her mother happily.

Zandorah left the chamber, planning to locate Armbruster and Aerianna. She wanted details about the events that had unfolded at the cabin. She also wanted to know what Gardone had done and how bad the situation had been.

Lorthana appeared at the Palace entrance, ready to discover what had transpired between Alexis and Gardone. She had no success in finding Gardone and assumed that was bad news. She felt there was nothing left of her marriage to Gardone. He sealed his future by kidnapping Alexis. Lorthana was heartbroken over this and knew she would never be able to forgive him. She worried Alexis would want to retaliate and seek revenge.

To some extent, she did not blame Alexis. But she also did not want Gardone dead. She wanted him to face a trial for his crime and deal with whatever punishment he received.

Lorthana requested that the Security Commoner find her daughter, the Queen. The Commoner informed her that he was unaware of the Queen's return. He did not even realize she had been missing. Shaking her head and feeling frustrated, Lorthana decided it was best to head toward the Queen's chamber to see if she was back in the Palace. If not, she would locate Zandorah and Lilah and wait.

Florenzzah, Yarlen, and Armbruster headed to the Security Command Chamber. Pauto stayed outside the chamber doors, talking with Aerianna. He wanted to ensure she was okay after all that had happened.

After a few minutes, Aerianna decided it would be best to head back to her chamber to clean up and meet Alexis. They would have to discuss Yarlen. After all, he had previously escaped his prison chamber in the High Tower. Now, he was a hero, assisting in the rescue of the Queen. There would have to be some meaningful conversation about what to do and how to handle the entire issue with the old Warlock.

Aerianna left to spend time alone, contemplating Pauto's proposal. She was caught off guard when he offered a Ceremonial Exchange. In a way, she felt it was a bit too soon and maybe too spontaneous. Aerianna wanted to marry Pauto, but at the same time, she did not want to rush into anything so important. She figured it would be best to consider the entire process and decide if she still wanted to pursue marriage.

Alexis held Lilah, feeling a sense of completeness and happiness. She was also very grateful she had been rescued from

Gardone's clutches. Alexis considered his whereabouts and wondered if she would ever see him again. She figured he would not appear in the Palace as Armbruster would have him arrested immediately.

Gardone would have to stay away and live out his life as a fugitive, which saddened her. Unfortunately, she knew things would never be the same, and she felt awful for her mother, Lorthana.

Once Lorthana knew all he had done, she would be devastated. Alexis realized she had to be careful and thoughtful in how she broke the news to her. It would not be easy. Zandorah acted strangely ever since her return. Alexis had no idea why and planned to speak with her to get to the bottom of it.

Zandorah changed into clean clothes in her guest chamber, choosing a burnt-orange cloak. She looked in the mirror, scowling, not happy about what had happened. She loved her dad, Gardone, and wanted to see him. She felt Alexis would never allow that to happen. She also wanted to speak with her mother, Lorthana.

She looked outside, standing in front of the large, oval window in the room. The weather outside was beautiful. Large, fluffy clouds filled the sky, the twin moons sparkling bright. The Valley of Grandu looked beautiful. The fields leading to the valley were colorful and filled with Bloommitz, orange, and yellow—fall was here. The Trimbers changed colors as well. Tullah Mountain resembled a quilted blanket, with shades of green, orange, red, brown, and yellow.

A few Trimbers were bare without leaves, while others were full of orange, red, and yellow leaves falling to the ground. Zandorah adored fall, loving the weather and scenery. She was glad Alexis had allowed all four seasons to return to Alstromia. It was a chant she knew Alexis did not want to cast. However, she did it to appease the general public. She wanted everyone on Alstromia to feel welcome and happy.

Zandorah stepped away from the window and walked to the full-length mirror by the door. She looked at herself and thought about Alexis, wondering if she should confront her, feeling that Alexis was responsible for the kidnapping to some degree. She made enemies and never seemed to take responsibility for her actions.

Gardone must have had a good reason for doing what he did, or so Zandorah believed. Zandorah felt Gardone was not the only one to blame for the entire fiasco. The more Zandorah contemplated it, the angrier she became at Alexis. She sighed heavily and decided the time had come. She would find Alexis and confront her. They would discuss Gardone, Yarlen, and what had occurred. She planned to involve Lorthana as well. She wondered if Lorthana knew about Alexis's return to the Palace. Did she realize what Gardone had done to Alexis?

Zandorah decided it was time to confront them all. She was not ready to give up her father or allow Alexis or anyone else to take him away from her. She would do whatever was necessary to find Gardone and protect him.

Yarlen sat quietly in the Security Command Chamber chair, waiting to learn about his fate. He was worried, rocking back and forth in the chair, feeling anxious. Armbruster, Pauto, and Andreh discussed how to handle the situation with Yarlen.

Ultimately, they knew Alexis would have the final say. But they wanted to present a straightforward course of action to her and give her options for dealing with Yarlen.

Andreh wanted him returned to his prison chamber immediately. He felt Yarlen should be kept there until he could face another trial for escaping.

Pauto agreed with Andreh. Armbruster was not so sure about the proposed actions.

He felt Yarlen proved his loyalty to the Queen and Alstromia by aiding them and rescuing her.

Armbruster wanted there to be some consequence for his escape. On the other hand, he felt there should be compensation for his assistance. He insisted on giving Alexis clear guidance, seeking out the law by talking with Head Legal Counsel Jamessihn Shorttar—Yarlen's previous attorney. Maybe Jamessihn Shorttar would have an appropriate punishment in mind, given that Yarlen aided the Queen. It seemed like a fair consideration.

They continued to debate options for a while. Yarlen looked on without saying anything, nervous and uptight. He worried he might be sent back to the dreadful prison chamber. Yarlen preferred to die rather than return there. He watched the others huddled around the large table, deciding his fate and future. He felt helpless.

Alexis entered the chamber with two security members on her heels. She quickly approached and sat in the chair at the table's head, looking directly at Yarlen.

"So, what is the verdict? What punishment will we enact against Yarlen?" she asked Armbruster.

"We have had a lengthy conversation about this, Alexis. I feel we should speak with Jamessihn Shorttar and seek his guidance. Pauto and Andreh feel Yarlen should return to the prison chamber to await a new trial. Ultimately, it is your choice, dear."

Armbruster tilted his head, staring at Alexis, hoping she would give Yarlen a break and not confine him to the prison chamber. He realized she was still agitated with him for all that had happened in the past.

"I see. So, what do you want me to do? You expect me to let him go? You want me to forget about his previous betrayal? Hmmm, I am not sure I can do that." She tapped her long nails on the table, staring at Yarlen, considering all options.

In a way, she felt she owed him a lot. He had been there to help her, one of the only ones who came through for her. *'Is he trying to get back on my good side? Is it just a ploy? Is he sincere?'*

"I'll tell you what. I am incredibly grateful. I would not be here if a few individuals had not gone above and beyond to help me. Yarlen is one of those individuals. Loyalty is everything to me. You all know this. I propose allowing Yarlen to return to his chamber in the Palace. He will be allowed to stay on a temporary trial basis. We will speak with our legal team and seek their guidance. We have to do what is fair and what is right. It is not just about what I want to do. Other Clan members will not be happy if we let Yarlen get away with the escape. I am unsure if a new trial is fair or not. I want to allow our legal team to address those questions. As far as I, the Queen, I temporarily allow him to resume his job as Head Seeier. I believe he has more than earned it." She stood and walked toward Yarlen. He jumped out of his chair when she approached. He bowed his head respectfully. She looked at him and smiled.

"Yarlen, I can never fully repay you for your loyalty and aid. However, I promise you that I will be fair. Justice will prevail. I hope you trust me and know I will do everything in my power to ensure your safety and fair handling of this matter. I am in your debt and grateful, thank you." She shook his hand and nodded.

Yarlen was shocked. He did not expect her to act so graciously and kindly. He was thrilled to resume his job as Head Seeier, even if it was just for a while until a potential new trial. He was not worried, figuring it would work out in the long run. Before Alexis left the chamber, Yarlen spoke up.

"My Queen, I know I can never fully make it up to you for what has happened in the past. Please be assured that I was never unfaithful or disloyal. I helped Armbruster. I realize now that I approached it incorrectly, and I apologize for my mistake. I will spend the rest of my life making it up to you, remaining loyal by your side. I promise!" He bowed and remained quiet with his head down.

Alexis tapped him on the shoulder, and he looked up. She could see it in his eyes. He told her the truth. "Yarlen, we will work it out. Continue to stay devoted to the kingdom. Do your job, and we will talk again soon." She turned and planned to exit the chamber. Armbruster leaned against the door frame, watching her interaction with Yarlen.

"You made the right choice, dear. Yarlen deserves a second chance." Armbruster smiled at her and observed her as she left the chamber without a response. He knew she had done the best she could. She was not one to become too mushy with feelings, though he knew she was thankful for Yarlen's heroic actions.

Alexis was happy with her decision. She felt it was fair and kind, given what Yarlen sacrificed to help her. He came to her rescue, while many others did not. Now, she wanted to find a way to speak with Andreh about his role in her rescue. She knew they had to talk, but it would need to wait.

First, she wanted to find Lorthana and Zandorah. They would have to speak about Gardone and what had happened at the cabin on Tullah Mountain.

Lorthana sat on the cold stone bench on the Landing Deck. She felt the warm breeze and loved the surroundings. The Valley of Grandu was a spectacular sight, especially this time of year.

Alexis prepared the Palace for the Harvest Festival, followed by the Battle Rounds. It was one of the most sought-after events on Alstromia. Many Witches, Wizzards, and Warlocks, came from different Clans and planets to try out and compete in the event. Alexis planned to compete again this year. Lorthana wondered if Zandorah would compete. She had not competed against Alexis in years.

Zandorah stepped onto the Landing Deck, hoping to find Alexis and Lorthana. She spotted her mother sitting on the bench, facing Tullah Mountain. Zandorah approached quietly, not wanting to interrupt her. She looked deep in thought.

"Hello, Mother! How are you? Isn't it a beautiful day today? I just love it. Look at that mountain." She pointed to Tullah

Mountain, which was a colorful and gorgeous sight.

"I know it is a spectacular sight this time of year. Where is your sister? Have you seen her?" Lorthana inquired, hoping the three Witches would have the opportunity to discuss Gardone.

"Last time I saw her, she held Lilah in her chamber. I left her alone. Perhaps she will be here soon. Mom, we need to talk about Gardone."

"Yes, we do. I need to know the details about what Gardone has done. I feel sick to my stomach. I have only heard snippets of information. I need to know everything. I deserve to know."

Alexis finally made her appearance on the Landing Deck, holding her Ceptre, looking regal. She wore her Grand Cloak, indicating she wanted everyone to know she was back and in charge. Surprisingly, she did appear happy. Her face was expressionless, and she was not alone. Two security members stood behind her, keeping watch.

"I am so glad I found you both. We need to talk. I guess we might as well conduct our discussion out here. There is no one else around." She turned and asked the two Security Commoners to leave. They nodded and headed back inside the Palace.

"Mom, I must tell you what occurred at the cabin. I know you are curious and want to know all the details. Please try to remain calm. I know you will not like what you hear. It was quite a horrible experience. I am lucky to be alive! I also hope that you—Zandorah—are ready to hear it too. Okay, here it goes...."

Alexis spent almost twenty minutes on the Landing Deck, providing detailed information about what had happened on Tullah Mountain inside the cabin. When she finished speaking, she cried, sitting next to Lorthana, holding her hands.

Zandorah stood up and walked to the Landing Deck's railing, choosing to look out onto the valley, ignoring Alexis. She did not believe everything Alexis told them. She knew there was much more to the story, and Alexis was probably leaving out some crucial details. There was no way Gardone could have been so heartless. Zandorah did not believe it, not for one second. However, she planned to interrogate Alexis and get to the bottom of her lies.

Gardone and Korbin teleported to the hut on Earth. No one was there when they arrived. Gardone released Korbin's hand, looking around. He knew they could not stay there, and someone would come to find him. He would run away to his secret place. No one knew where that was.

Gardone prepared the place a long time ago in the event that his plans to kidnap Alexis failed. He was a firm believer in a backup plan. Korbin stood by the front door, unsure of what to do. It felt awkward to him, as if his life was over. He would never be able to go back to the Palace. He would miss his friends. Luckily for him, all his family was dead, and no one would miss him.

"We need to stack the trunks into a pile. It is easier to transport them that way. Are you planning to come with me, or do you wish to stay here on Earth?" Gardone asked Korbin, gathering his pre-packed items.

"Sir, there is no place for me to hide or go! If I can be of assistance to you, I would appreciate it if you could take me with you. I promise to be your humble servant."

Gardone nodded. "Very well, I shall take you with me. Let us gather the rest of the items, and then I will transport us and the items to my new place." Gardone could not wait to leave. He felt nervous.

Alexis would have her security scouts looking for him. Zandorah would likely involve her teams as well. He was a Wanted

Warlock, and time was ticking. He had to hurry if he was going to escape in time.

After a few minutes, the filled trunks were in a huge pile. Gardone looked around the hut one last time. Korbin stood next to Gardone and looked at all the trunks filled with Gardone's belongings. Gardone closed his eyes, waving his Ceptre around in a circular motion, chanting. A loud, buzzing noise filled the hut. Then, Gardone, Korbin, and the filled trunks disappeared, leaving an empty and quiet hut.

Yarlen accompanied Armbruster as they headed toward his chamber, grateful to be back in the Palace. At the chamber door, Armbruster placed his hand on Yarlen's right shoulder and looked him in the eyes.

"Yarlen, I wanted to thank you for all you have done. I have also sent word to Sonia. She has a right to know you are back at the Palace. Sonia has been worried about you! Please, be smart and make amends with her and your son. You have another chance. I suggest you don't blow it." Yarlen grinned and nodded in agreement. He opened the chamber door and entered, ready to start his new life.

Armbruster decided to forgo his conversation with Andreh for now. He planned to visit Lilah and find Alexis. It was time for healing. The family needed to pull together. Alexis was safe and sound, and there was much to celebrate. He wanted to make the Harvest Festival a giant celebration in honor of Alexis' safe return.

On the Landing Deck of the Palace, Zandorah felt she could not shut her mouth. She returned to the bench and stood before Alexis and Lorthana. "Alexis, you are full of yourself. There is no way that Daddy did all of that. There is more to what you are telling us. Why don't you just tell us everything? You are lying! Daddy may have kidnapped you, but he would never have hurt you. You are full of shit. I don't believe it. Mom, how can you sit there, watching her crying…which you know is just an act. How can you allow her to slander your husband's name?" Zandorah yelled loudly.

The Security Commoners overheard the yelling and came running onto the Landing Deck, ready to defend the Queen. Alexis pointed to the door, indicating she wanted them to return inside. They quickly departed the Landing Deck.

"Are you serious, Zandorah? Are you going to protect Dad? After everything he did to me? WOW! I knew you hated me at times, but now you've gone too far," screamed Alexis, standing face-to-face with Zandorah.

Lorthana stood up to jump between them. Alexis pushed her down onto the bench. "Mom, sit down and stay out of this. This is between us! Zandorah and I will work this out. Do not get involved." Lorthana stayed seated, watching.

"Alexis, I am sick and tired of you constantly playing the victim. When will you ever accept responsibility for your actions? You had nothing to do with what happened at the cabin, huh? Is that what you want us and everyone else to believe? Doubtful. Trouble should be your middle name. It follows you like some nasty disease. You are infested with negativity and bad karma. I wish you would see that there was a reason this happened." Zandorah continued to stare at Alexis. She refused to back down this time.

Alexis was furious. She could not believe her sister wanted to blame her for the kidnapping. It was absurd. She stood her ground, unmoving, ready to retaliate and present her case.

"Say what you will. I have witnesses. Daddy chose to do this. He wanted the kingdom and expected me to relinquish my crown. I told him over my dead body. His supposed followers failed him. If you choose to go down this path, siding with him, then we have problems."

"Alexis, are you threatening me? Be careful! You are not the only one with power. I will not allow you to bully me," Zandorah declared. She refused to let Alexis intimidate her. It was time for someone to stand up to Alexis Snipperdoom, and she was happy to be the one to do it!

"I am not threatening you. I am letting you know that we will be enemies if you stand by Dad. You better get your training on, Sis. The Battle Rounds are just around the corner, and I cannot wait to kick your butt!" responded Alexis.

"Oh, it's on. I will go one step further. If we cannot resolve this in the Battle Rounds, we can resolve it the old-fashioned way—WAR! Alstromia versus Iriss. How do you like that, Alexis?"

Zandorah knew precisely what she had just done, and she did not care! Lorthana stood up quickly and squeezed between the sisters, pushing them apart. "Girls, this is not how we do things in our family. STOP IT! We are family!" begged Lorthana.

"No, Mom, Zandorah is right. We will begin with the Battle Rounds, which are coming up. But if she refuses to accept that I am right and that Daddy is now our enemy, we will start a war. I am done with all of this. I will protect my kingdom and family. If Zandorah does not want to be part of my family, she is my enemy. It is as simple as that."

Alexis turned her back to Zandorah, her arms crossed. She refused to continue justifying her side of the story, especially since her sister had not witnessed the atrocity. Zandorah rejected the truth. It seemed their conversation was stalled. There was no point in continuing since it visibly hurt and upset their mother, Lorthana.

"Mom, choose a side. You must pick your allegiance. I'm sorry, but you have to..." Zandorah agreed. The time had come. There would be a battle and potentially a war. The Battle Rounds were the perfect time to get in shape and sharpen the skills needed for combat. She did not believe Alexis and was not intimidated by her.

"I will not choose a side. You cannot ask me to do that. I refuse! You are my daughters, and I love you. You two, work it out. I plan to find my son-in-law, Armbruster, and tell him what is happening. I suggest you talk this through before doing something rash that will affect all of Alstromia and Iriss." Lorthana walked away, leaving them alone on the Landing

Deck. Their backs were turned to each other, neither talking nor moving.

Alexis spun around and faced Zandorah. "Mom made her decision. It is fine with me. I have no issue with Mom staying out of this or staying neutral. You and I are finished. I am tired of you and your blatant inability to recognize what happened on the mountain. You want to believe Dad, and that is fine. I will see you in the Battle Colosseum. I cannot wait to destroy you! We will see who emerges from the *'battle zone'* and who doesn't. I tell you what…let's not play games. We both know what this really means."

Zandorah glared at Alexis, knowing the answer before she even said it. "Absolutely, Alexis—it means WAR!!!"

www.ingramcontent.com/pod-product-compliance
Lightning Source LLC
LaVergne TN
LVHW100506110826
845146LV00002B/535

* 9 7 9 8 9 9 2 6 7 3 2 7 2 *